THE HAND OF THE HUNTER

GORDON BONNET

The Communion of Shadows
The Scattering Winds
The Chains of Orion
In the Midst of Lions
Behind the Frame
Descent Into Ulthoa
The Shambles
The Fifth Day
Signal to Noise
Sights, Signs, and Shadows
Slings and Arrows
Sephirot
Lock and Key
Gears
Kill Switch
Lines of Sight
Whistling in the Dark
Fear no Colors
Poison the Well
The Dead Letter Office
Face Value
Past Imperfect
Room for Wrath
The Obituary Collector

Text copyright © 2024 by Gordon Bonnet
All Rights Reserved. Printed in the United States of America

Published by Motina Books, LLC, Van Alstyne, Texas
www.MotinaBooks.com

Library of Congress Cataloguing-in-Publication Data:
Names: Bonnet, Gordon
Title: The Hand of the Hunter
Description: First Edition. | Van Alstyne: Motina Books, 2024

Identifiers:
LCCN: 2024940098

ISBN-13: 979-8-88784-028-4 (paperback)
ISBN-13: 979-8-88784-027-7 (e-book)
ISBN-13: 79-8-88784-029-1 (hardcover)

Subjects: BISAC:
Fiction > Science Fiction > General
Fiction > Thrillers > Suspense

Cover and Interior Design: Diane Windsor

Deliver yourself like a gazelle from the hand of the hunter, like a
bird from the snares of the fowler.

Proverbs 6:5

PART 1
THE SETTING
OF THE
SNARES

CHAPTER 1

May 4, 1996

Dear Janina,

I do not have a great deal of hope that you will remember me, and even less if you do remember that you will want to help me. Many years have passed since we were acquainted, and after all you were so young then. So was I, although I didn't think then that I was. I was young and innocent, young and stupid.

I suppose everyone in the village has forgotten me or tried to. I haven't forgotten them—not a single person. I know all of their names. I know where they lived, worked, and went to church. Since I've been here, I've waited and watched for a sign that it was time to contact one of them, one of the ones who was there when it all happened. I had begun to lose hope that the sign would come, but I shouldn't have. I don't know why I picked you, but for some reason your name kept coming to mind. Perhaps that was part of the sign, too. I'll ask him when I see him.

If I am going to ask you for your help, I suppose I must tell you everything. They say that I am crazy, that what I am going to tell you is a lie or a delusion. All I ask is that you read this, and wait until the end to decide for yourself. You were a very headstrong and intelligent girl back then, and I hope that you still are. If you read this, and decide to help me, I will be more grateful than you can imagine. If you decide that I am crazy, I will understand.

April 1996

The sound of three bells echoed through the hall of J. P. McMahon High School, and the silence that had reigned only seconds before was shattered by a rising swell of hundreds of voices. Mrs. Vannoy, the choral music teacher, looked up at the clock in her room with an exclamation of dismay. Her planning period had vanished, sucked away by a visit to the counseling office, a brief and unpleasant meeting with the principal centering on the fact that she was a day late in turning in her final budget for the next school year, and a quick stop at the faculty restroom. How could that have taken up forty-five minutes?

She rushed about, collecting sheet music left on the stands by her select chorus two periods ago. The door to the choral room swung open to admit a small, dark-haired boy whose curls were held back by a faded blue bandanna. "Morning, Mrs. Vannoy."

"Good morning, Jason."

Jason tossed his books underneath one of the folding chairs in the bass section and sat down. Three girls and another boy entered, then two girls chatting and smiling, one very tall and blonde, the other tiny and sandy-haired. Gradually the room filled up, and only a couple of stragglers were left to hurry in by the time the late bell rang.

Mrs. Vannoy dropped the stack of sheet music onto a desk and went over to the old upright piano that stood in the middle of the room. Still standing, she played a C chord and looked at the chorus over the top of her wire-rim reading glasses, which had, as usual, slid down her nose.

The talking faded swiftly to a murmur. When she played the chord a second time, the room was completely silent. "Good morning. Let's warm up, shall we? Nine hundred...."

The routine was known by heart. The entire class, teacher included, took a deep breath and sang one of their standard warm-ups, "Nine hundred ninety-nine nuns interned in an Indiana nunnery." C-sharp chord. "Nine hundred ninety-nine...." D chord, and on up the scale, their voices filling the room with the nonsense words sung so often that they didn't seem funny or even strange any more.

They worked through scales and arpeggios, and then on into the pieces they were practicing for the next choral concert, scheduled for April 28. The spring sunshine streamed in through the window, although there were still patches of snow on the ground from the last snowfall two weeks ago. Spring came slowly in upstate New York. There could be squalls in early May, but it looked as if winter was at least considering abandoning its grip. The music swelled and flowed around them, as if it had its own strange, rhythmic, independent life, which would continue after they had all left the room and gone about their own business. When the bell rang, it always seemed like they had just begun.

"Are you coming to see the musical, Mrs. Vannoy?" It was Ellen, the tall blonde girl with the infectious smile who was one of the leads in the alto section.

"I wouldn't miss it. It opens in two weeks, doesn't it?"

"Yes. I can't decide whether I'm happy or terrified."

Mrs. Vannoy laughed. "Exactly how I felt when I was in

plays and musicals. But my fear always vanished as soon as I walked onto the stage."

Ellen gave her a grin in return. "Me, too. I'm a ham."

"You have to be if you're an actress."

"I guess you're right...." She looked up at the clock. "Crap, I've got to get to biology class. Ms. Caldwell threatened to dissect me if I'm late again. Bye, Mrs. V."

"See you tomorrow, Ellen."

The door shut.

Mrs. Vannoy took a deep breath. Forty-five minutes to buy lunch from the cafeteria, go down to the faculty room, and eat. She briefly considered people like her sister-in-law, Maria, who worked at what she referred to as a "boring desk job." Teaching definitely wasn't a boring desk job. Most days, it was more like running a race. She pictured Maria calmly and quietly sitting behind her desk, all day every day, answering phones and typing letters, and for a moment she couldn't figure out whether she felt pity or envy. Finally, she sighed and walked out of her classroom, locking the door behind her.

The faculty room was full of the usual crowd. Teachers were eating lunch and socializing with one another not because of common interest but because they were thrown together into the same lunch period by the vicissitudes of scheduling.

At the large table in the center of the room sat Janina's usual group of lunch mates. Lucy Donahue, the Honors History teacher and the resident intellectual. Wanda Corliss, the keyboarding teacher, who had a taste both for gossip and junk food. As a result, both she and her conversation were on the heavy side. Doris Harnaway, the daffy old-timer who had been on the English faculty for thirty years and had achieved notoriety among both students and staff earlier that year by coming to school wearing shoes from two different pairs.

Others came and went. There were the four men, teachers of physics, history, math, and P.E., who spent every lunch period playing bridge at a table in the corner of the room. Chris Franzia, one of the two biology teachers, came into the faculty room wearing his stained white lab jacket, heated up some lasagna in the microwave, and left without saying a word. The buzz of conversation rose and fell. One of the card players burst out laughing at some joke. It was a typical day in the J. P. McMahon High School faculty room.

"Janina." It was Wanda, the keyboarding teacher. Janina turned away from a conversation with Lucy about a performance of *The Pirates of Penzance* they'd seen in a theater in Colville the previous week. "Did you see that the old Christian house is up for sale? That's not so far from where you live."

"No, I hadn't noticed."

"I wonder who owns it. It's been abandoned for years."

"I don't know. Some family member, I suppose. Someone always hires a kid to mow the grass in the summer, but I never heard who it is that takes care of it."

Wanda took a bite of the pizza she was eating and gestured at Janina with what was left of the slice. "I certainly wouldn't want to live there."

"Oh, don't be superstitious," Lucy said archly.

"Would you?" Wanda opened her eyes wide, her eyebrows riding up on her broad forehead.

"Oh, I don't think it would bother me. Any ghosts who lived there would certainly have become bored and changed their venue long ago."

"Horrible place, I say." Doris's voice was husky from years of smoking, a habit she'd only recently abandoned. "I wouldn't buy it."

"I've always thought it a rather nice house," said Janina. "A coat of paint and some strong hands, and it could be beautiful." Her voice became thoughtful. "It was, once."

"I wouldn't be able to sleep knowing what had happened there," said Doris flatly.

"What happened where?" Alice Jackson, who taught math, set down her cafeteria tray and pulled up a chair.

"Oh, they're just rehashing old dirt about Kathy and Tom Christian," said Lucy. "Well, I've heard the story before, and I have twenty essays to correct by tomorrow morning. I'd better get started." She stood up and folded her lunch bag. "You ladies let me know if you reach any new conclusions," she added, with a pointed glance at Wanda. She slipped her folded lunch bag into the pocket of her purse, pushed her chair in, and left.

"What's wrong with Lucy today?" Doris frowned vaguely after her through her thick spectacles.

"Oh, she always did have a bee in her bonnet about this subject." Wanda leaned forward and dropped her voice. "She thinks Kathy Christian was innocent, that she was covering up for someone."

"Who?" Janina realized the sharp note of interest in her voice, and she felt her cheeks warm. She did not usually participate in the lunch hour gossip, and she actually liked Lucy much better than she did Wanda.

"Well, I'm not sure, really. But we all know how Lucy likes to get the last word in, so I'm fairly sure she doesn't know either."

An uncomfortable silence descended. Janina, not able to think of anything to say, looked down at her lunch tray. Wanda, however, continued on undaunted.

"And now the house is up for sale. I wonder if it's one of Kathy or Tom's relatives who's selling it, and who's kept it up for all these years. It must be... oh, twenty years since it all happened."

"Twenty-five," said Janina quietly.

"What?"

She looked up. "It's been twenty-five years. Or, rather, it will be. It happened in the summer of 1971."

Wanda looked at her, open-mouthed, but said nothing.

"I was ten years old. I remember it."

"I didn't know that you...."

"My parents bought the house on McAllan Street when I was twelve," Janina said. "The one Jim and I live in now. Up to the time I was twelve, though, we lived on King Street." She looked at Wanda, silently daring her to question further. Finally, the other woman's gaze dropped, and she said nothing. "The Christians were our next-door neighbors."

CHAPTER 2

I suppose, if truth be told, the real beginning of it all was a month before what finally happened. It was a sunny day, just a few puffy white clouds. A perfect summer day. Seems like it was yesterday, in some ways, and in others like a day from someone else's story, someone who lived and died a thousand years ago. Didn't seem like a special day then, but the real pivots in our lives probably never do. It's only in cheap novels that the turning points are accompanied by omens and foreshadowing.

Maybe you'll remember it, if you try. Where were you that day? I remember where I was. It was a sunny summer day, and I was working the counter at the hardware store. The day Justin Lazarus walked into the store, my life changed.

July 1971

"Janina!"

Maddy Starcevich's powerful voice rang out from the front porch, and Janina, who was ten years old and soaking wet, winced. "Uh-oh." She slowly turned her head, expecting her mother to be glaring in her direction. Janina had been warned not to play in the pond that morning, but her endless fascination with frogs and toads had proved impossible to ignore. If her mother saw her now—dripping with pond water, the lower half of her spattered with mud—there would be a very tiresome lecture, and perhaps all outdoor activities suspended for the afternoon. Fortunately, when she looked, her mother was nowhere to be seen. Still out of sight standing in the front doorway, in all likelihood.

"Yes, Mom?" Janina shouted, trying to sound like a sweet, clean, dry girl so as not to invite suspicion.

"Your lunch is ready."

The screen door slammed.

A close shave. Now all she had to do was sneak in and change without being seen. Not easy but possible. Of course, her mother would have to find out sooner or later when the wet clothes were discovered. But with a little careful planning, that might not be until evening, and then, who cares? By then she'd be going to bed anyhow. What worse could her mother do?

She walked cautiously back to the house, taking care to keep out of sight as much as possible. Her father, a fanatical gardener, had filled up the yard with shrubs and gardens, so it wasn't difficult to flit from shadow to shadow. Actually, this was kind of fun. She hadn't even gone ten yards before she'd forgotten about her mother and begun pretending she was on *Mission: Impossible*. Janina, Secret Agent, trying to get past electrified security gates, ferocious guard dogs, and a mine field to enter a top criminal's house. If only the squelching of her sneakers didn't give her away to the highly sensitive sound sensors in the walls!

"What'd you do, Janina, fall in?"

Janina looked around frantically, nearly fainting with fright. She finally located the source of the voice—her older brother, Doug, who was grinning down at her from a perch high in a walnut tree. Doug was thirteen and alternated between hating his younger sister—usually when his buddies were around—and being a co-conspirator in whatever Janina was up to. Janina looked up, her face a mask of anxiety. "Shut up, Doug, okay?" she said in an intense whisper. "Why'd you yell like that for?"

"Mom'll kill you if she sees you like that."

"I know. Why do you think I'm trying to sneak in without being seen?"

"Ah. Now I get it."

"Please don't rat on me, Doug. She'll kill me. She truly will."

Doug considered for a moment. "I've gotta go get some lunch anyhow." He began to descend the tree, swinging down the branches with a lean, sinuous grace that had only recently begun to replace a coltish clumsiness he'd suffered from since babyhood. "I'll keep Mom occupied in the kitchen while I fix myself lunch. That'll give you time to get inside." He dropped from the lowest branch onto the ground. "But you owe me one."

Janina gave a sigh of relief. "Okay. Thanks, Doug."

Doug trotted off around the front of the house. Janina waited for about a minute and then resumed her cautious approach to the house. She ran lightly to the back door, let herself in, and closed the door silently, turning the handle and easing it shut.

Ten minutes later she was sitting, dry and comparatively clean, at the dinner table eating a peanut butter and jelly sandwich. Maddy was stirring bread dough in a mixing bowl and chattering in her typical, rather distracted way. Telling them that their father was only working a half-day at the Shur-Save grocery store that day and would be home at one o'clock. Perhaps after he was home and they'd all eaten lunch, they could go out to the pond and see if any of his prize waterlilies had bloomed yet. Such a shame how no one took any notice of the pond except when the waterlilies were blooming. It seemed almost a waste to have it the rest of the year. Doug, nearly finished with a tuna salad sandwich, looked across at his sister and slowly closed one eye. Janina grinned, and then turned to look out of the window so that her mother wouldn't notice and wonder what was so funny.

Her father returned right on schedule at about ten minutes after one. Very little could keep Leonard Starcevich inside on a sunny summer day. There were always yard chores to be done, and failing that, a few hours simply poking about in the garden were enough to keep him happily occupied. As soon as he ate a light lunch, he was ready to don his gardening gloves and work boots and head outside.

Janina was up in her room when she heard his car drive up, and shortly afterwards there was a call from downstairs. "Doug, Janina! Either of you want to go down to the hardware store with me?"

Doug didn't respond—he was in his room with the radio turned up with John Fogarty belting out *Down on the Corner*.

He wouldn't have wanted to go in any case.

Janina shouted, "I'll be down in a minute." She dropped the book she was looking at, popped on a pair of slip-on shoes, and clattered down the staircase with a few seconds to spare.

"Just going to pick up a pair of loppers. Want to come along?"

"Sure, Dad."

Maddy clucked disapprovingly. "Turning that child into a tomboy, Leonard. She likes the hardware store better than the toy store. She'll grow up to be a plumber, you see if she doesn't."

"And she'll make a damn sight more money than I do if she does," Leonard retorted. This, too, was an old argument, replayed so many times that the participants had lost all their fire and enthusiasm for the topic. Maddy, however, had never been known to let go of a disagreement once she'd stated her opinion.

"Leonard, that yard is becoming an obsession." Maddy shook her head in a faintly disapproving way, not looking up from kneading her bread dough. This comment had also been voiced nearly every clement day in the past fifteen years, but she showed no signs of letting up.

"Now, Maddy, if I don't go and cut back the viburnums, who will? I know you're not anxious to get out there and do it."

"No, you're right about that."

"And the handle of my loppers split last week. Split right down the middle. I have to go down to the hardware store and get a new pair."

"They don't make things like they used to," said Maddy, still not looking up.

That truism hardly needed a response. "So, we'd best get going."

"All right, then." Maddy still sounded disapproving, but then, she always did.

A few minutes later, Janina and her dad climbed into the car and headed off for the hardware and feed store up on Main Street. Leonard chatted happily about loppers, shears, and quality tools while Janina sat happily listening. Janina loved her dad's boundless enthusiasm for his gardens. She felt the same kind of enthusiasm welling up inside her at times, although it wasn't stirred by flowers. She hadn't quite found what her passion would be yet. She had the feeling, however, that when she found out it would take over her life the same way her dad's life was constantly wrapped up in his plants.

They pulled into the parking lot at the hardware store, and after a cursory look at the trays of brilliant annuals beside the front entrance, they went into the brightly-lit store. A few familiar faces were there. Dane Crawford from the farm up near the county line was buying a set of Allen wrenches. Audrey Perry was buying a thirty-pound sack of cat food for her six feline companions. Frank Letts and his teenage son were looking at chain saws. And, of course, Kathy Christian stood behind the counter.

Janina thought Kathy Christian was the most elegant woman she'd ever seen, and her elegance—far from seeming out of place in a rural hardware store—made the store itself seem like something out of the ordinary. She was very tall and slender with jet black hair tied in a neat bun, and her eyes were such a dark brown as to look nearly black. Her movements were unhurried and graceful, and her smile gave her face a nearly unearthly radiance. She was an accomplished pianist and singer, and her paintings had been displayed at the nearby Art Conservatory. Janina had heard her mother—never the most charitable of people—wonder at how Tom Christian had ever caught her eye. Tom was a kind enough person but was unremarkable in looks and was also a serious and unsmiling man whose life revolved around his hardware and feed store. Not at all the type one would have expected Kathy to have married. Janina wondered that Tom had a romantic side that only his wife knew about. Maddy, less kindly, had speculated that there might be something unsavory in Kathy's past that had made her settle for a country hick like Tom.

Janina wandered up and down the aisles, leaving her father to peruse the various makes and models of loppers before selecting one, a procedure which could take fifteen or twenty minutes. Kathy was running up a bill for Dane Crawford just as Janina reached the end of an aisle. She ran her hands along the tops of bins of rabbit food and cracked corn, gradually making her way to the big central check-out counter.

"Have a good day, Dane." Kathy handed him a small bag with his Allen wrenches.

Dane Crawford nodded in acknowledgement, mumbled, "Afternoon, Miz Christian," and walked out of the store. The bell above the door rang out shrilly to signal his exit.

"Well, Janina, how are you today?" said Kathy, resting her elbows on the counter and looking at Janina at eye level.

"Fine, thank you, Mrs. Christian."

"You here with your dad?"

Janina nodded. "He's over there looking at loppers."

"Your dad sure does have a beautiful yard."

Janina grinned and was about to answer when the bell jingled again. Kathy looked up, and Janina half-turned to see who had just opened the door. Both frowned momentarily before turning back to their small talk, although Janina was conscious that Kathy was looking past her.

Finally, she straightened up, smiled, and said, "Can I help you?"

Janina turned to find a young man standing behind her. She had never seen the newcomer before. His looks weren't striking—a young man, about twenty-five, with a tousled mane of too-long sandy hair, a few stray freckles across the bridge of a straight, narrow nose, and wide gray eyes. He was dressed in jeans, a dark green t-shirt, and a pair of disreputable sneakers. Janina looked at him closely and then back at Kathy. There seemed no hope of their private conversation being continued. Janina allowed herself a momentary scowl at the interloper before settling down to listen to their conversation.

"I saw your help wanted sign," he was saying to Kathy.

"You'd have to talk to my husband. He's the owner."

The young man frowned and glanced down at his clothes. "Do you think I should come back when I'm better dressed? I happened to be passing by, and I saw the sign...."

Kathy laughed. "Oh, no, Tom won't care about that. He cares more about the condition of your muscles than your clothes."

The young man's face was illuminated by a relieved smile. "When can I meet with him?"

"He should be back in about an hour. By the way," she said, extending her hand across the counter, "I'm Kathy Christian."

He took the hand in a firm grip. "I'm pleased to meet you. My name is Justin. Justin Lazarus."

CHAPTER 3

He wasn't really much to look at. Just another young drifter looking for work. But there was something about him that made you look again and again. It kept you up at night trying to figure out what it was that was different about him—what it was that set the whole village on its ear over the next four weeks with every gossip speculating on who he was and why he was here.

I'm getting things out of order. I did eventually find out the answers to both of those questions, but that was only near the end. For a time, he spent his days working at the hardware store, hauling around sacks of feed and bales of peat moss for Tom. He rented a small apartment above Lars Nilsson's bicycle shop, although I heard from others that he didn't spend many nights there. Where he was on the nights he was away, I didn't know and still don't know.

All that time I didn't realize what was coming. I'd go home after closing up the store, fix dinner for Tom and me, and read or paint or play the piano for a while. Then, I'd go to bed and do it all again the next day. It seemed so repetitive then, so endlessly dreary, like a hamster on a wheel. Now, of course, I'd give anything to be back there again, in our house doing our own routine.

I have a friend here, one of the male nurses. His name is Leo Carson. He finds out information about people in the village for me, and then comes and tells me about it. That's how I got your address, and in fact he's the one who has agreed to mail this letter for me. He found out that our old house is still standing, and that Tom's sister and her husband have kept it up. I would love to see it again, but I don't think that will be possible.

☆☆☆

"Mail call." Janina stepped over a backpack that had been dropped carelessly in the doorway and walked into her living room. "Sarah, you got a letter from Grandma." She tossed the card to her twelve-year-old daughter, who was lying on the floor reading a book.

Janina resumed flipping through the stack of envelopes. "A bill from Sears. A bill from the phone company. Brendan, somebody's trying to sell you more baseball cards." Brendan, who was nine, responded with a joyous exclamation of "Yes!" He grabbed the catalog from his mother, and disappeared into his bedroom.

"AT&T wants us to switch. Citibank's trying to give us another VISA card. Just what we need. *National Geographic.* That's all."

"Aw, Mom!" Seven-year-old Katie scowled at Janina. "I don't ever get anything."

"Neither do I, sweetie. All I got was bills."

Sarah had ripped open the letter from her grandmother and waved a five-dollar bill in the air. "If you'd write to Grandma occasionally, maybe she'd write to you. She always sends money, too."

"I'm gonna go write her a letter right now." Katie, still scowling, stomped off toward her room.

Janina tossed the rest of the mail onto the coffee table and then walked into the kitchen. As usual, the children had not washed their plates, bowls, and glasses after their afternoon snack. Janina considered briefly calling them all back into the kitchen and demanding that they clean up after themselves, thought better of it, and began to wash the dirty dishes.

The window above the sink looked out across the driveway to the house next door. Mary Ann Sovinsky, their next-door neighbor, was an amiable woman in her thirties whose job as a social worker at a nearby halfway house kept her away from home far into the evening. Janina looked at the empty house. What was there about an empty house that seemed so different from one that was lived in? It was more than just the lack of a car in the driveway. There was some indefinable air of loneliness about an empty house, even one which had been well maintained. Mary Anne's house wasn't exactly empty, of course, but her frequent absence from it gave it a hint of that desolation.

The Christians' old house, on the other hand, was permeated by it. Almost against her will, Janina had driven home after school by way of King Street just to take a look at it. She'd passed it a number of times since her family had moved, but it seemed to her that this was the first time in years that she'd really looked at it.

It needed a coat of paint, but other than that, it was in fair shape. Wanda had mentioned that a window had been shattered by vandals the previous summer and had been quickly repaired but didn't know who had fixed it. A tangible cloud of sadness hung about the house, which the "For Sale" sign in front did nothing to disperse. Janina wondered if a place could remember the people who had once lived there.

She had driven almost all the way home before she realized

that she'd looked more closely at the Christians' old house than at the house next door, the one she'd grown up in. She felt a momentary pang of annoyance with herself. Had she become just another rubbernecking village gossip of the likes of Wanda Corliss?

Janina's reveries were interrupted by the sound of the front door opening and voices in the living room.

"Hi, Sarah."

"Hi, Daddy!" A clatter of footsteps sounded down the hall. Janina smiled and pictured her husband giving their daughters one of his huge bear hugs. Jim Vannoy was a big man, well over six feet tall, fair skin and blond hair obtained honestly from his Norwegian father, and a ready smile that came from his Irish mother. His classmates in high school had nicknamed him Paul Bunyan, and the name still seemed apt.

Janina dried her hands on the tea towel and went into the living room. Jim stood, and Janina reached up on tiptoe to give him a kiss. "How was your day, honey?"

"Fine. Joe Marks's dachshund is over the worst of its pneumonia. I think old Heinz is going to be with us for at least a little while longer. Mrs. Brooks brought in her pet parakeet to have its beak trimmed, and she hovered around me to make sure that I didn't hurt her 'poor little birdie,' as if this had never happened before, instead of every six months. I keep telling her to get the poor thing a cuttlebone, but she's too damn cheap."

Janina glanced at her husband's huge hands and didn't wonder that old Mrs. Brooks had feared for her little bird's safety. She knew her husband to be a gentle man and a dexterous surgeon, but it was easier to imagine Jim doing veterinary work on cattle and horses than on parakeets.

"I was about to get started on dinner," Janina said. "I wouldn't mind some help, if you're not too tired."

"Sure. Let me just wash up first. I'll be there in a moment."

Jim appeared in the kitchen a few minutes later with Katie in tow. "I'm writing a letter to Grandma," Katie was telling him. "Sarah got a letter from her and it wasn't fair because I didn't get one. So, I'm going to write to Grandma, and she'll send me a letter some time when Sarah won't get one."

"Sounds like a good plan. What are you going to tell her?" Jim picked up a cucumber and began to peel it.

"I'm going to tell her about the field trip we took to the Science Center, and how we learned all about astronauts and saw pictures of the International Space Station. Also, how I'm going to be an astronaut when I grow up."

Janina grinned at Jim. "I wonder what your grandma will think. I don't think she approves of girls doing jobs like that."

"Why not?"

"Oh, Grandma thinks that girls should have girl jobs. You know like seamstresses, librarians, and second-grade teachers."

"Mr. Kellogg isn't a girl, and he's a second-grade teacher."

"I know."

Katie considered this for a moment, the scowl reappearing on her face. "That's silly," she finally announced.

"I think so, too, sweetie," said Jim. "You become an astronaut if you want to."

Katie looked down at her half-finished letter. "Of course I will," she said with finality.

"That's exactly what I was like at her age," said Janina quietly to her husband.

"Whew. I didn't know there was another one like her."

"Oh, yes. I gave my poor mother a run for her money. She didn't quite know what to make of me." She sighed. "Still doesn't, actually."

Jim picked up his stack of sliced cucumber and added it to the salad Janina was assembling. Janina glanced over at him, and said, trying to make it sound off-hand, "Did you see that the old Christian house is for sale?"

"They're selling the church?"

"Cute. You know what I mean."

"No. I hadn't noticed."

"I wonder who's been taking care of it all of these years." Then she winced. "Jeez, I sound exactly like Wanda."

"The Wandamatic been recycling ancient history during lunch again?"

"How did you guess?"

Jim snorted. "That woman wants to live in a soap opera. If nothing off-color happened, she'd make it up. I think her skull contents are split evenly between mud and hot air."

"She was talking about Tom and Kathy over lunch. It got me to thinking about it all."

"Now, don't you start worrying about all of that. It's all done and settled, years ago."

"I wonder whether Kathy's still alive."

"Never heard about if she died."

"If who died?" Katie asked without looking up from her letter.

"Someone I knew a long time ago, honey," Janina said.

"Oh."

There was a pause. "It bothers me." Janina picked up a tomato and began to slice it into chunks. "I'd like to know."

"I don't know what difference it can possibly make," said Jim.

"You're probably right. It's all over and done with. No sense stirring it all up again."

"None."

Janina turned back to the tomato she was slicing and bit her lip. She did not typically keep secrets from her husband, but today she hoped she could unobtrusively sneak out to her car to hide the note she'd left on the seat—a small square slip of paper she'd used to copy down the name and phone number of the realtor who was handling the Christians' house. She probably wouldn't call him anyway. No, she was sure she wouldn't. But still, there was no use worrying Jim. If he saw the note, he would surely worry about her. He'd wonder why it mattered so much for her to find out who was selling the house and why, and what had happened to the woman who had once lived there.

CHAPTER 4

I guess it was near the end of July before I began to sense that there was something different about him, something more than the youth and unfamiliarity that fed the gossips' fires. Maybe in the years since, you've had the experience of knowing that something was different about a person without being able to put your finger on it. That's how Justin Lazarus struck me. Not anything bad, just something wasn't quite right, if you know what I mean. He was dependable and honest as far as I could tell. It was more like the feeling that everything wasn't what it seemed, similar to looking at an optical illusion before you've figured it out.

I tried to explain it at the trial, how it seemed. Of course, the prosecution ignored it, and my lawyer tried to use it to show that I was crazy. Honestly, Janina, that trial was a nightmare. I felt like both sides were against me, and I didn't have a defense lawyer. It was all prosecution.

It was July 31, the day of the Guildford Summer Fair, and Tom was mowing his lawn.

To Janina, this was unthinkable. Tom had closed the hardware store early—a nearly unthinkable occurrence—not because he was going to the fair, but because the route of the parade went right past the store. It would be impossible for customers to get into his parking lot unless they walked. Janina approved wholeheartedly of this acknowledgement of what was, to her, one of the high points of the year. The amazing thing was that, once freed from minding the store, Tom didn't avail himself of everything the fair had to offer. How often, she thought, did you have the chance to ride the Scrambler and eat cotton candy? As soon as her father got off work—in about a half-hour, she had just checked the clock five minutes ago—her entire family would be going to the fair. Her brother Doug was one of a group of teenage boys chosen to ride on one of the antique fire trucks in that afternoon's parade, which in Janina's eyes was an opportunity of nearly mythic proportions. Everyone in the town, she had believed as recently as that morning, went to the Guildford Summer Fair.

But there was Tom walking his ancient push mower across his lawn, his sneakers gradually brightening from dingy gray to brilliant green as he walked heavily along in the freshly cut grass. Tom was a dark, square-faced man with short, medium brown hair and deep-set hazel eyes. The combination might have seemed less formidable had his face occasionally been graced with a smile. It almost never was, though. Janina stood in her driveway, astride her bicycle—the latest model, bright cherry red with a banana seat and flat plastic tassels hanging from the handlebars—and watched him. At his closest approach, he met her gaze levelly, neither friendly nor unfriendly, and then he turned and began another row. His broad back receded across the front yard. Janina wanted to ask him why he wasn't at the fair. Would he maybe go later? If not, why? But even had he not been mowing the lawn, she would not have dared to interrupt him. He reminded her of a draft horse plodding, single-minded, down a field.

Her father returned right on schedule, his car scrunching up the gravel driveway amid whoops of joy from Janina.

Maddy opened the door and walked out onto the deck. "Heavens above, Janina, quiet down. You sound like a savage." Janina ignored her completely and ran to her father, nearly bowling him over as he climbed out of the car. "When can we go to the fair?"

Leonard grinned. "As soon as I've had a bite to eat."

After a brief lunch, and with a wistful look at his flower gardens, Leonard ushered his wife and daughter into their Oldsmobile station wagon. Doug had already left on his ten-speed with two of his buddies who were also to be in the fire-engine brigade. As Maddy and Janina were climbing into the car, Leonard noticed Tom pushing his mower, now silent except for the rattle of its wheels, toward the storage shed in his back yard.

"Going to the fair today, Tom?"

"Don't think so," Tom answered.

"Nice day for it, though," said Leonard pleasantly.

"It is that."

"Well, enjoy the day anyhow."

"I will, thanks."

Leonard climbed into the driver's seat and shut the door. Tom disappeared around the back corner of his house.

"Why on earth do you bother?" said Maddy acidly.

"Bother with what?" asked Leonard.

Janina rolled her eyes. How could her dad not know what that meant? Even *she* knew what her mom was talking about.

"That Tom Christian is about the most unfriendly person I know. Why do you bother trying to make small talk with him?"

"Oh, well, I don't think he's so bad."

Maddy humphed.

"What's he ever done that's so bad?" Leonard persisted.

"That much I certainly don't know," said Maddy darkly.

"He's always been a good neighbor."

Maddy humphed again, and this time Leonard didn't respond.

Janina tended to agree with her father—she usually did when her parents disagreed. Tom Christian certainly wasn't friendly in the conventional sense, but he seemed solid, plain, and honest. Her mother had once described him as "down-in-the-dirt country," and had meant it as an insult, but Janina agreed with the description, if not with its pejorative nature. In Janina's mind, there was nothing wrong with dirt.

All thoughts of the Christians, however, flew right out of her mind when her father turned their station wagon onto Main Street. Already she could see signs of the parade scheduled for later that afternoon. Horse-drawn wagons filled with hay, a truck loaded with farmyard props that would carry a bevy of nervous preschoolers dressed up like various farm animals. Christine Denzler, a dazzlingly beautiful high school senior who was to lead the school's senior marching band, talking to one of the parade coordinators. A shiny Model-A Ford, parked by the side of the road, waiting for the arrival of the mayor some hours later. It seemed like it would take forever.

Leonard paid for tickets for the three of them, but that was the last time he took a leadership role that afternoon. As soon as they entered the fairgrounds, Janina led her father by the hand and coaxed him aboard one ride after another—complex and noisy contraptions bearing frighteningly suggestive names—the Scrambler, the Orbiter, the Zipper, and her own personal favorite, the Tilt-a-Whirl. Leonard looked more than a little green in the face when he exited the latter, refused Janina's request in an uncharacteristically curt fashion when she asked for a second round, and ignored Maddy's clucks of disapproval at her husband's childlike participation in the fair.

The afternoon went by in a frenzy of rides, soda, hand-pulled taffy, muttered words from tattooed and sleazy-looking carny operators, joyful meetings with school friends, and the general all-consuming noise of a typical fair. Five o'clock approached, the time for the *pièce de résistance*—the parade. Janina would have been hard pressed to explain why the parade was her favorite part of the fair, but it was. Even better than the Tilt-a-Whirl. Something about it seemed grand and beautiful. It was like folklore come to life.

The real parade fanatics left the fairgrounds at four-thirty to set up lawn chairs along the curbs so as to get a completely unobstructed view. These were fairly few in number, though. Everyone else began collecting along the edges of Main Street at about fifteen minutes till five, and by five till, nearly the entire town, with the exception of a few acknowledged oddballs such as Tom Christian and his wife, were assembled along the parade route. A few stragglers waited until they heard the volunteer fire department's fire siren sound at five sharp to run up to the street, but by that time there was little space for any newcomers to squeeze in.

The Starceviches had come reasonably early and been rewarded with a good location near the corner of Main and Oak Streets. Janina stood with her back to the cold, ridged metal pole of a stop sign. Street signs, so familiar to her when she was riding, always looked odd to her at close quarters. At the moment, though, she liked being able to claim this one as her own personal spot.

The first car was, of course, the Model-A bearing Mayor Charles "Chuck" Upshaw III. The Mayor was a large, red-faced man whose smile revealed what seemed like an inordinate number of teeth. He was immensely unpopular, despite his occupancy of a position that had been his for years, as well as his father's and grandfathers' before him. He had been re-elected three years ago, and villagers still discussed, over fences, dinner tables, and glasses of beer in Cooley's Bar and Grill, how on earth he had ever obtained a majority vote. Even Leonard, who hardly ever said a bad word about anyone, referred to him as "Shaw Upchuck" and threw away mass mailings from the Mayor's office unopened.

The mayor moved in and out of view, showing off his dental prowess and waving pontifically to the crowds. He was followed by the Guildford Volunteer Fire Department, then by the high school marching band. The band, though loud as only a high school marching band can be, could scarcely compete with the whistles and hoots of admiration caused by Christine, dressed in a white mini-skirt that left very little to the imagination, marching backwards while conducting the band with a flourish and the ghost of a smile.

Then there came a line of five antique fire trucks. Doug was on the second one, tossing candy to the crowd. Janina jumped up and down and yelled, "Doug! Doug! Hey, Doug!" Doug, even though in the company of his buddies, had been put into such a good humor by his position as candy dispenser that he grinned at his little sister and even gave her a wink.

It was immediately after Doug's truck passed that Janina noticed someone else looking at her. Across the street, a young man with sandy hair was looking at her with an oddly piercing gaze. She knew he wasn't a villager, and yet he looked familiar. It took her a moment to realize that he was the young man who had come into the hardware store two weeks earlier asking for work. He was the one who had interrupted her conversation with Kathy Christian. It struck Janina as odd that he would be here. He didn't belong. This wasn't his parade. She thought this without any rancor. It wasn't that she disliked him or people from elsewhere in general. It simply struck her as strange that someone from another place would even *want* to be at the village parade.

Yet there he was, not only looking at her but staring at her, boring holes into her skull with his eyes. And then she noticed that he was pointing down at her feet. He was mouthing some words—they couldn't be heard over the clamor, of course, but she still somehow knew what he was saying. It was as if all of the other hundreds of voices had been pushed aside.

Down. Look down. Down on the ground.

She frowned at him, and shook her head. He continued to stare at her and point. She stared back, her perplexity deepening to a cold flutter of fear. She didn't want to look down. What would be down there?

It only took a moment for her curiosity to overwhelm her. She gave in and looked down. There was nothing there but a squashed cigarette package, a gum wrapper, and... was that it? Sitting on the curb was a piece of hard candy thrown by one of the boys on the fire engine. How could the man have seen that from all the way across the street? Even if he had, why would he care? Nevertheless, she leaned over to pick up the candy, as the fifth and last antique fire truck passed her by.

With no warning at all, there was a crack like the report of a rifle, followed by a sharp *ping* from somewhere right above Janina's head. Janina gave a little shriek and jumped up. The rear passenger-side tire of the last antique fire engines had blown out. The truck sat on one flat tire, and already its passengers were climbing out to survey the damage.

Maddy grabbed Janina roughly. Janina started to object but then turned and looked up at her. Maddy's broad face was pinched with fear, and this was so unexpected that she simply stared at her in silence. "My baby, are you all right?" Maddy said thickly.

"Yes, I'm fine, why...." She turned to look at her father for some sort of explanation as to why her mother was acting so strangely and saw that he too was white in the face. Then, he stepped into the street and picked up a small black object from the pavement. He walked back and held it out to his wife.

"Oh, my dear God," she said.

Sitting in the callused palm of Leonard's hand was the metal nozzle from the tube of the blown-out tire.

Leonard looked at the dull gray metal of the stop sign pole that his daughter had been standing in front of. There, right at the level of Janina's head, was a bright silver dent. And suddenly, Janina understood.

She turned to look back at the young man across the street, her mind rolling with a hundred conflicting emotions, but he was already gone.

CHAPTER 5

The lawyers thought I was crazy. They thought that what I said about Justin just meant I had lost my mind. I kept telling them, "Call some other people from the village, they'll tell you that I'm telling the truth." They wouldn't do it, of course. It wouldn't have changed the outcome anyway. What did anyone but Tom and me ever actually see that would have been accepted as hard evidence?

Justin somehow knew things. That's the only way to say it. He'd tell Tom that we needed to reorder herbicide and white clover seed, even though the supply wasn't all that low, and the next day, Doug Bysinger would come in saying he'd decided to spray one of his fallow fields and seed it with a cover crop of clover for the fall. He'd walk in to the store on a sunny day carrying an umbrella, and we'd laugh, but the times he did, there would always be a thunderstorm at quitting time.

Finally, we stopped laughing. It may seem strange, but at first, we never questioned it. It was always little things, things that weren't obvious or didn't seem to matter. People talked about him, but mostly it was just small-town gossip about a new person. I'm sure that you know what that's like. Stories get inflated or invented, and half the time you can't sort the truth from the fiction. The real strangeness about him, I believe, no one ever saw except me and Tom.

"Can I help you?"

Janina jumped as if stung and turned around to see a slender, immaculately dressed young African-American woman smiling at her quizzically. "I... I'm just... yes."

The offices of Madsen and Harcourt Realty were housed in a huge old Victorian-style mansion in Colville, ten miles south of the village of Guildford. Before entering, Janina had stood on the sidewalk and stared up the broad flight of stairs that led up to the front porch of the building, her face a study in ambivalence. People passed her—mostly heading to or from the Colville Public Library, which was right next door—a few of them looking at her curiously. Finally, she had ascended the steps. She was certain that Wanda or one of Wanda's network of gossip-informers would see her, and that during Monday's lunch period she would be asked ever-so-innocently whether perhaps she and Jim were considering moving. She turned the old-fashioned brass doorknob and pulled open the door before walking into the dimly-lit foyer.

The interior of the house matched the exterior—massive, old, and immaculately maintained. A pair of doors with intricately carved glass panes stood half open across a wide reception area, giving a glimpse of a long wooden table within. Obviously this was where papers were signed and deals concluded. The reception room itself was floored with polished hardwood, but a beautiful Persian rug graced an area off to the left that contained armchairs and a coffee table littered with magazines.

It was empty of people. A receptionist's desk sat in the center of the foyer, blocking further entry into the house, but it was unoccupied. Janina spent a few minutes scanning a free-standing cork board near the front door that held a veritable collage of pictures of homes ranging from cheap shoebox-sized ranch style houses—there were few of these—to outlandishly expensive luxury homes in the fine old neighborhoods of Grove Hill and Foxcroft. It was while looking unsuccessfully for a photograph and further information about the Christian home that she had been surprised by the young woman's question.

"My name's Lynda Rogers," the woman said, smiling broadly with an offered hand held out.

If the woman recognized how nervous she was, she was hiding it well. Janina consciously tried to stop her hand from shaking as she briefly clasped Ms. Rogers's hand. "I'm Janina Vannoy."

"Our receptionist is at lunch, and the realtors take turns at her desk," Lynda continued. "I had just stepped out of the room for a moment or I'd have been here to greet you more properly."

"It's quite all right," Janina assured her.

"Now." She seated herself primly at the receptionist's desk. "What can I do for you today?" She motioned Janina into one of the antique chairs that sat in front of the desk.

"I saw a sign in front of a house up in Guildford," Janina said. "On King Street. A big, white gabled house with a large picture window in front."

"Oh, yes." Lynda smiled even more broadly. "I showed a young couple that one just two days ago."

"I'm interested in finding out a little more about it," Janina began tentatively.

"It's beautiful inside. Solid oak floors." She pulled open a drawer in the desk, retrieved a large book, and immediately began to thumb through it. "Let me see, it should be right around here somewhere. Ah. Two and a half baths, four beds, living room, finished basement...." She paused, looked up, and the smile flashed out again. "Do you have kids, Ms. Vannoy?"

"Three," Janina said.

"Perfect play room or game room. Conveniently close to the school, grocery store, PO, and bank. Four blocks off of Route 84." She looked up again, the litany concluded. Janina didn't say anything for a moment as the two women simply stared at one another.

"Are you interested in seeing it?" Lynda asked, her smile dimming somewhat.

"No, not really. I'm more interested in finding out about the seller."

"The seller?" The voice held a note of incredulity, and the smile dropped a few more degrees.

"Yes. Who is selling the house?"

"If you're not interested in the house, then why do you want to know?"

"Is their last name Christian?" Janina persisted.

"Mrs. Vannoy, I really don't think...."

Janina took a deep breath. "Look, Ms. Rogers, I used to live next to this house. No one's lived in it for years, but someone's always kept it up. I just want to know if it's being sold by relatives of the family I knew who lived there." Her forehead creased. "I know it sounds weird, but I'm not trying to find this out for any kind of shady reason. I cared about... about a person who lived in that house a long time ago. I just want to see if I can find out if she's still... still alive."

Lynda Rogers looked at Janina for a moment in silence, and then her face relaxed slightly. It lost its saleswoman's brightness, but at the same time her smile became, by an almost imperceptible change, more sincere and less forced. "Well, I guess it's not illegal, but still, my boss wouldn't be very happy to know this is how I'm spending my time," she said, her voice low.

"I know." Janina lowered her own voice. "If you really can't, I understand...."

"Just be glad that it was my turn at the front desk." She looked back down at the book, which was still open to the entry for the old Christian house. "Looks like it's being sold by a J. Carignoli. I don't see any mention of anyone with the last name of Christian."

"Does the seller live in the area?"

Lynda looked up at Janina sourly. "You're really trying to get me in trouble, aren't you? Oh, well, it's too late now anyway. No, it looks like Mr. or Ms. Carignoli lives up near Syracuse. 315 area code. And that's positively all I'm going to tell you."

Janina stood up and smiled herself for the first time. "Thank you. You've been very helpful."

"Don't you try to buy this house out from under us, now," Lynda said, but a faint smile had returned to her face, too.

"Oh, I would never...." Janina began.

"No, you probably wouldn't. Good luck with whatever it is you're trying to find out."

"Thanks."

Janina exited the office quickly and nearly ran back to her car. She had the inexplicable and ridiculous feeling that she had just shoplifted something, and that if she turned, Lynda Rogers would be pursuing her, shouting, *Give it back! Give me back that information! Police, help!* Her heart was pounding by the time she climbed into the driver's seat of her car and pulled the door shut. She forced herself to drive away without a backward glance at the forbidding double doors of Madsen and Harcourt Realty.

CHAPTER 6

Since you were so young, if you even remember him at all, I doubt whether you saw him as strange. Probably few people did. For us, it began with his uncanny foreknowledge of all sorts of small things, but it didn't end there. There was a rumor that people sometimes saw oddly-colored lights flashing in the night from his apartment above Lars's bicycle shop. Most only thought he was watching television or maybe had one of those psychedelic lights that were so popular back then. He had an odd effect on animals too. Our cat loved him, even though most people were beneath her contempt. Justin's walk from the store back to his apartment took him past Phil Lee's place. You remember his rottweiler? It used to bark at everyone but not at Justin. I think it would have eaten out of his hand.

It was like I said. Nothing alarming, nothing so unusual that we sat up and took notice. He came to us long before we would have thought of going to him.

Janina lay in the dark of her bedroom, staring at her ceiling. The feelings of delight that had filled her earlier had evaporated entirely, leaving behind confusion. She had not told her mother and father about the role that Justin had played in that day's events. She doubted that they would have believed her if she *had* told them. When it came right down to it, she wasn't sure what she believed either.

Growing up in a small village had its advantages. Janina had grown up with a static set of built-in playmates with whom her acceptance was never an issue. The village kids were just kids, of course. There were the inevitable squabbles, cliques, and fights, but there was an underlying permanence that was immensely comforting. There was little crime, the streets were safe, and everyone knew everyone else. Life flowed along like a placid river. No sharp bends, no rapids, and no rocks.

Her narrow escape from injury that afternoon had kicked the props out from beneath her sense of security. She was old enough to know that she would one day feel secure again, but at the moment that thought provided no comfort at all. Other thoughts—picturing that horrid metal tube piercing her eye or fracturing her skull—effectively blocked everything else out.

But it wasn't only the thought of the injuries she might have sustained that robbed her of her sleep. Unbidden, the image of the young man with the tousled blond hair and worn clothes rose before her mind, his eyes boring into hers, and saying to her, *Look down.* Janina was certain that he'd known what was going to happen.

Ever since she was old enough to follow a story, Janina had insisted on knowing whether or not it was "real." For as long as she could remember, the distinction between fact and fancy had been almost more important than the story itself. A bit of fantastical fiction might be entertaining, but a true story was something to marvel at. It had really happened. Even as a three-year-old, she had driven her mother crazy at the grocery store asking, "Is the Trix rabbit *real*? Is the Gerber baby *real*? Is that a picture of a *real* cat on the package of cat litter?"

She had read stories about people who could see into the future. Each of them had had that one important little word down at the bottom, near where the price was printed. "Fiction." She'd figured out what that word meant early on. It meant it wasn't *real*. It can't happen. It doesn't happen.

But now, Justin had taken away the comfort of that certainty too. If fiction could be true, then all bets were off. Anything could happen now.

It was a long time before Janina's small body finally relaxed enough that her fatigue could overtake her. Her sleep was restless and filled with confused dreams where she ran through the village streets searching for something she couldn't find. As she reached Main Street there was a grinding, mechanical noise, and a fire engine bore down upon her. Tom, grinning maniacally, was at the wheel. Her last thoughts before sinking down into a dark realm beyond the reach of dreams was that Justin had warned her to watch out for fire engines, and now it was too late.

✩
✩ ✩

The next morning Janina woke to the sun streaming in through her window. She was normally an early riser, but the little clock on her bed stand read, amazingly enough, 10:35. She looked at it three times before she was convinced that she had read it correctly.

Janina pushed herself into a sitting position. She was snarled in a tangled twist of blankets, and Neeno, her stuffed bear, was lying face down on the floor. Extricating herself from the blankets, she restored Neeno to his rightful place next to her pillow. Then, she yawned and stretched luxuriously, her back arching like a cat's. The sunshine, combined with the resiliency of youth, had already washed out last night's fears—for the moment, at least—and Janina got dressed before padding barefoot down the stairs.

Doug and her father were already long gone by the time she arose—Doug to go fishing with a friend and her father to work. Maddy was usually bustling about by eight o'clock with laundry and other household chores. As a result, breakfast in the Starcevich household was often a catch-as-catch-can affair, but this morning Maddy was solicitous and doting. Janina didn't especially appreciate her mother hovering over her, but blueberry pancakes were a rarity that such a bounty should not go unappreciated.

"Mom, do you know where that guy lives who works for Kathy and Tom at the hardware store?" Janina asked, in a sticky voice. Then added, "And can I have another pancake?"

Maddy's immediate response of, "I'm not sure, why?" left Janina in doubt as to which question was being answered. She looked up. Maddy's eyes were filled with curiosity and a hint of suspicion, but she nevertheless dutifully added a pancake to her daughter's plate.

"I saw him at the parade yesterday. I was just curious."

The mention of the parade seemed to reset Maddy's expression into one of motherly concern. "Actually, I think that he might be rooming over the bicycle shop. Georgia Petrie told me that someone had moved in there, and I think she said something about some young worker that Tom had hired."

Janina knew her mother well enough to realize Maddy had certainly learned more from Georgia Petrie—the head librarian and one of the village's chief gossips—than she was telling. However, she knew better than to ask any more questions. To show further interest would result in an interrogation regarding how she knew Justin and why she cared. In regards to the latter question, she certainly didn't want to get into that. In the end, she simply said, "Oh."

She looked up from the remains of her breakfast and waited a seemly amount of time before asking, "Can I go ride my bike?"

One respect in which Janina and her mother were similar was their curiosity. It was no more in Janina's character to let go of an interesting line of thought than it was in a dog's character to stop worrying at a soup bone. It was inevitable that less than half an hour later, Janina should find herself pedaling down King Street toward the village, red handlebar tassels flying in the wind, her tire bumping over cracks and uneven edges in the cement sidewalk. She wasn't supposed to cross Main Street on her bicycle, but she had already decided to overlook that rule for today. Lars Nilsson's bicycle shop was across Main Street, right in the middle of the village, so she would have to cross carefully while trying to avoid being seen by anyone who might report her misconduct to her parents and hope for the best.

As it happened, the only cause for concern was a curious glance from Mark Dempsey, a friend of her dad's who worked for the telephone company. Mark gave her a quizzical grin, then waved. Janina waved back cheerily, attempting to look like a child who has every right to be bicycling across Main Street. With luck, he wouldn't mention it to her parents.

But then she realized that even if he did, she was already on her way. It was too late to stop her.

Those thoughts took her across the busy street and up onto the opposite sidewalk. She stopped beneath a green-and-white-striped awning that shaded a dusty glass-fronted shop window and looked at a dim reflection of herself superimposed upon a row of shining bicycles receding into the shadows within. The words "Nilsson's Bicycle Shop" were stenciled above the window in green to match the awning.

The owner was nowhere to be seen, and that was all for the better. Lars was a gruff, blustery Dane long on sarcasm and short on patience. He had sharp blue eyes framed by masses of sandy hair and a long curling beard. He always reminded her of a picture of a Viking from a book on Ancient Explorers she'd checked out of the elementary school library the previous school year. She pictured him wearing a hat with horns on it like the Viking in the book, and snickered a little despite her caution.

The bike shop occupied the last of a row of buildings of late nineteenth century vintage, built of brick and slate. The occupants were the usual mix of typical small village businesses—a lawyer's office, an arts and crafts store, a laundromat, a cafe, a used-goods store, and Lars's bike shop. Each shared connecting walls with its neighbors, fronted right on the street, and contained an apartment above—sometimes occupied by the business owner's family, sometimes rented out.

Janina slipped around to the back of the shop. Here she realized her luck again, because the apartment above Nilsson's Bicycle Shop was probably the only one into which it was possible to see—if not exactly unobtrusively, at least not blatantly—by climbing a walnut tree that grew behind the shop. And if she got caught, she could say she was just climbing the tree, and they wouldn't know she was spying.

She parked her bike beside the shed at the back of the shop before walking over to the walnut tree. She was not easily visible from the street where she stood, but she would certainly be once she was up high enough.

Oh, well, she was already there, and the desire to see into his apartment overrode the worry about someone finding out what she was up to. If she was seen, she was seen.

With the agility born of long practice, she swung up into the lower branches of the tree and then hoisted herself up further. From where she was sitting, the angle wasn't right. She was still too low, and the sun was reflecting off the window in such a way that all she could see was an annoying glare. She pulled herself onto the next tier of branches and slipped along the branch until she was almost level with the window. The branch was also thin enough at that point to bend alarmingly, but she wriggled further out thinking again that she hoped none of her mom's friends saw her. She'd get chewed out good if her mom got wind of this.

The second-floor window was partially covered by a pair of cream-colored curtains, but from her vantage point Janina could see directly into Justin's apartment. There didn't seem to be much in it. She made out part of a bed and what looked like a desk. Boring furniture, nothing interesting. What exactly had she been expecting?

She shaded her eyes with one hand. As she let go of the branch, it swayed and creaked, but she gave it little attention. There seemed to be something on the bed, but she couldn't quite figure out what it was. All she could tell was it was something small and rounded. She leaned out farther. Suddenly, the branch she was sitting on bent double. Janina slithered off, uttering a little shriek of dismay, and caught herself just in time to save herself a fall of about fifteen feet. She gasped and scooted back along the branch toward the trunk.

Janina squinted upward. Just above her previous vantage point was a longer and somewhat thicker branch, and undaunted, she made her way up to the next higher tier. More carefully this time, she wiggled her way out onto the branch as far as she dared, then laid flat along it on her stomach with her legs draped on either side. Only then did she look down into the window.

She was immediately amazed at how much better she could see into it. With a flutter of her heart, she realized that the rounded thing on the bed was clearly someone's knee.

It had not occurred to her that Justin might be home—if it was indeed him. She scooted cautiously further out, and slowly, the entire person came into view.

Justin was sitting on the bed cross-legged, clad only in a pair of old blue jeans. His eyes were closed, and his face completely expressionless. He looked as if he were unconscious or asleep.

What was he doing? Why would anyone be taking a nap on a beautiful summer afternoon? And in any case, who would sleep sitting up like that? He must be sleeping. No one who was awake could be that still.

She lay there, as motionless as he was, for nearly five minutes, when she suddenly realized that she was frightened. His immobility was unnatural. His smooth, tanned chest did not even seem to be rising and falling with his breathing. Alarm grew within her.

Was he even breathing?

Why had she come here? Suddenly, all she wanted to do was get down out of that tree, get home, and never see Justin Lazarus again.

She was lifting herself up, ready to turn around and climb down, when without warning, Justin's eyes snapped open. There was still no expression on his face. His eyelids opened as smoothly and suddenly as the shutter of a camera, and he was staring straight at her. Panicked, Janina swung from the branch she was lying on down to the branch below. At this angle, the sun caught the window, and a flash of brilliance seemed to blaze from the young man's eyes. Then, she was swinging down the walnut tree like a monkey, her heart slamming against her ribcage. She was on the ground in a matter of seconds, ran to the shed, and leaped astride her bicycle. She heard Justin's voice from the window, "Hey! Are you okay? Don't be scared!" But she was already pedaling as fast as she could down the sidewalk. She turned into the crosswalk without a glance for traffic, and an old man in a rusty Oldsmobile with Pennsylvania plates had to slam on his brakes to avoid hitting her. "Reckless kid!" he shouted in a rasping snarl, but she barely heard him. All she could hear was an endless hollow echo in her mind, "Hey are you okay don't be scared hey are you okay don't be scared hey are you okay...."

CHAPTER 7

It was one day in the late summer—I don't recall the exact date, but it was one of the hottest days I can remember—when Justin came to me to ask about bringing some bales of peat moss out from storage. He'd been working for nearly an hour unloading sacks of chicken feed from the supply van, and it struck me suddenly that he wasn't at all sweaty. You know how people smell when they've been out in the sun? It's not sweat, or it's not just sweat, anyhow. It's the smell of sun-warmed skin, or something like that. In any case, he didn't have it. He didn't smell like anything.

"My goodness, Justin," I said. "If I'd been out there, I'd be soaking wet, and you're dry as a bone!"

His reaction—how can I describe it to you?—he looked scared. Suddenly, he looked like a frightened rabbit. Then he smiled, but it was forced. "It's not so hot, Mrs. Christian," he said and went back outside. That was rubbish, of course. It was easily ninety degrees without a breath of air stirring. The next time he came inside, there were dark sweat stains under his arms and down the middle of his back.

Janina sat in the music office at the high school, staring at the wall while her hand rested on the telephone sitting on her desk. Twice she had picked it up, dialed a few numbers, and then replaced it before it was answered. She did not have a moment free in her schedule until fourth period, and it was all she could do to keep her mind on her classes until her free period.

Then she was going to call this J. Carignoli to see if she could find out what happened to Kathy.

It wasn't because she was obsessed.

Curious. That was it. She was just curious.

But when fourth period arrived, she was reluctant even to call the Syracuse directory assistance to find out the number. It seemed like an invasion of a stranger's privacy. Even if she never called Mr. or Mrs. Carignoli, whichever it was. Just having wheedled information out of a real estate agent and using it to find the owner's telephone number seemed like a tremendous act of disrespect.

"You're being silly," she said out loud as she picked up the telephone. This time she dialed directory assistance before she could stop herself.

"What city?" said the inflectionless female voice of the operator.

"Syracuse."

"Go ahead."

"J. Carignoli. I'm not sure what the first name is, but it starts with a 'J.'" She spelled the last name.

"There's an Anthony and Joanne Carignoli on Markham Street."

"That must be it."

There was a click, followed by an even more inflectionless female voice—the computerized number-reciter chanting out the telephone number in a nasal monotone. Janina wrote the number down on her note pad and hung up.

She stared at the number for a moment, her pulse racing, and then lifted the receiver and dialed. There was one ring, two, and then simultaneously a voice on the other end said, "Hello?" as a much more familiar voice behind her shrilled out, "Janina!"

Janina gave a little shriek, and the receiver dropped from her hand. It bonked once on the desk, fell over the side, and bounced lazily at the end of its cord. Janina whirled around in her chair. Wanda was standing at the door of her office, smiling. Another woman, blonde and slender but mostly hidden behind Wanda's rather formidable bulk, was behind her.

Janina sat gasping, unable to speak, while a tiny, disembodied voice on the phone twittered, "Hello? Hello?" She snatched up the phone and replaced it on the receiver. Wanda watched all of this with some degree of eagerness. Odd behavior was Wanda's meat and cheese, and Janina had no doubt that her skittishness had been duly noted to be brought out in conversation with anyone should the need ever arise.

Wanda stepped aside, still beaming, and motioned toward the figure standing behind her with one chubby hand. The woman stepped forward. She was a petite woman of about twenty-five with straight blond hair pulled back into a knot, clear green eyes, and wearing a flowered print skirt and a white blouse. "Janina, I'm introducing my student teacher to the other members of the faculty. This is Martha Alport. She's going to be working with me for the next ten weeks. Martha, this is Janina Vannoy. She's our choral music teacher."

Janina reached out a hand and managed a smile. "I'm glad to meet you."

"Likewise." Martha returned the smile. Her face had a sweet-ly innocent air about it, which her smile did nothing to diminish. "I'm sorry we startled you."

"No problem. I wasn't expecting someone to speak out right

behind me. I guess I was deep in thought."

Wanda's grin widened. "Well, Janina, you must apologize to whoever you were speaking to. I'd guess they were as surprised as you were."

Janina didn't know how to respond to that, and an awkward moment passed. Martha looked away uncomfortably.

"I hope you enjoy your stay at our school," Janina finally said.

"I'm sure I will," Martha responded, her face relaxing into a smile again. Janina decided that she'd look for a sudden upswing in the number of boys vitally interested in keyboarding over the next week or two.

"We don't want to take up your whole free period," said Wanda. "There are a lot of other folks I want Martha to meet. See you later, Janina."

Janina forced a smile, then tried to force it not to look forced. It didn't work. "Later, Wanda. It was nice meeting you, Martha."

It took a few minutes after the two women had left for Janina to get control over her thudding heartbeat. She cursed Wanda under her breath. If it weren't for her, the call would already be made. Now here she was, still sitting there, trying once again to make herself dial the number.

Really, why was she so determined to call these people? None of it was any of her business. She should be working, prepping for her next class, and here she was wasting her free period chasing phantoms.

The clarity and rationality of that objection was immediately obvious, but it wasn't the first time this particular argument had been offered by her subconscious. With an effort, she silenced it.

She wanted to know. No, more than that, she *needed* to know.

She winced. So, she was obsessed after all. Wasn't that what an obsession was? A desperate fixation on something for no rational reason? She didn't need to call the Carignolis, she needed to call a therapist.

"Now that's a fine idea," said Janina sourly and picked up the telephone receiver. Her hands were shaking as she punched in the numbers, but years of vocal training allowed her to consciously, and successfully, will her voice to remain steady.

There were three rings, then a click. "Hello?" said a female voice. An older voice, Janina could tell that. A little rough around the edges.

"Hello, may I please speak with Anthony or Joanne Carignoli?"

"This is Joanne speaking."

Janina had rehearsed this speech a hundred times. Lying sleepless in bed at night, driving to school, even while teaching class, the flow of the lesson proceeding on autopilot while her brain coursed along on its own, completely unrelated track. She took a deep breath.

"My name is Janina Vannoy. I'm a music teacher at the high school in Guildford. I'm trying to find out some information about some people I knew while I was growing up, and a... a friend of mine gave me your name and told me you might be able to help." Janina hoped the woman hadn't noticed the hesitation. Try though she might, she hadn't been able to prevent it. Friend? More like a total stranger, and she'd wheedled the information out of her. And most likely she could get in trouble for it, too.

Some friend.

A pause. "I don't think I know anyone who lives in Guildford." The woman's voice sounded guarded. Non-committal. Not cold but not friendly.

"They don't live there anymore. When I was growing up, I lived next door to a couple named Tom and Kathy Christian."

Another pause. "Tom Christian was my brother," came the reply finally.

"Oh." Damn, why hadn't she expected something like that? "I'm sorry."

"What information did you want?" Now the guarded tone

was gone, and so was any trace of warmth. Joanne Carignoli's voice sounded flat and cold.

"I'm trying to find out what happened to Kathy. If she's still alive. If so, where she is."

There was a hissing intake of breath. "I have no idea. Nor do I care. Young woman, I have no wish to spend my time discussing this with a total stranger."

"Please." Janina was a little shocked at the vehemence with which she had said that single word, and it cut through the flow of the other woman's voice as if it had been shut off with a switch. "I was very young when your brother died, and I just want to know what happened. I mean, what became of Kathy. We lived next door to them."

"Why do you want to know?"

"My family knew them well. It's always bothered me that I didn't know."

"It's no business of yours," responded the other woman flatly, and then stopped, as if daring Janina to push further.

"It's just that... I cared about them. Kathy was my friend, and I always felt so bad about what happened."

"I'm sorry about that." Mrs. Carignoli sounded anything but sorry, but at least this time she kept talking. "I don't know what became of her other than that she was sent to an asylum. She should have gone to jail after what she did, but the judge said she was crazy. I suppose she was, but still. Murder's murder."

"And you don't know which asylum...."

Mrs. Carignoli cut her off, her voice icy and bitter. "No, Mrs. Whatever-Your-Name-Is, I never bothered to keep in touch with Kathy." She spat the name out. "At first, I wished her dead. Now I hope she's still alive and still rotting in whatever madhouse they sent her to."

For a moment, Janina was struck silent by the hate in the older woman's words. Then, she said quietly, "I'm sorry I disturbed you." Without waiting for a reply, she set the receiver back gently into its cradle.

CHAPTER 8

Something must have really scared Justin about that incident, because later that day he stopped me as I was locking up the store. Tom was around back, locking all the outbuildings. Justin came in looking serious. That caught my attention. He ordinarily had a relaxed, easy manner, and his face was usually kind and open. That afternoon, though, he looked different. Worried, tense.

"Mrs. Christian," he said, "can I talk to you for a moment?"

I said sure, why, what's up? He said he had a problem. He thought it best to talk to me first, but that he'd talk to Tom too if I thought it was okay.

"What's on your mind, Justin?" I asked.

"I don't know quite how to say it, Mrs. Christian," he said. "The folks here in Guildford have been really friendly considering I'm a stranger, but...." He stopped like he didn't know what to say.

"You can tell me," I said to him.

"It's just that people are beginning to talk about me," he said. "They think I'm different. I don't want to attract attention,

but somehow I do."

The thought crossed my mind, you are different. Anyone who doesn't sweat until someone notices it is definitely different. But then when I thought about it, I began to wonder about my own memory—if I was remembering correctly, if we'd really had the conversation about why he wasn't sweaty. It suddenly seemed to me like that hadn't happened, that it was something I had made up. My brain just felt totally stuck for a moment, like I couldn't sort truth from fiction.

After a little bit, I said, "Oh, you shouldn't worry about that," or something like it. "You know small town tongues. They flap like a flag in a gale. You're a novelty. It'll wear off."

"It's more than being a novelty. Just yesterday, a little girl climbed a tree outside my room to try to see inside. I tried to talk to her afterwards. She seemed scared. I don't think it helped. I don't know why people find me so interesting. They stare at me on the street."

At that moment he seemed so vulnerable, so young. I smiled at him—I swear, Janina, I did it out of kindness, at that point that was all it was—and he looked up, those clear gray eyes seeming to connect with mine. And I tell you, at that moment, I knew that I was caught.

Janina pelted up her driveway so fast that the tassels on her bike handle stood out nearly horizontal. She was so winded that she felt dizzy, but she knew better than to go into the house. If her mother saw her in this state—especially after yesterday's close call—she would be lucky to be allowed to go out again that afternoon. Even if Janina didn't say what she had seen from up in the tree, which she was certainly not foolish enough to do, her mother would know that something was wrong and badger an explanation out of her. Heaven only knew what would happen after that.

She left her bicycle leaning against the wall in the garage, went around the side of the house into the back yard, and down the hill to the pond. There she could hide so her mother couldn't accidentally see her from the window and come out to investigate. She didn't want to be seen at the moment. She could feel the hot tears at the back of her throat but held them in until she plunked down on the ground with her back to the willow tree at the pond's edge. Then, she broke into helpless sobs.

Even as she sat crying, a small part of herself remained detached. What was she so upset about? She'd seen a guy through an apartment window, and she'd almost fallen out of a tree. It wasn't the first time either of those had happened.

She was being a baby.

But then, she realized it was more than that. She had a good reason to be afraid. She hadn't just seen a guy. He'd looked at her and pushed her with his eyes. His eyes had flashed at her. Like a torch. Like lightning.

Rational explanations simply didn't work. It couldn't have been the sun. The light had come from inside the room, not outside. Which was impossible, wasn't it?

Apparently not. It had happened.

At this point, Janina cried even harder, and her sobs drowned out both of the arguing internal voices.

After some time passed, her tears diminished, but she still felt no inclination to go inside, or indeed, to go anywhere. She sat looking at the inverted reflections of the surrounding trees in the still water of the pond. A dragonfly lighted on a reed, and the reed bent under its slight weight until it nearly touched the water. Then, with a jewel-like flash of green and blue, the dragonfly was gone. The waterlilies bloomed pink and white in the summer heat. All was as it always was, but in a very real way, everything was different. Janina felt very alone and very unsafe. The reasonable, stable world she had known suddenly felt very unreasonable and unstable. The borderline between reality and fiction was blurred. She seemed to have wandered into a fantasy story, and she didn't like it. She had always been game for adventure, but at the moment, her desire for excitement was ebbing fast. Even her mother's dull world of housework, taking care of the family, and complaining, as tiresome as it seemed to Janina, now looked comfortable and safe.

What to do now? She considered. She had no desire to ride her bike any more, but none of the usual indoor activities, usually reserved for rainy days, seemed at all appealing. Unbidden, her mind kept returning to her vision of the man in the apartment. It was the only thing she could focus on. When she closed her eyes, she could still see his cross-legged form, stone-like in its immobility. She remembered everything about him—every contour of his old jeans, the narrow, graceful bare feet, the overlong sandy hair brushing his smooth, sunburned shoulders, and the deep, deep tranquility of his still face.

But mostly, the eyes. Gray eyes that flashed when they opened. And they *had* flashed. It wasn't the sun. It....

"Hey."

She turned. And she wasn't really surprised to find that it was him. Some part of her expected it, knew that he would find her. He was still wearing the old jeans, but now he had on sneakers and a worn t-shirt with an outline of a mountain printed above the words "This T-Shirt and I Climbed Mt. Washington." She felt curiously numb. She couldn't have run even if she'd been inclined to.

"Don't be scared, okay?" He was smiling, this strange young man. Everything about him was so normal.

But if he was so normal, what was so wrong about him?

"I'm not scared." She spoke calmly and quietly, almost in a whisper. She hoped it sounded more truthful to him than it did to herself.

"I've seen you and your dad a lot in the hardware store." His voice was a clear, pure baritone, a gentle voice. "I knew your dad's name, so I asked Lars in the bike shop where you lived. I found out your house was only a couple blocks away, so I walked up here. I wanted to talk to you."

"Okay."

"I saw you up in the tree outside my window. I thought you might have gotten scared, and I wanted to say that I was sorry if I scared you. And...."

He paused, and she looked up. That was when she suddenly realized that she wasn't the only one who was scared. He was scared, too. She was sure of it. He was hiding it well, but he was scared. Why?

He seemed uncertain about what to say next.

"What?" prompted Janina.

"You were the one I saw at the parade, too, aren't you? The one who almost got hit by the tire nozzle."

"Yes."

"I... I'm glad you didn't get hurt."

"Me too."

Her clipped answers seemed to disconcert the young man. He stammered a little as he said, "I hope your parents weren't too worried. Your mom looked like she might faint."

She felt a surge of anger. "What is it you want? I know you didn't only come here to apologize."

He gave her a half smile, but he now seemed genuinely uneasy. "Okay. You're right. I guess I wanted to ask you for a favor."

Janina's stomach did a flip. The words *He's going to ask me to do something that will change me forever* slipped across her mind, almost too fast for her to acknowledge, certainly too quick to understand. Suddenly, she was dreading whatever it was that this young man had to say. "What is it?" she asked in a strange, flat voice.

Her mom always said don't talk to strangers, because they'd do bad things to her. Was this what she was talking about? She fought to stem a rising panic.

"I think…." He swallowed and paused for a moment as if trying to think of what to say. "I think you might have the idea that I told you to duck, and that's why the tire nozzle didn't hit you. I… saw how scared you looked when I looked at you through the window today and thought you might have… I mean, I didn't want you…." He trailed off.

Suddenly Janina knew but had no idea how she knew or what her knowledge implied. "You don't want me to tell anyone."

His eyes met hers. This time there was no lightning flash, but she sensed the intensity behind them. "Yes."

"Why? What difference does it make?"

He looked away, scanning the pond and then gazing out across the field toward the tree-lined horizon. "I can't tell you that. You wouldn't believe me anyway if I did."

"What are you scared of?" she asked suddenly.

His gaze snapped back into hers so quickly that she blinked. "What makes you think I'm scared?" he said, his voice almost a whisper.

"I can tell when someone's scared," she said, a little scornfully. "I'm not stupid."

"But I'm…." he began, and then stopped. "I'm not really…."

"Yes, you are," she interrupted. "You're scared silly."

"Is it that obvious?"

She shrugged and gave a little lift of her eyebrows.

He looked away again. "Look, can I trust you not to mention what you've seen to anyone?"

Janina considered. Who would she have told in any case? No one, probably. If she tried to tell her father, he would be troubled and concerned in his vague, gentle way, and then think that she was remembering a nightmare or still upset about her near accident. Her mother, on the other hand, would think she was just trying to get attention. Her brother Doug wouldn't believe her, pure and simple. Who did that leave? She wasn't especially close to other children her age. She played with them some, but there were no bosom buddies—she remembered the phrase from reading *Anne of Green Gables* earlier that year—with whom to exchange secrets. No, she wouldn't have been likely to tell anyone in any case, but this stranger's mysterious fear had struck a compassionate chord in her. For some strange reason, she found herself liking him. With a degree of surprise, she found that her own fear had evaporated.

"Okay, I promise," she said. "I won't tell anyone."

He closed his eyes. "Thank you. I really appreciate that. I'm sorry I scared you today and at the parade. I couldn't let you get hurt...." He stopped suddenly and looked up at her.

Janina frowned. "So, you really did warn me about the tire blowing out? How did you know?"

He shook his head. "I just know things sometimes."

She raised an eyebrow. "Look, if whatever you're scared of is smarter than a kid, you'd better start being more careful about what you say. I hope that you haven't been talking like this around everyone in the village."

"I haven't."

"Good. What's your name?"

"Justin Lazarus."

"Mine's Janina. Janina Starcevich. I've decided you're okay, by the way."

A smile like sunlight spilled across his face. "I'm glad. Can I come back and visit again?"

"Sure. We're your boss's next-door neighbor. Did you know that?"

"Mr. and Mrs. Christian live next to you? Really?"

She pointed. "That big white house over there, past the hedge."

He turned his gaze toward the house for a long time. "Do you know them well?"

"Sure. We've known them forever."

"Do you like them?"

It seemed a strange question, but then, nothing about this entire day had been ordinary. "Sure," she finally said.

"Do you think they're trustworthy?"

"Yes," she said, and then, after a moment's pause, "Well, I know that Mrs. Christian is just about one of the nicest people around. I'd trust her with about anything. Mr. Christian is kind of strange—quiet and serious—but I think I'd trust him, too." She looked at him quizzically. "Trustworthy about what, though?"

"Oh, I don't know," he said. She immediately realized that this was the first lie he'd told her. She hoped he was not planning on lying a lot, because he was lousy at it. But she didn't push him to tell her more.

"I should be going," he said abruptly, standing up. "I have to be at work at eleven."

Janina stood, too, and her sudden motion startled a goldfinch that had been perched in a nearby tree. It was only later that it occurred to her to question why the bird had reacted to her movement but not to his. "I'll see you later," she said.

Justin smiled slightly. "Yes, you just might."

CHAPTER 9

I think I must have gaped a little. Somehow, he knew that something had changed. It was one of those electric moments. It seemed to last far longer than it really did. I think that if, at that moment, he'd asked me to leave everything and run away with him, I would have.

He really wasn't that much younger than I was. I was only 28 then, and Justin was certainly no younger than 23 or 24. I'm not trying to excuse myself, understand. I still loved Tom, and I still do, really, despite all that has happened. But looking into those clear gray eyes, still as a dark pool, I suddenly felt that I was with someone I needed. And someone who needed me, that was clear. He was scared about something.

"Well," I said, "I'm sure that it's no more than seeing a handsome but unfamiliar face that makes people in the village look at you twice."

"So, you and Mr. Christian think I'm... odd?"

I laughed. "Odd? You just seem honest, hardworking, and polite to me." And a lot more, but I didn't say that. "I mean, you do seem to have an unusual bit of intuition, you might say. I've heard that mentioned."

His wary expression deepened. "By who?"

"Oh, I don't recall. People just notice things, that's all. You do a good turn for folks, and they remember it. It's things like last week when you loaded up the bags of topsoil near the front door, and Mrs. Wardlow drove up five minutes later needing ten bags of topsoil. It's as if you know about things people need and see to them before they even ask."

His eyes widened. His wariness had become fear, pure and simple. "I don't really know things ahead of time. I don't. Is that what they're saying?"

I laughed again. "No, nothing like that. It's just friendly talk, you know—'That boy up at Christians' Hardware, he sure has a good sense about what everyone needs.' Nothing more serious." I looked at him curiously. "What are you afraid of?"

At that moment, Tom walked in the front door. "Justin, go lock up the front gate," he said as he tossed him the key. Tom continued around behind the counter where I was standing. "Haven't you got the till shut down yet?" he asked me. It sounds bossy, what he said, when I write it down, but he didn't say it that way. He was just like that, if you remember—straightforward. He didn't say anything more or less than what he meant.

"Oh, Justin and I have just been having a chat. I'll only be five minutes." Justin looked at me, and his look told me he was about to say something. I gave him a little shake of my head, too small for Tom to see, as if to say, Don't say anything to Tom about this. He understood. He turned and left without saying anything more.

Janina couldn't sleep.

Jim's warm, comfortable bulk lay stretched out motionless at her side. Even allowing for his size, he took up a significant percentage of the bed, and he was breathing deeply and slowly. She envied him his ability to go to sleep quickly and easily. She had always been a restless sleeper, a dreamer of confused dreams whose point seemed solely to disturb her sleep. While she'd never suffered from insomnia, exactly, going to sleep was not the simple release and drop into unconsciousness that it was for her husband. She found herself irritated by his relaxed breathing and submerged a sudden impulse to elbow him in the ribs.

Instead, she rolled over and began mulling again the same thought that was responsible for delaying her sleep. She had dealt with plenty of angry people during her adult life—angry parents, angry students, angry administrators. Sometimes it seemed to her that as a teacher she was actually nothing more than a glorified peacekeeper. In none of those encounters, however, had she ever come across the kind of cold, bitter hatred that she had heard that day in Joanne Carignoli's voice. It had stayed with her all day, haunting her as if she herself were its object, as if this woman hated her for simply bringing the topic of her brother's death to light.

She found herself wondering, for the hundredth time, where Kathy Christian was tonight. They had always said that Kathy had killed Tom, but Janina had never been told the details, not in so many words. Everything she knew—if information of such dubious genealogy could be called *knowledge*—came from listening in on gossip from her parents and parents' friends. Tales about what had happened varied. Tom had caught Kathy with another man, and her lover had shot him. Kathy had caught Tom with another woman, and Kathy had killed him out of jealousy. The hardware store was going down the drain, and Tom went crazy causing Kathy to kill him in self-defense. Other stories, even less likely. Of what came out in the trial, Janina didn't know. Apparently nothing definite. The case got notoriety enough that, had there been anything proven, it would have become common knowledge.

Janina raised her head slightly. The digital clock read 12:24. She put her head back on her pillow with a little sigh. At least tomorrow was Saturday, and maybe she could sleep in. She rolled onto her back again and frowned at the dark ceiling. An idea was forming in her mind. The library was open on Saturday. She'd heard that they had archives of old newspapers on microfilm there. Maybe that would clear some of this up.

The word came back to her. *Obsessed.* And for no good reason.

Why did she care so much about this? It had all happened decades ago. It was over. There was no reason for her to care.

"But I do," she whispered to the darkness. "I just do."

She woke up the next morning unable to recall how or when she had finally gone to sleep. Jim had risen before her. This was not an unusual occurrence—he was a morning person and was frequently up and around by seven-thirty even on Sundays. On Saturdays, however, he spent a half-day on walk-in cases as well as attending to the needs of his various inpatients. Glancing at the clock, Janina knew that he was probably already gone.

Of their three children, only seven-year-old Katie had inherited her father's tendency to wake early. Sarah, the oldest, might be awake by now but would certainly still be in bed reading. As for Brendan, the middle child, he was the type who had to be physically dumped out of bed if he had to be ready before ten o'clock. Janina lay back, cupped her hands behind her head, and considered how she would be able to go to the Colville Public Library and be back by the time Jim returned, usually around twelve-thirty.

She pulled back the covers, stretched, swung her legs out of bed, yawned, and then stood to rummage about in her dresser for something to wear. She settled on jeans and an old sweatshirt. She ran a brush through her hair, slipped a barrette into it, and padded downstairs barefoot.

Katie, as predicted, was already up, though still pajama-clad. She was sitting on the living room floor, frowning at a partially completed jigsaw puzzle of a coyote. She looked up when her mother entered the room and gave her a reproachful eye.

"I've been waiting for you to get up. I've been up forever."

"I'm sure you have, sweetie. Thanks for playing so nicely and letting me sleep. When did Daddy leave?"

"Not long ago. He said he'd be back early if Mrs. Stenning doesn't bring in one of her cats." This was a running joke, and Janina smiled. Mrs. Stenning was an elderly widow with three overfed Persians, and she had an uncanny knack for walking in five minutes before closing time with some feline distress that had to be seen to immediately.

"Katie, would you like to go to the library with me this morning?"

Katie scowled. "No."

Janina sighed inwardly at her youngest daughter's lack of tact. There was no mystery about which side of the family she'd gotten that from. "Well, what if we stop at Mr. and Mrs. Lee's house on the way back? I saw Mr. Lee in the grocery store a couple of days ago, and he said that his golden lab's puppies were getting old enough to handle. He wondered if maybe you'd like to see them. He said that any time this weekend would be fine."

"Oh, okay." Katie brightened up just as fast as she had scowled. "Would Sarah and Brendan have to come along?"

"Not if they don't want to."

"I hope they don't want to. I'd like to go just the two of us."

Janina smiled. "I think that's pretty likely. Last night at dinner Brendan said that he and some of his pals were getting together to play baseball. I expect that's what he'll do, if he can ever drag himself out of bed. And Sarah will probably just want to hang out around here, if I know her at all."

So, it was forty-five minutes later when Janina and Katie were heading south toward Colville. Katie was working on a drawing of the planet Saturn, carefully balancing paper resting on a book and colored pencils on her lap. While Janina would not exactly have minded chatting with her daughter, at the moment she was glad that Katie was not a chatter, as both of her siblings had been when they were her age. Unless something specific was on her mind, Katie was usually content to stay within her own thoughts and keep them there. This morning, the silence was a welcome companion. It gave Janina time to think.

This nonsense was getting unhealthy. It was interfering with her life—her job, her parenting, her home.

She frowned. But where had the obsession *come* from? It wasn't as if she hadn't thought about Tom and Kathy over the years, and certainly she had heard people talking about them more than once. It was the only village scandal in recent memory, so it was bound to come up here and there.

When Wanda brought them up, though, in the faculty room, it was like something had switched on in her brain that caused everything else to be switched off.

With some alarm, she realized that she had not even put on any music the previous evening, and around the Vannoy house, there was seldom a moment when there wasn't some kind of music playing. It was Janina's great love, and it filled the house to overflowing. One night it would be Natalie Dessay singing French operatic arias, another night spare, cerebral Bach cello suites. Sweet, danceable Schubert quintets one day, and the harsh dissonance of Schönberg's *Verklärte Nacht* the next. The fact that she'd forgotten to pop a CD into the player would not have struck anyone else as odd, but to her, it was like a breath of cold air down her neck. It was indicative of how deeply she had been taken over by this pursuit of hers.

"What's wrong, Mom?" Katie asked with a suddenness that made Janina jump.

"Oh, nothing. Why?"

"You look funny today."

Janina smiled at her daughter's choice of words. "Oh, I'm just thinking about something that happened yesterday. I had to talk to a lady who wasn't very nice, and it kind of upset me. I'm not upset any more, really, but I was thinking about it and wondering about how people can sometimes not be very nice to each other."

She winced inwardly. Good cover. Now she was even being evasive with her daughter.

Katie, however, seemed satisfied and went back to her drawing. Five minutes later they were pulling up alongside the Colville Public Library. Janina tried not to look at the offices of Harcourt and Madsen Realty next door. She hoped that Lynda Rogers wouldn't glance out of a window and notice her there.

Of course, what would Lynda do, even if she saw her?

What on earth was she so afraid of anyway?

They walked up the wide stone stairs in front of the library, through the automatic doors and the theft-sensor gates, and into the lobby. Once inside, Janina bent over and said quietly to her daughter, "Now, Katie, you know where the kids' section is, right?" Katie nodded solemnly. "I'm going right over there." She pointed to the reference desk. "You see that big sign that says 'Reference and Information?' You can see it from anywhere in the library. If you need to find me, just look for the sign and that's where I'll be."

Katie seemed totally unconcerned. She said, "Okay, Mom," and trotted off toward the children's section, sat down at a small, brightly colored table, and began thumbing through a picture book someone had left sitting on it. Janina watched her for a moment, then turned and headed towards the reference desk.

A young woman smiled up at her as she approached the desk. She was very small and slender with straight black hair pulled back away from her round face into a sleek pony tail. She wore a tag that said, "L. Sakai. Assistant Reference Librarian."

"Can I help you?"

"Yes," said Janina quietly. "I'm trying to find old microfilmed newspapers from the summer of 1971. *The Colville Times*, or whatever local paper you might have on file."

"We have the *Times* microfilmed back into the sixties," said the librarian. "It's month by month. What months were you interested in?"

"July and August of 1971."

"Okay, just wait here a moment, please, and I'll get them."

Janina stood fidgeting at the desk, getting more nervous every moment—for no reason she could put her finger on—but the librarian was gone no more than three minutes before she returned with two spools of film.

"Do you know how to use a microfilm reader?"

Janina nodded.

"Okay, then, here they are. Just return them to me when you're done."

Janina thanked her and walked across the aisle to a row of microfilm readers and sat down at the nearest one. She slipped the spool over the pin on the left side of the reader, threaded the film through the platen, and wound it over another spool on the right-hand side. Then, she clicked the light on and began to wind.

July 1971 passed her by in a whirlwind. She thought that Tom had died sometime around the end of July or beginning of August, but she wasn't entirely sure of the date. The words, "Communists Pushed Back in Laos," whizzed past. She slowed down near the end of the spool, and the history of twenty-five years ago began to unwind more slowly—slowly enough to read the headlines clearly. July 25—the headline announced that Dr. Christiaan Barnard of South Africa had done a successful heart/lung transplant. The twenty-sixth was full of news of the launching of Apollo 15. Nothing about anyone killed in Guildford. By the thirty-first, the only thing mentioned of local interest was a brief blurb and a photograph of the Guildford Fair. The bulk of the newspaper was still with the Apollo astronauts, describing their successful landing on the moon and detailing how they were preparing to deploy the land rover. She glanced through the pages without much real interest, and then they ended. Janina rewound the film onto the spool, pulled it off the pin, stuck it in its box, and replaced it with the film for August.

More news about the Vietnam War and war between Pakistan and India. More news of the astronauts as they explored the moon. She realized how unaware of all this she had been at the time. It was only later, when she was a teenager, that the war began to have any impact on her. When she was ten, all she recalled were long, peaceful summers, and longer, but also peaceful, school years. Weird to think that, as she was playing and exploring and sitting in class, people had been fighting and dying or walking on the moon.

Then, she got to the front page of the *Times*, August 7, 1971.

The headline jumped out at her: "Guildford Man Slain in Home." Eagerly, she sharpened up the focus and began to read.

Police report that Thomas Christian, age 30, of 38 King Street in Guildford, was killed yesterday evening in his home by an unknown assailant. Neighbors had reported the sounds of a fight late that afternoon, and the police responding had found Christian unconscious in his living room, bleeding heavily from a gunshot wound to the chest. He was rushed to Colville Area General Hospital where he was pronounced dead upon arrival.

It is reported that the dead man's wife, Katherine Christian, age 28, has been taken into custody. At this time, it is not certain if she will be charged with the death or is only wanted for questioning.

The Christians are both well-known members of the Guildford community. Mr. Christian was the owner and manager of Christian's Hardware and Feed Store on the north end of Guildford village. His wife is a familiar face at the store and is also a respected artist and musician in the community.

Police report that there seems to have been nothing taken from the house. At the present time, no motive for the slaying has been offered.

Janina flipped through the rest of that day's newspaper, and in fact was turning the handle of the spool so quickly that she zipped past the front page of the August 8th edition. Backing up, she saw a second article. Not a banner headline like the first but still on the front page.

WIFE CHARGED IN GUILDFORD SLAYING

Police authorities announced early this morning that they have arrested Katherine Christian, 28, for the brutal slaying of her husband, Thomas Christian, 30. Few details have yet surfaced regarding the death, which has shocked and dismayed the inhabitants of this sleepy farming community.

"It doesn't seem real," neighbor Leonard Starcevich told reporters earlier today. "Kathy and Tom were just regular folk. The kind you see every day, meet on the street, sit next to in church. I can't believe it."

These sentiments were echoed by other members of the community. Guildford's mayor, Charles "Chuck" Upshaw, made a public statement yesterday commenting that this is the first murder in Guildford in over fifty years. "The people of Guildford are at a loss to understand how this could happen to a fine, upstanding man like Tom," the mayor told reporters. "Such a thing has never happened here within anyone's memory."

Days flipped by. On August 9th, the front page had reverted to news of the recently returned astronauts and to the various wars here and there. A short article on the first page of the "Local and Regional" section mentioned the case, stating that Kathy Christian was apparently maintaining silence about the entire affair. It also stated that police were looking for a young man named Justin Lazarus, twenty-two or twenty-three years of age with sandy hair and a slender build, for questioning. There was a hint that he might not be traveling under that name.

Janina frowned. *Justin Lazarus?* That name sounded strangely familiar, but try as she might, she couldn't put a face, nor any other information, together with it. How did he, whoever he was, fit into all of this?

There was nothing further until the eighteenth, but it was well hidden behind a long, fairly self-congratulatory-sounding feature about desegregation. It described how Governor Wallace of Alabama was refusing to comply with integration orders and how much more enlightened everyone was here in the Northeast. The article, a mere two paragraphs at the bottom of the second page, stated simply that Kathy had been brought up in front of district court and was being charged with murder. There was some reason, though, to believe that she may not be fit to stand trial.

The rest of the spool provided nothing of any interest to Janina's search. She returned the films to Ms. Sakai, and after a quick check to make sure that her daughter was still happily occupied with Dr. Seuss in the children's area, she requested the ones for September and October.

She turned through September and found little mention of the case. Funny how today's headline is forgotten tomorrow. Besides brief blurbs to the effect that Kathy had refused the opportunity to hire a lawyer and was being represented by the public defender, and that jury selection was scheduled to begin in October, there was nothing.

She rewound the film and placed October's on the pin. A paragraph on October 2nd stated that jury selection had begun. The trial was scheduled to begin in mid-October, and another brief on the fourteenth stated that this had, in fact, happened. It wasn't until October 31st that the case jumped back onto the front page.

CHRISTIAN'S WIFE FOUND NOT GUILTY BY REASON OF INSANITY

Judge H. Terrell McKeown of Stephens County Court ruled yesterday that Katherine Christian, 28, of Guildford, was not guilty in the slaying of her husband, Thomas Christian, 30, by reason of insanity. Mr. Christian was found unconscious with a gunshot wound to the chest on the evening of August 7th and died in the ambulance on the way to Colville General Hospital.

Mrs. Christian was arrested for the killing the following day. Informed sources report that she brought much suspicion upon herself by refusing to talk to the police. Since her arrest, and especially during her trial, she has exhibited a great deal of bizarre and erratic behavior. The judge's ruling yesterday made it clear that he believed her responsible for her husband's death, but psychiatric testing indicated that she was sufficiently out of touch with reality to render her unable to understand what had happened.

The judge's ruling was met with anger from Joanne Christian, the dead man's younger sister. "She knows perfectly well what she did," Miss Christian told reporters outside the courthouse yesterday afternoon. "That woman has everyone fooled. She's no more insane than I am. She's covering for someone."

It is widely believed that a second person, a drifter traveling under the name of Justin Lazarus, was somehow involved in the slaying. Lazarus was in the employ of Mr. Christian and disappeared immediately after Christian's death. Inquiries were made, but there has been no information regarding Lazarus's whereabouts. Police report that there is no direct evidence to connect him to the killing, but he is still wanted for questioning.

Judge McKeown has recommended that Mrs. Christian be institutionalized at Hazleton for an indefinite period.

Janina leaned back in her chair. So, that was where she ended up. Hazleton Hospital. The local answer to the crazy house. Twenty miles out of Guildford, up near the army depot, surrounded by fences topped with razor wire. Kathy had been in there all that time? It didn't bear thinking about.

"Well, hi there," said a friendly voice behind her. Startled, Janina turned around, and in a swift, almost reflexive motion, simultaneously switched off the light on the microfilm reader.

Martha Alport, Wanda's student teacher, was standing there, smiling, with a stack of books tucked under her arm. "I'm sorry, I didn't mean to interrupt you."

Janina managed a smile. Why, why did she have to look like a frightened mouse every time she was around this woman? "Oh, no, I was just deep in thought. Actually, I'm done, so you didn't really interrupt me. I've got to go collect my daughter, anyhow. I'm surprised she wasn't here ten minutes ago tugging on my sleeve."

Martha laughed. "I just thought I'd say hi. I'm trying to learn everyone's name, so when I'm out and I see one of the faculty, I just have to stop them and practice. You're the music teacher, right? Mrs... don't tell me. Mrs. Vannoy."

"You get a gold star," said Janina. She felt herself relax, put at ease by Martha's guilelessness. "But call me Janina. Oh, and here comes my daughter." Janina signaled to her, and Katie, arms loaded down, tottered up and dumped a brightly-colored variety of books unceremoniously onto the floor.

Martha laughed again. "You must be quite a reader." She leaned over and extended a hand. "I'm Martha. I'm working at your mom's school."

Katie shook her hand solemnly. "My name's Katie."

"Nice to meet you, Katie. I must be going. I'll see you Monday, Janina."

"Enjoy the rest of the weekend."

"You too." Martha strolled off toward the circulation desk.

"What a weird lady," remarked Katie, after Martha had gone out of earshot.

Janina looked at her daughter in perplexity. "I think she seems rather nice. What's weird about her?"

"I don't like it when people read over my shoulder."

"She wasn't reading over your shoulder. What are you talking about?"

"No, not me," said Katie, slowly and deliberately, her brown eyes looking up into Janina's. "*Your* shoulder. She was looking at you for a long time before you turned around. She was standing there while staring at you almost the whole time you were sitting there."

CHAPTER 10

I knew that Justin was hiding something. This, somehow, made him even more attractive to me. I couldn't imagine that it was something bad. There was something about Justin that was so innocent, so sweet. I thought he was probably in trouble, and all I wanted to do was help him.

I thought that Justin should talk to Tom, because I knew that Tom wouldn't have understood if he knew that I'd been talking to Justin behind his back. Tom wasn't a jealous man, exactly, but he didn't think it was proper for me to have male friends. And before Justin talked to Tom, I wanted to know more details, not only to satisfy my own curiosity, but also so I could advise Justin on how to approach the subject.

I felt that if Justin was on the run from the police, or something, Tom might actually help him if he felt that Justin had been dealt with unfairly. Tom always had a very strong sense of fair play, and if he thought Justin had been accused wrongly, he'd risk a lot to help him out, especially since Justin had been a good, hard working employee, even if it had only been a few weeks. I figured that was probably it—that Justin had run afoul of the law. Over drugs, maybe. That was a big deal back then. Still is, I guess. Or maybe he'd gotten some girl pregnant, and her family was looking for him. I couldn't imagine that it was anything more serious than that.

Janina sat by the pond for nearly an hour after Justin had left her. She was no longer afraid, but she still felt restless. She had come to the conclusion that Justin was not some kind of evil magician, which was how she had pictured him before. After talking with him, she found that he seemed almost—although not *quite*—like any ordinary guy. He certainly was friendly and kind. She felt, however, a strange magnetism about him. She was old enough to recognize that he was not what most people called handsome. He was too small, a little on the thin side, and didn't dress or wear his hair like the male models in the magazines her mom read. There was something, though—in his eyes, she thought—that made her remember him, remember every detail.

Janina walked around the side of the house and almost ran into her brother, Doug, who was unstrapping a sack of cat food from the rack on the back of his bicycle. She followed him inside.

"Janina, where on earth have you been?" demanded their mother without preamble as they walked into the house. She was sorting laundry, and as she talked, the tempo of her movements never faltered. "I saw your bicycle in the garage, but I didn't know where you'd gone. Doug, make sure that you don't spill any food as you pour it into the canister, and the empty bag goes into the trash. Don't leave it on the floor like you did last time."

"Okay, Mom," said Doug without looking at his mother as he

proceeded to open the sack of food and pour it into the cat food canister.

"I was out by the pond," Janina said. "Why didn't you just call for me?"

"Well, I didn't know where to call since you didn't tell me where you were. I could hardly call all over the neighborhood. You could have been anywhere."

"I wasn't. I was out at the pond. I didn't think I needed permission to go there."

Doug looked at his sister and rolled his eyes.

"Don't get sassy with me, young lady," Maddy warned.

Janina scowled. "I'm not being sassy."

"I'll be the judge of that." Maddy turned back to the laundry. Janina made a face at her mother, which Maddy either chose to ignore or didn't see. In order to forestall any further sparring, Doug straightened up, still holding the empty sack of cat food, and interjected a cheerful comment.

"Mom, have you met the new guy who works for Mr. Christian?"

Maddy and Janina both looked at Doug. Maddy swiveled her head slowly, but Janina snapped her gaze around at her brother, eyes wide with alarm.

"Georgia Petrie mentioned him. I haven't met him. Why?" Maddy looked curiously at Janina. Janina realized she must look as startled as she felt and wondered if her mother remembered that she'd asked her almost this exact question that morning over breakfast.

"I talked with him a little when I was leaving the store with the cat food. He knows everything about bicycles. He looked at my bike and told me that my handbrakes needed adjusting. He even showed me how to do it. He's cool."

"Cool," repeated Maddy with some distaste. "I suppose that means he wears his hair like a girl and dresses like a tramp."

Doug grinned. "Come on, Mom. There's nothing wrong with

that. When I go away to college, I'm gonna grow my hair really long. Down to my waist."

"I'll send you a nice dress to go with it."

Sarcasm was as close as Maddy ever got to humor.

Doug didn't respond to that. Janina marveled at his ability to bait their mother without either of them getting really angry.

"Well, maybe I'll make a point of going to meet this 'cool' young man down at the hardware store," Maddy said. "Your father mentioned last night at dinner that he was out of rose fertilizer. Perhaps I'll go pick up a box for him."

Janina looked at Doug, who glanced back with a little smile. Both knew that if their mother was going to make a special trip to the hardware store for fertilizer, it was motivated by curiosity rather than by any desire to save her husband trouble.

"Can I come along?" asked Janina in a small voice.

Maddy gave her daughter another curious glance. So did Doug, who then looked thoughtful and went to the trash can to dispose of the empty cat food bag.

"I don't see why not," said Maddy. "We can go when I've finished putting away the laundry." She stood, carrying a stack of impeccably folded clothes, and walked out of the room.

Janina watched her mother go, and then just stood there looking down the hall, a distant expression on her face.

"Okay, kid. Give," said Doug suddenly.

Janina started, then turned to look at him. "What?"

"What do you know about the new guy at Christians'? You got this funny look on your face when I was talking about him. Like you'd just been thinking about him, or just seen him, or something."

Janina didn't answer.

"I thought so," her brother said, satisfied. "So, what's with him?"

"I can't tell you."

"Why not?"

"Oh, Doug, don't ask."

Doug stopped, his easy grin fading as he realized that Janina was genuinely upset. "What's the matter?"

"I don't know. I don't understand anything." Janina took a deep, hitching breath, then scowled.

"Look, don't be mad. I didn't mean to make you mad."

"I know. I'm not mad. And it isn't you. It's... everything."

"Okay, whatever." Doug shrugged, but his face still registered concern. "Look, if you want to talk about it…."

Janina cut him off. "I don't."

"Okay," Doug said again. He seemed about to say something more but changed his mind. Any opportunity for conversation was cut off as Maddy reentered the room.

"Are you ready, Janina?"

Janina nodded, gave her brother a quick and somewhat ambiguous look, and followed her mother through the door into the garage.

Car trips with Janina and her mother—even long ones, which this one was not—were usually fairly quiet. Somehow, when forced into close quarters, neither of them seemed to be able to think of anything to say unless they were quarreling.

"Looks like George Flynn is having his roof replaced."

"Mmm-hmm."

There was a long pause.

"How many weeks till school starts again?"

"Four, I think."

Another long pause ensued.

"I expect your father will be surprised when he finds out I got his rose fertilizer for him."

"Mmm-hmm."

It was a relief to both of them when they pulled into the parking lot of the hardware store. Janina looked out of her window as her mother eased into a parking space between a battered pickup and a maroon station wagon. Justin was standing near the front door of the store using a garden hose to water the trays of annuals that Janina's father had admired several weeks ago.

Maddy and Janina both got out of the car. Maddy looped her purse over her arm and made her way to the front door. She kept her eye on the young man with the hose.

Justin looked up, recognized Janina, and smiled. Janina smiled back, a little wanly.

Maddy walked toward him and stopped very deliberately in front of the plant trays. She picked up a flat of marigolds and looked at it critically. "Isn't it a bit late to be planting out annuals?" Maddy said with an air of superiority but without looking up.

Justin gave her a sweet smile, which she ignored. "I'm not planting them, ma'am, just watering them."

Maddy set the flat down and picked up a second one. She still didn't look at him but examined a flat of zinnias with exaggerated interest. "I'm Mrs. Starcevich. Thank you for helping my son with his bicycle today."

"No problem, ma'am. He's a nice boy."

Maddy's right eyebrow rose a fraction of an inch. She looked up at Justin. Janina had been listening to them both—her mother's haughty comments, Justin's innocent replies—and wondered how long it would take either for her mother to accuse the young man of disrespect or for Justin to get fed up and tell Mrs. Starcevich to mind her own business.

Neither happened. Maddy froze, whatever sour response she'd been intending to make caught on her lips, as their eyes met. It only lasted a fraction of a second. Then, Maddy's open mouth shut suddenly, and Justin, unaffected, returned to watering the plants.

Maddy's superior stance was gone. She fumbled with her purse strap, cleared her throat, and said, "Well, thank you for helping my son with his bicycle today."

"No problem, ma'am. He's a nice boy," said Justin.

Janina's heart skipped a beat. Hadn't she just lived through this moment in time?

Maddy attempted an ingratiating smile, failed, and turned away toward the front door. Janina followed, throwing a frightened backward glance at Justin who was looking at her with a thoughtful expression.

Kathy was at the counter, as usual. "Hello, Mrs. Starcevich. Janina," she said as the bell on the door jingled. "How are you both today?"

"I'm fine, thank you." But Maddy sounded anything but fine. Her voice was tentative, and her face was pale. Janina, for once, hoped that Kathy wouldn't speak to her directly. She felt like if she tried to talk now, she'd squeak like a mouse.

Maddy and Janina walked down toward the garden tools. Maddy suddenly stopped, and said, more to herself than to Janina, "I've completely forgotten what we came here for."

"Rose fertilizer," said Janina, and was glad that, despite her worries, her voice sounded normal.

"Of course." They proceeded towards the aisle with the fertilizer, selected a box of it—Janina wondered how her mother, who never touched anything connected with gardening if she could help it, would know the right kind—and brought it to the counter.

Kathy rung up the purchase. While Maddy was paying for it, she said, "Keep those roses blooming. Your yard is the talk of the neighborhood."

Maddy worked up a weak smile. Janina wondered what could have happened that had destroyed her mother's usual self-possession. Kathy seemed to have noticed it, too.

"Mrs. Starcevich, are you all right? You look a bit faint. Do you need a drink of water?"

Maddy seemed to pull herself together, and her voice regained a bit of its old asperity. "No, I'm fine. I assure you. The sun is a bit hot today. I'm not used to it, that's all."

Kathy thanked her and handed over the receipt. She looked rather perplexed, though, by Maddy's odd behavior. So, for that matter, was Janina, although she had an inkling of what—or more accurately, who—was responsible for it. She began to wonder if her first estimation of Justin as being innocent and harmless had been correct.

The bell jingled as Maddy and Janina walked out of the store. Janina looked over toward the rack of flowers, but Justin had evidently finished watering them and was nowhere to be seen. They climbed back into the car, and Maddy backed out into the parking lot without saying anything.

"Well," said Janina finally, in a small voice. "What did you think of him? That guy who was watering the flowers?"

Maddy frowned slightly. "Oh, yes," she said, as if she'd been thinking of something else entirely—or perhaps of nothing at all. "Very nice young man." She cleared her throat. "It was very kind of him to help Doug with his bicycle."

CHAPTER 11

I guess it was more serious than all that, though, because one day, some men showed up at my house. It was a Monday morning, I remember that, and Tom had already left for work. These men claimed to be from the FBI and said that they were looking for Justin. They wouldn't tell me what they wanted him for, but it scared the life out of me. All of a sudden, Justin's concerns about fitting in and not attracting attention made sense.

Then, they went to talk to Tom, and he believed them completely. Suddenly, he became convinced that Justin was some kind of desperate criminal, even though the FBI men never told us why they were looking for him.

Justin didn't show up to work that day. We didn't see him the next morning, either, when he was supposed to start his shift. Instead of being mad, Tom felt it was good riddance to bad rubbish, especially after he found out that these FBI men had been asking about Justin all over the village. Then came the evening of August 7, 1971.

It was a sullen, muggy sort of day. Everybody was on edge

already. Right after dinner, the doorbell rang. I got up to answer it.

Justin was at the door. He looked terrified. I didn't know what to say, but my heart just ached to see him looking so afraid. I asked him what it was all about, quietly, hoping that Tom wouldn't hear us talking and come to find Justin at the door. I had a feeling that I knew what would happen if he saw him.

And then, Justin told me... oh, Janina, you'll think I'm crazy, I know you will. He said that the FBI men weren't FBI men at all. He said he was being hunted by some people who wanted to hurt him, maybe kill him. He said that they had already killed most of his friends and family, and he thought he'd be safe in Guildford because it was so remote. He had been terrified that they'd eventually catch up with him.

And now they had....

✩✩✩

It was a typical Tuesday morning. Janina taught music theory first period, and it was populated by the typical weird array of rock guitarists, aspiring musical dramatists, and classical musicians that the course always seemed to attract. When the bell rang, the first students to enter were Jim Lacy, arrayed in dreadlocks and a tie-dyed t-shirt, and his girlfriend Amy McCaffrey, resplendent in a scarlet pullover and a cream-colored cotton dress. Next came Steve Michaels, wearing jeans, a button-down plaid shirt, and wire-rim glasses. Janina smiled. There was a complete microcosm of high school music theory, personified. But how many would guess who was which? Jim certainly didn't look to be the aspiring actor he was. His frizzed hair, when pulled back into a rough ponytail, had looked strangely apt for his role as the embattled John Proctor in last December's performance of *The Crucible*. He sang as well as he acted, and he had easily garnered a lead in the spring musical, which opened in only a few days. The elegant Amy was a superlative pianist and aspiring composer. And Steve, despite his lack of flamboyance, was the lead guitarist in an alternative rock band called "Cholera" that had played for two years running at the annual Colville Music Fest.

"Have you met Mrs. Corliss's new student teacher?" Steve was saying as they entered.

"Yeah, she's hot," responded Jim with gusto, which elicited a playful slap from Amy.

"You gotta admit, she's better than the Great Pumpkin," said Steve.

Janina swallowed a snicker and turned to straighten up the papers on her desk so that her students wouldn't notice that she had not only overheard them but found them funny. She had heard this nickname for Wanda before and had to admit it was all too apt.

"She's too nice," said Amy, her expression thoughtful.

"What do you mean by that?" Steve asked. "How can anyone be too nice?"

"It seems fake. Like there's something hard underneath it." She shook her head. "I don't know."

Any further analysis was cut off by the noise of other arriving students, and then the late bell. Janina found that she couldn't keep her mind on her lesson—of course, that was not anything unusual lately. Stray thoughts kept getting in her way.

Someone else besides Katie thought Martha was weird. But why? She seemed perfectly okay.

Although, had Martha really been behind her the whole time at the library, reading over her shoulder? If so, why?

Then, from somewhere deeper in the recesses of her brain, the obsession pushed its way back in.

What was Kathy doing right now?

She gave an inward wince. At that moment, she decided

she'd have to tell Jim about all of this. She never hid anything from him, and here she was being secretive.

It was too much like lying for her comfort.

Afterward, maybe she could forget about it. She'd found what she wanted to know—where Kathy was. That was enough. It *had* to be enough.

If it wasn't, the next step was to call a psychiatrist.

She actually did a fair job of forgetting about it for the remainder of the day. She threw herself into directing her select chorus. They sounded great, which was a good thing since they only had a week to go before the spring concert. Maybe they really could pull off the *Geographical Fugue.* It was such a crowd pleaser, but it had to be nearly perfect, or it didn't work at all. Today it had worked, but up on the stage in front of an audience—well, she'd just have to wait and see.

During lunch she watched Martha closely, looking for signs of the interior hardness that Amy had noticed. She saw none. Martha sat next to her master teacher, at first listening politely to Wanda's nonstop stream of conversation, talking very little. What she said was always clear and pertinent. Then, she had found a common interest in Shakespearean tragedy with Lucy Donahue, the honors history teacher, and they chatted for a while about Kenneth Branagh's *Hamlet.*

The four card-players in the corner of the faculty room spent the entire lunch period trying to watch Martha without being obvious about it. As a result, it was obvious to everyone. When Lucy left, she swept past them with one eyebrow arched and said, "I'm sure the nurse has some liniment you could apply to those nasty cricks in the neck you gentlemen all seem to be suffering from," to the general amusement of everyone else in the room. Martha herself laughed merrily and seemed quite cognizant of the effect she was having. Still, Janina reflected, it was nothing very unusual for a beautiful young woman to be well aware of the fact.

Janina returned to her classroom further determined not to worry herself about the Christian affair, or anything else besides her family and her work. When the final bell rang, she was in a much more cheerful state of mind than she had been in weeks. She drove home to the music of one of Haydn's symphonies and arrived before her children's bus did. The silence which greeted her when this happened was always welcomed. She walked to the end of the driveway to fetch the mail—it turned out to be quite a stack today—went inside, and popped a CD into the player. Something by Mozart. She hardly even looked at the label, because anything by Mozart was fine by her. Then she put on water for tea.

She began to flip through the mail. Village of Guildford water and sewer service bill. A catalog advertising fall bulbs. "You're just a tad early," Janina said aloud, placing it in the discard stack. Advertisements from J. C. Penney and the local grocery store. A letter from her mother addressed to "Miss Katherine Vannoy." Katie would be elated. She finally received a letter from Grandma. Lastly, a legal-size envelope, quite full, with no return address.

She glanced at the cancellation to see where it was posted from, and her heart did a back flip. It was postmarked Hazleton, NY.

"No," Janina said. "No. Dear God. It can't be."

She tore open the flap of the envelope. Inside were a number of sheets of long, close-ruled yellow paper covered back and front by a neat, regular handwriting that showed little regard for margins. It ran nearly from edge to edge, top to bottom for six pages, back and front.

She read the first lines.

May 4, 1996

Dear Janina,

I do not have a great deal of hope that you will remember me, and even less if you remember you will want to help me. Many years have passed since we were acquainted and after all you were so young then....

"No," she repeated, her voice almost a whisper. "It can't be."

Hands trembling, she turned the letter over and began to read the last paragraphs.

And so, Janina, I don't know what else I can say. What I have written will have to stand on its own merit. I fully realize that there is nothing, really, that I can offer to convince you that what I've said is true, if you're not already convinced. I don't have a shred of evidence. All I have— literally all—is my memory of what happened, which is still as clear as a cloudless sky. I swear to you that I have reported the truth. My writing of it may be rambling or less than coherent, but everything in this letter is the truth. Where I am now, there is no need to lie.

I don't know why exactly I'm asking you to do this. I don't know what it could accomplish, even if you succeed. But I knew I had to connect with you, somehow. I don't know why, but I'm sure that you are the one who can help me. I believe you are, or were, selected. Perhaps just as I was.

Think this over. You are married now and probably have children. I realize that you have many responsibilities and must think of the people you care about first. But I also know that I must get back to Guildford somehow. I know I can't do that if you don't help me. You are truly my only hope.

Please don't try to write back to me. I hate to think of what would happen if this letter, or any letter you wrote answering it, were to be intercepted. There are people here who are untrustworthy—if that is the right word! It would be easier if you contacted Leo Carson, who is a nurse here who can be trusted. I've told him you might call him. He lives in Emerson, a little village north of here.

As I said before, I will try to understand if you cannot, or do not, help me.

Thank you for reading this.

With love,
Katherine Raynes Christian

Janina stared at the signature for a few seconds, and without warning, she began to cry. Her whole body was racked by great, gasping sobs while sweet, light Mozart serenades shimmered around her. All she could do was stare at that signature—that neat, elegant signature that was the embodiment of the Kathy Christian she remembered. Finally, still weeping uncontrollably, Janina ran to her bedroom, stuffed the letter into the bottom of her underwear drawer, and collapsed onto the bed.

Fortunately, she had gotten somewhat better control over herself by the time the kids arrived. The older two immediately disappeared into their rooms. Only Katie hung around, fiddling aimlessly with things and several times looking over at her mother with a frown.

Finally, Katie gave an exasperated sigh. "Mom," she said, in a scolding tone, "you're just angry all over!"

Janina's smile was a little forced, but at least she smiled. "Why do you say that, sweetie? I haven't yelled at you, have I?"

"No, I don't mean at me. You're angry everywhere."

That was accurate enough. She *was* angry. Angry at how she'd been caught, almost against her will, in this crazy web. Angry at the letter, and its careful, reasonable-sounding prose.

Angry at mental institutions, gossips, policemen, and strange drifters who cause trouble.

But most of all, angry at memories that wouldn't leave her alone.

Janina knelt down and reached out her arms. Katie came over and leaned against her mother, but she was still scowling and unmollified.

"Katie, honey," Janina said, soothingly. "You're right, in a way. I've had a lot on my mind. I am angry—angry at the way people treat each other sometimes. But I don't want you to think I'm mad at you or that it has anything to do with you, Brendan, Sarah, or Daddy. It's just something I have to think through. I'll get over it, okay?"

Katie nodded but didn't look particularly cheered up.

Jim arrived home at about five-thirty, and when he walked into the kitchen, Janina was adding chopped green peppers to a pot of chili. She gave him a smile and a kiss, and they chatted about his day at the clinic—the familiar, warm, sweet routine. It seemed cheering, somehow, and she knew that she couldn't tell Jim about everything that had happened yet. She would. She would have to eventually, of course, but not now.

She turned back to the chili, and Jim came up behind her to wrap his arms around her waist. She leaned back against him and closed her eyes with one hand still on the wooden spoon. She simply enjoyed the feeling of contact with her husband. Everything about it, from his radiant warmth and gentle touch down to the faint antiseptic smell that was so characteristic of him—that he could never quite get rid of—she loved.

"Lousy day at school, eh?" he asked, in a quiet voice.

The tears jumped back into her eyes with an alarming speed, but she forced them away. How did he always know? "Yeah," she said quietly. "I suppose it was."

"Like to talk about it?"

"Well... no." He didn't respond, and she continued. "Not yet.

Please don't be worried. It's nothing, really. I just don't feel like talking about it right now. It's almost dinnertime, anyways, and I don't want to explain it to the kids if they overhear...."

"Hey, it's okay." His voice was still gentle and soothing. "I was just a little concerned."

She turned and rubbed her cheek against his shoulder. "I'm fine, so don't worry. I'll tell you about it, I promise. But not now."

Later, she was lying in bed—once again unable to sleep—cursing Kathy Christian and the whole situation. Over the past few weeks, how many hours of sleep had she lost because of this? Why couldn't she let it go? Her husband and children were starting to figure out that something was wrong. How soon would it be before they became really worried? Before Jim suggested psychiatric help?

Janina crept silently out of bed. Jim didn't stir but continued to snore softly, his head and one bare shoulder poking out from under the blanket. Janina padded over to her dresser and pulled open the top drawer. After a moment's fishing about in the dark, her hand closed on the letter.

She crossed the floor and opened the bedroom door silently before walking down the hall. The entire house was completely quiet except for the ticking of the clock in the living room. She went into the kitchen, the blue and gray tile floor cold beneath her feet, and she sat down at their dining table.

The clock on the stove read 12:42. She wouldn't have the luxury of sleeping in tomorrow morning like she did last time. She knew without a doubt, though, that she wouldn't sleep—couldn't sleep—before she'd read this whole letter and found out exactly what strange story Kathy had to tell.

She pulled the letter out of its envelope and began to read.

PART 2

THE

HUNT

BEGINS

CHAPTER 1

Silverware clinked against plates. A bowl of mashed potatoes hit the table top with a hollow clunk. A throat was cleared as a chair leg squeaked across the floor. The silence in between was almost shrill. It seemed so full of tension that if someone spoke the air itself would shatter.

Janina knew what was wrong. Indeed, she was probably the only one who did. Doug was looking worried, but he probably thought someone was mad at someone, most likely their mother at their father for one of the hundred obscure reasons she always had at hand, so the family was being given the silent treatment. Leonard, on the other hand, seemed blissfully unaware of anything the matter. He normally didn't talk while eating anyway and acted as if he were enjoying the unusual silence almost as much as he was enjoying the food.

Maddy was the problem. It was Maddy who kept the flow of talking going in the house. The kids talked if they were excited about something. Leonard talked when the subject was gardening and sometimes about the latest idiocies perpetrated by Mayor

Upshaw. But Maddy talked about anything as long as she had an audience that was willing to respond with more than a nod or a grunt.

Tonight, however, she had stopped talking. She didn't seem angry. She seemed bemused, almost dreamy. When Leonard had gotten home, he had asked her how her day was.

"We went up to Christians' Hardware and met Tom's new helper." Maddy's voice was vague and toneless. "He's a nice boy. He helped Doug with his bicycle."

When Janina had heard that, she had wanted to scream, to run up to her father and make him understand that that "nice boy" had somehow hypnotized her mother, or something. One look and Maddy's brain had been wiped clean. Janina wanted to warn him about Justin.

Don't trust him. Don't look at him. He's dangerous.

How would her father respond to such an outburst? Gentle puzzlement was the strongest emotion he ever seemed to feel. There was no way she could have communicated the panic she felt, at least not in such a way as to make him understand. In the end, she said nothing.

☆☆☆

The next day dawned dark and thundery. No prospects of outside play today. Maddy seemed to be back to her former self. Over breakfast, she made an acidic response to Leonard's thankfulness for rain. Usually her mother's sharp tongue irritated Janina on her father's behalf, but today she felt almost happy about it. It seemed like the family she knew had returned.

Leonard went off to work, and Janina was left indoors to play with toys that were suddenly dull and lifeless as the rain swirled down in veils and ribbons. The wind threw an occasional spray across her window, and thunder rumbled in the distance. She rarely sought out her mother's company while playing indoors, and today she felt even less like being around her. Neither, however, was she comfortable being alone. She moped about in her room until lunch time, ate a sandwich and a piece of fruit, then returned to her room as the afternoon hours stretched out in front of her, seeming ten times longer than they really were.

She drew pictures for a while without any real enthusiasm, looked through a book on dinosaurs that she was no longer very interested in, and then finally, in desperation, she began rummaging around in her desk. After pulling out most of the contents of the top drawer, she found the little white Panasonic AM/FM radio her Grandma Larkin had given her for her last birthday. At the time, she had not found it a particularly appealing gift. After leaving it on her desk until her mother had forgotten about it and therefore could not accuse her of being ungrateful, she had thrown it into her drawer and forgotten it as well.

Now, stuck inside with no company except her own unsettled thoughts, she took it out and began to fiddle with it. The batteries were old but still had enough juice in them to produce a crackle of static as soon as she turned it on. She dialed across music, blips of newscasts, commercials, and more static.

"... back to back hits... Apollo astronauts report that the mission seems... sale today at ShopRite... peace activists march protesting Vietnam...."

And then, near the upper end of the dial, the static gave way to a sudden swell of music, enticing Janina to stop, transfixing her.

It was like nothing she had ever heard before. Her brother always had his radio on the rock stations—her mother called it loud trash, but that had as little impact on Doug as everything else she said. To Janina it was just "Doug's music" and had become nothing more than background noise. Her father occasionally listened to Lawrence Welk, but that had never excited any real interest in either Janina or him. But this... this was magic. It was as if she were a bowed string, and the music had set her vibrating in resonance.

Then, the singing started, and Janina's mouth fell open in an expression that would have been comical had the moment not been so solemn. She sat, unmoving, hardly breathing, until the music ended. A voice spoke from the radio, and it said to her—at that moment, it seemed to speak to her alone in the universe—"The opening chorus of the *Magnificat in D*, by Johann Sebastian Bach. We have just heard the London Baroque Orchestra alongside the English Philharmonia Choir."

Janina closed her mouth and took a deep breath. She was near tears and near laughing at the same time. Such an intensity of emotion flowed through her that she could not comprehend it. At that moment, she knew that she would do anything to be able to produce music like that and to be a part of that incredible interweaving of sound. All her troubles, including the mysterious Justin, were swallowed up in the grandeur of music.

Mozart followed Bach, Haydn followed Mozart, and Sibelius followed Haydn for another three and a half hours. Janina hardly moved a muscle. She had happened upon the one station in range of her little radio on the one afternoon a week that it played classical music. Somehow, she knew this was a watershed moment, a turning point, something that would change her life forever. She couldn't have explained how she knew, but it was certain.

In that moment, nothing else mattered but her and the music.

Janina could not find herself worrying about much of anything for the rest of that day. Her father returned, dinner was placed before her and duly eaten, and she responded to questions and comments in a manner as bemused as her mother's had been the previous day. No one seemed to notice except possibly Doug, who once or twice gave her a peculiar glance at the dinner table.

Chores done, Janina once again retired to her room trying vainly to find another classical music station. All she heard were news reports, rock-and-roll, and a station or two playing forties-style big band music. None of it seemed to call to her in the way the other music had. She went to bed exhilarated and a little frustrated but did not give a thought to Justin.

☆☆☆

The weather cleared the next day. After another unsuccessful session with her radio, Janina went outside and was practicing roller-skating in the driveway when Tom Christian left for work. He gave her an unsmiling but not exactly unfriendly nod before getting into his car. She found herself momentarily thinking of the hardware store and Justin. At that moment, her left skate skidded on a pebble eliciting an unceremonious fall onto her hands and knees. The sharp, angry pain from a pair each of scraped palms and scraped knees drove the thought away. She sat up, glancing at her hands. The skin was scuffed on the right one and actually broken on the left. Three drops of bright scarlet blood beaded up, glistening on her palm. She sucked on the injury briefly, scowled away any desire to cry, and resolutely got back up again. Justin was once more banished from her mind.

The day crawled by like only midsummer days can crawl. The dusk at bedtime faded into a night so short that it seemed that morning came in the closing of an eye. Her dreams were filled with snippets of music, and she felt she was chasing them like a kitten chasing falling leaves. It was a dream filled to the brim with the intense frustration that had filled her day. She had come back to the radio over and over during the past twenty-four hours, but the music was gone. Gone forever, perhaps—but that did not bear thinking about. She could not leave the radio alone. It was a magnet pulling her back, teasing her with its promise of beauty. Shortly before going to bed, she had been so frustrated that she had almost thrown it against the wall, but that of course would end any chance of ever finding the music again.

It never occurred to her to share this discovery with her parents. She loved them both, but even at this age, she had discovered that there was an unbridgeable gulf between her and them. She was sure they wouldn't understand how the music had conquered her. She was even uncertain that they—her mother, really—might not forbid it. Far better to keep it secret. Secrecy was a reflex, a response to protect something she felt to be more valuable than anything she had ever experienced.

Still, the walls of her bedroom were beginning to tire her, and she asked her mother after breakfast the next morning if she could go to the little park on Lawrence Street near the public library. Her mother acquiesced—somewhat suspiciously—and after a stern injunction to be home by lunch, Janina took off on her bicycle. She was wearing a little green backpack where she had stowed her radio, a packet of graham crackers pinched from the kitchen when Maddy wasn't looking, and Neeno, her stuffed bear.

It was a warm morning, promising a hot day. The ride to the park left her sweating even though it had been shaded nearly all the way by the huge sugar maples that lined the village streets. The park was nearly empty. A pair of young mothers pushing toddlers in the swings and two shirtless high-school age boys throwing a frisbee were the only people visible. She coasted onto the grass, then walked her bike over to a big fir tree in the middle of the park. This tree was one of her favorite spots. It had branches that swept the ground, but the interior was hollow and formed a gigantic, cool teepee the sunlight flickered through when the branches were moved by the wind. Janina nudged her kickstand with her toe, propped her bike, and disappeared into the tree. She took off her backpack and sat down with her back to the massive trunk as she pulled out her precious radio and turned it on.

Nothing but the usual. Not so many news reports, but still nothing aside from rock, big band, and commercials. She shut it off in disgust. Then she found herself wanting to cry but got out a graham cracker and nibbled at it instead.

"Hi again," said a voice.

She looked up, startled, and saw Justin peering through the branches at her.

Panic flashed across her mind. Why had she left her house where she was safe?

Then, an even more disconcerting thought occurred to her. How on earth had he found her?

"I saw your bike," he said, smiling easily at her, as if in answer.

"What do you want?" Her voice was thin and reedy in her own ears.

"Just to say hi. This is a great place you've got here."

Janina stared at him. It was amazing how she could feel terrified of this strange man one time, totally at ease with him the next, and then be terrified of him again. "What did you do to my mother?" she said, her voice still high and squeaky. "Did you hypnotize her or something?"

Justin's smile faded. "What are you talking about?"

"Don't ask me that!" Janina shrilled. "You know what I'm talking about. You know just what I'm talking about, so don't lie!"

The rest of his smile dropped away. "I didn't hypnotize her," he said, his voice inflectionless and weary. "I turned her thoughts away onto a different track."

"Why?"

"Because she wanted to ask me questions I couldn't answer."

"How did you know that?" she asked, her voice bitter and accusing. "And how did you know I'd be here, and how did you find me that day by the pond? And about the truck tire on the day of the parade? How did you know?"

"I don't know how. I just do."

Janina considered this. "Well, whatever, what do you want? I know it isn't to say hi. You're a terrible liar."

The smile broke out again, sweet as sunshine after rain. "I know."

"So, what do you want?"

"I wanted to talk to you. Look…." He parted the fir branches and stepped inside, then hunkered down beside her. "You ask me how I know things sometimes? Well, I know I can trust you. Don't ask how, but I know. I'm here to ask you for a favor."

"I already gave you one." She scowled at him. "I promised not to tell anyone about you. And I haven't, either."

"I know. This is a bigger favor." He looked at the ground. "I wish I could explain everything to you, but it wouldn't be safe. For me or for you. But I'll tell you this, I'm in a lot of trouble. Not trouble like you'd usually think of, but I'm in danger. Bad danger, and I'm afraid that other people might get hurt. I have to leave soon. All I'm asking you is this…." He reached out his hand and touched Janina's forehead. Suddenly, her hazel eyes went blank, and the taut muscles in her face relaxed. The angry scowl smoothed away leaving in its place a look expressionless as a doll.

Justin moved his face close to hers, and his voice dropped to an almost inaudible murmur like the wind in the fir branches. "I may need help. It may be soon, or it may be later, much later. All I'm asking is that if I need help sometime, you'll try to help me. I swear to you that I am not trying to hurt anyone. I've never wanted to hurt anyone. But I've been alone for a long time, and I need someone who I can count on to help me when the time comes. Will you do that for me, Janina? Wait, listen, and help me when I need your help?"

Without blinking or moving, Janina whispered, "Yes. I will help you."

"Good. Thank you." He touched her forehead again, and she blinked, looked confused for a moment, then looked up at him. The scowl returned, but there was a measure of ambivalence in it now.

"What's that you got?" he asked brightly.

She looked down at her hand, still holding the partially eaten graham cracker, and frowned. He laughed and pointed. "No, that, silly."

"It's my radio."

He picked it up, smiling. "You like music?"

Even her distrust of Justin couldn't mask her intensity on this topic. "Yes." The word came out like a plea.

"When I was growing up, we always had music. If you know what station to tune in to, you can sometimes find music like it on the radio. Let me see." He began to turn the tuning dial. There was the familiar static and blips of other radio programs, and then, spilling out from the speakers was the most beautiful music she had ever heard. It surpassed even the classical music of two days ago. It was as if the stars and the sun themselves had acquired voices. It brought tears of sweet, painful joy to her eyes. Justin smiled at her a little sadly before setting the radio down on the soft, needle-strewn ground. Then he was gone.

The music ended after minutes or hours—Janina could not be sure which it was—without any announcer's voice to give it a name. Silence followed it, many minutes of silence broken by nothing but the wind, the birds, and the voices and laughter of the two boys playing frisbee. Finally, when she was sure that no more music was forthcoming, she picked up the little radio and looked at it.

The radio's switch was set to "off." Somehow she knew it would be. When she switched it on, she was greeted by a crackle of static that seemed to her to be the most empty, despairing sound she had ever heard. There was a dry little click as she shut it off. Then, still clutching the radio in her hand, she wept bitterly.

CHAPTER 2

Janina felt like she had just closed her eyes when her clock radio went off at six o'clock. As always on work mornings, Jim was already up. Janina, on the other hand, had not only slept right through Jim's alarm clock but through the inevitable blanket tug-of-war that happened when he got out of bed. She yawned and stretched, resisted the urge to hit the snooze, and pulled her unwilling body out from under the covers. At least now that spring was here, it was beginning to be warmer in the mornings. Getting out of bed to face an upstate New York January morning was nothing short of brutal.

By the time she was up, showered, and dressed, Jim was alrcady sitting at thc brcakfast tablc, rcading thc *Colville Times*, and finishing his second cup of coffee.

"Anything interesting happening in the world?" Janina asked as she walked into the room.

"Well, Senator D'Amato says that in order to fix the schools, there need to be more requirements for teacher certification. He's suggesting so many graduate courses every five years, or your certificate lapses."

"Ah," said Janina. "So, if I take a three-credit summer course in the structure of fourteenth century Gregorian chant, it'll make me a better high school chorus teacher."

"That's the idea."

"God, what a brain wave. I wish I'd thought of that myself. It could revolutionize education nationwide."

Jim gave her a genial smile. "Biting sarcasm becomes you, my dear. Especially given such a deserving target."

Janina smiled back and poured herself a bowl of cereal. "Well, *really*." She added milk to her bowl, served herself orange juice from a yellow pitcher, and then sat down.

Jim glanced at his watch. "I've got to go." He folded his paper and drained the last of his coffee. "Hate to get up just as you're starting breakfast, but I've got two dogs to spay this morning, and I've got to get things ready. Plus, I think Mrs. Warren is bringing Mitzi-Pie in early, and heaven above help me if I'm not there to meet her." He stood. "Coffee breath," he warned, then leaned over and kissed Janina anyway.

"No problem, I'm used to it." Janina reached out and touched his arm. "Jim?"

He paused, and turned to look at his wife questioningly.

"I know you don't have time now, but I need to talk to you about something. When do you think you'll be home?"

"Well, provided everything goes as planned, I'll probably be back at my usual five or five-thirty. Is this a let's-talk-while-making-dinner thing, or a wait-till-the-kids-are-in-bed thing?"

"Oh, I think we can talk it over while making dinner. As long as we don't have all three of them hanging on my every word or clamoring for attention. That won't happen, of course. It's nothing secret, anyhow. I just need your opinion about something."

"Okay, no problem." He kissed her again. "Have fun today."

"Always do. Don't be too mean to Mrs. Warren's baby

doggie."

Jim laughed. "Oh, I won't. But Mrs. Warren's baby doggie is gonna be a little surprised to find out that I intend to take most of the zip out of her sex life."

Janina finished her breakfast, gave her own cursory read-through to the article on education, and responded to the honorable Senator D'Amato's ideas by jamming the newspaper with unnecessary vigor into the recycle bin. By this time, all three children—even Brendan, miracle of miracles—were up, dressed, and mostly ready to catch the school bus. She gave each a kiss and a quick barrage of questions—"Everyone got lunches? Backpacks? Homework? Teeth brushed?" After receiving a chorus of affirmatives, she saw them out the front door. She then stuffed some errant papers into her own book bag, grabbed her sweater, and rushed out herself.

The drive to school was short, but normally it was a time to quiet her mind in preparation for the day's classes. Today, however, it refused to be quieted. The contents of Kathy's letter had filled it to overflowing, and it simply would not quiet down. Questions kept coming to her mind, questions with no real answers.

Was Kathy actually crazy? No one not in her right mind could write a letter that lucid.

Right?

But even if Kathy wasn't crazy, how could Janina do what she'd asked? It was illegal, not to mention dangerous.

No, more than that, it was impossible.

But if Kathy were telling the truth, how could she do otherwise?

There had to be someone else she could talk to. She'd already decided to tell Jim, but maybe someone else who had no vested interest in what she did?

Maybe Lucy Donahue would listen. Lucy had better sense than just about anyone else Janina knew. And she was honest. If Janina was being an idiot, Lucy would have the guts to tell her so.

She pulled into the school parking lot, parking her little blue Volkswagen between the principal's flashy red Saab and the hulking Dodge van belonging to Mrs. Cavanaugh, who taught ninth grade history and had eight children.

That was it, then. She'd talk to Lucy first chance she had.

As luck would have it, Janina saw Lucy in the main office as she was checking her teacher's mailbox. Lucy was standing at the photocopy machine glowering at the screen in a most uncharacteristic fashion. "This machine is possessed by Satan," she pronounced darkly, sounding for all the world like the Grand Inquisitor at a medieval heresy trial. She knelt in front of it, yanked open the doors, twisted a mysteriously marked lever, and the guts of the machine spilled open. She began to pull out handfuls of jammed paper from within.

Janina smiled in sympathy and went over to stand next to her as she peered into the dark interior of the photocopier. "Can I help? I've had a few fights with this one myself."

"Not unless you know of a good exorcist," murmured Lucy grimly. She plunged her hands inside once again. "There." She pulled out a blackened and shredded piece of what had once been paper. "Got you!" She began to close the machine up. Her hands were sooty with toner, but her face was triumphant.

"Lucy," said Janina as the other woman stood and prepared to attempt making her copies once more. "I was wondering if you'd like to have lunch with me in the music office today."

There was no hesitation. "I'd love to."

Despite the ease with which Lucy had agreed, Janina felt the need to explain. "Actually, I need your advice about something, and... well, I...."

Lucy nodded sagely. "Say no more. I spend too much time in the faculty room as it is. It's been a long time since I've made it down to your end of the building." She lowered her voice. "Walls may not have ears, despite the cliché, but people do. And some have bigger ones than normal, I might add."

Janina smiled. "Thanks."

"I'll see you then."

☆
☆ ☆

The morning crawled by, and Janina was more preoccupied than ever by lunch time. She had just returned from retrieving her lunch bag from the refrigerator in the little kitchen area behind the main office when Lucy came in carrying a cafeteria tray. Janina motioned her to sit down at the big table in the center of the music office, which was still cluttered with stacks of sheet music.

"What's up?" Lucy asked, as soon as they were both seated. "I've worked myself up into quite a passable imitation of Wanda this morning wondering what was on your mind."

"Well, it's pretty strange." Janina consciously kept her voice light. "Wanda would love it, you can bet that." She took a deep breath. "You remember that conversation we had in the faculty room a week or two ago about Tom and Kathy Christian?"

"I believe I walked out in the middle of it, but yes."

"After that conversation, I couldn't stop thinking about it. It was on my mind pretty much constantly, but I wrote it off as a silly obsession. Finally, yesterday I made the decision to put it all out of my mind. Then, yesterday afternoon, guess what was in the mail?"

"A letter from someone asking about the Christians?"

"Better. A letter from Kathy Christian herself."

"No!" Lucy set down her fork looking genuinely taken aback.

"Yup."

"So, she's still alive. Where is she?"

"Hazleton."

"My goodness. Well, I suppose she would be. Somehow, one just never thinks of someone being sent to a place like that and just... going on and on. It's like it's over, they're gone and forgotten."

"It seems she remembers me and decided to write."

"That's curious." Lucy picked up her fork and took a bite of her cafeteria spaghetti. "You must have been very young when she was sent to Hazleton. It's interesting she remembers you."

"Oh, I suppose you weren't there for that part of the conversation in the faculty room. I grew up in the house next to the Christians' house. Kathy knew me quite well. I was ten when Tom died."

"I never knew that. Did she say why she chose you to write to?"

"Well, yes and no. I guess she remembered me fondly, but that wasn't it. She seemed to think I was... chosen somehow." Janina blushed, expecting Lucy to laugh at her.

Lucy didn't laugh. "Poor woman."

"Anyhow, she's asked me to come up to visit her. I suppose I could do that. I'd guess that you can visit people there, same as in a prison, right? But actually, I'm wondering if I should get involved at all. I mean, the woman actually killed her own husband."

Lucy looked thoughtful. "So they say."

Janina set down her chicken salad sandwich on the table and leaned forward, a hint of eagerness in her voice. "Did you know Kathy? Before her husband's death?"

"Oh, yes." Lucy's light blue eyes met Janina's levelly. "I

didn't know her well, of course. But I grew up in the village, you know. I was maybe twenty years old when the whole incident occurred. But before that, I spoke with her many times. She's what I'd have called a good acquaintance."

"And you don't think she killed Tom?"

"I rather think I have suspended my judgment on that." Lucy took another bite of spaghetti and shook her head. "The judge obviously thought she did."

"But you didn't," persisted Janina.

"Let's say that I never could quite see Kathy in the role of a murderer. But I'm no jurist, and I certainly don't know all the facts. People do strange things sometimes."

"So, who killed Tom, then?"

Lucy's right eyebrow rose a notch. "Now, don't jump to conclusions. I never said she *didn't* do it. I simply have never been completely convinced. For all I know, she may well be as guilty as sin. As for who else might have done it, that I don't know. Somehow, I always got the idea that there was someone else involved, but it was only intuition, if you will."

"She never said in the letter that she was innocent."

"Absence of evidence is not evidence of absence, remember. Who was it that said that? Bertrand Russell or someone of that ilk. Or maybe it was just Sherlock Holmes."

Janina finished her carton of milk. "In my place, what would you do? Would you go visit her?"

"I hate to sound mean-spirited but probably not. She sounds delusional. How much of a bond of any sort could there be between her and a woman whom she knew only as a child twenty-five years ago?" Lucy gave Janina a thoughtful frown. "But that's not all she asked you to do, is it?"

"Well... no, it wasn't." Janina looked away. Lucy's perceptiveness could be intimidating at times.

"What does she want you to do?" Lucy asked, her voice gentle.

"It's too weird. I'm almost embarrassed to explain it, much less to justify why I'm even considering believing it." Janina paused and glanced out of the window, which overlooked the front sidewalk. Students were sitting on the steps and around the base of the flagpole, eating lunch and chatting and enjoying the sunshine. Here in her classroom it felt dark. Dark and confused and with no certain way to get out. "Let me just say that she wants me to bring her something," she finally said.

Lucy's eyebrow went up again. "Well, that would settle it for me. I don't know for sure but bringing her something that hasn't been approved by the warden, or director, or whatever the CEO of an asylum is called, is probably illegal and possibly dangerous. If you want my advice, that's it."

"I just keep thinking about the poor woman, locked in that horrible place...." Janina's voice was fervent, but she faltered and fell silent.

"It's all right to be sympathetic," said Lucy flatly. "Although if she actually killed her husband, she certainly isn't all that deserving. Don't put your own safety at risk, though."

Janina looked searchingly at Lucy for a moment, her forehead creased. Then her face relaxed suddenly, and she felt a surge of relief. "Okay, you've settled my mind. I don't need to get involved with this." She took a deep breath. "Thanks. I think I've been waiting for someone to tell me that. I'm glad I talked to you."

Lucy smiled. "So am I. For a moment, I was worried about you." She arranged her silverware on her tray and stood up. "In any case, how strange it is you received that letter so soon after the conversation in the faculty room."

"It *is* strange. Strange in a lot of ways."

Any further conversation was interrupted by the three bells that signaled the beginning of seventh period. "Good timing," said Lucy.

"Thanks again," said Janina. "See you later."

Janina made sure that she arrived home before the kids' bus that afternoon. She wanted some time simply to relax and think. She got the mail, which thank heaven included no more missives from psychiatric hospitals, and upon returning to the house, went to the CD rack to select some music. Something to match her mood. Something minor key and a little sad. Beethoven's *Pathétique Sonata* was perfect.

She dropped the CD into the player, pressed "Play," and without warning the speakers burst into the wildly triumphant violins and trumpets of the opening chorus of the Bach *Magnificat in D.*

"My God," Janina exclaimed and snatched up the CD case. No, it said Beethoven, all right. She must have accidentally switched the discs the last time she had played them. She quickly located the case for the *Magnificat* and opened it, and of course, there was the Beethoven CD.

However, she didn't turn the music off. The crescendo of voices began, each one overtopping the other, "Magnificat, magnificat, magnificat anima mea Dominum...." There was something about this piece of music that made her stop with her mouth opened slightly and a frown on her face. She knew it had been the first piece of classical music she had ever heard, and it had held a special place in her heart ever since. She had played it thousands of times and performed it as part of her college chorus. But today there was something else. Another memory of music, of a swell of glory from the tinny speakers of a radio... of a fir tree, and someone's face... someone....

The door burst open before Katie, Brendan, and Sarah piled noisily in with backpacks, shoes, and windbreakers flying into heaps on the floor. Janina stared dumbly for a moment and then touched a button on the CD player. The music stopped and silence fell. All three children swiveled around and looked at their mother.

"Why'd you turn it off?" asked Brendan. "I thought that was your favorite piece of music?"

"It is," Janina said. The kids continued to stare at her. Finally, she swallowed, and found her voice again. "I... uh, it was in the wrong case. I wasn't meaning to play that one, and it sort of surprised me." She turned to busy herself with switching the CD in hopes the children would not begin to ask questions about why she was acting so strangely. She pressed "Play" again, and the piano began to caress Beethoven's notes into life. The kids seemed satisfied that whatever it was that had happened wasn't serious. They began to chat again and went into the kitchen for snacks.

Janina stood there for a moment, trying to recapture the thoughts that the music had brought up from the deepest wells of her memory. She had almost grasped them, but as her hands closed about them, they had turned to smoke and drifted away. All she was left with were fragments as meaningless as three random pieces from a thousand-piece jigsaw puzzle.

A face. A face, and a fir tree. And a promise.

☆☆☆

"Anything new and interesting down at the clinic?" Janina asked Jim later that afternoon as they worked on dinner preparation. Jim had arrived home at five o'clock, given his wife and kids his usual warm greetings, and then dutifully submitted to being chief chicken-chopper for a pot of chicken stew.

"Oh, nothing of much import. Of course, Mrs. Warren was horrified at the stitches in Mitzi-Pie's belly. She all but accused me of outright butchery. Nothing I didn't expect, of course. Fortunately, Carla Wainwright was much more pleasant. Did I tell you she was having Bubbles spayed? I guess three batches of seven puppies each was sufficient. In any case, she and Mrs. Warren were both there this afternoon at four-thirty to pick up their dogs. After Mrs. Warren nearly took my head off, Carla remarked that I'd 'done a really neat job and was such a good man with animals.' Mrs. Warren hadn't left yet, and she about froze Carla solid with a glance. I almost laughed out loud. They say animals are funny, but for sheerly weird behavior I'd put my money on human beings every time."

"You got that right."

The vigor with which Janina voiced her agreement seemed to jog Jim's memory. "Here I've been yapping away about spaying dogs, and there was something you said you wanted to talk about. Is now a good time?"

"Sure." Janina was not quite sure how to begin and took a moment to select her words. "You remember how we were talking about Tom and Kathy Christian a while back?"

"Yup."

"Well, yesterday I got a letter from Kathy in the mail."

Jim stopped cutting for a moment and turned and looked at her, his face as astonished as Lucy's had been earlier that day. "You're kidding! No wonder you were so distracted yesterday evening."

"It's a pretty strange letter. If I let you read it, you'd probably think she's crazy."

"I pretty much already do," Jim remarked, returning to his work. He scowled down at the cutting board. "You know, cutting up a chicken properly is more of a pain than doing surgery."

"The letter sounds crazy on the surface, but there's something about it that makes some weird kind of sense. I'm not convinced she's actually crazy. And... Jim, she wants me to come visit her."

Jim picked up a double handful of chopped chicken and

dropped it into a pot of steaming broth. It was a moment before he spoke, and when he did, his voice was level. "Are you going to?"

"That's what I wanted to talk about. Should I?"

"I don't like giving you advice."

"I know. But I need it."

"Do you want to go visit her?"

"Well, part of me wants to. But part of me is frightened of her and of getting involved with... with her," she ended rather lamely.

"Maybe I should read the letter," Jim suggested.

"I'd really rather you didn't. I mean, it's so strange. I don't know why it's upset me so much. It's just a letter from some strange woman in an asylum...." She paused, her words catching in her throat. She was perilously near tears.

"So, that's all she wants? Only one visit?" Jim moved to the sink and began to wash his hands.

Janina hesitated. "No. She wants me to bring her something. Something she says she left in her house twenty-five years ago. Something she says is still there."

Jim looked up sharply. "What sort of thing?"

"A necklace. I don't understand why she wants it. I mean, she tried to explain. Something about a sign... receiving a sign that she needed it back, and that I was the one who could find it."

"She wants you to break into her old house, find this necklace, and bring it to her?"

"Basically, yes."

Jim washed his hands, dried them on a tea towel, and went over to put his arm around her shoulders. "Look, Janina, I understand why you feel upset about this. If I'd known her when I was a kid like you did, and admired her maybe, I'd feel bad about her being locked up, too. But you've got to remember what she did, how she ended up where she is. And now she writes to you, and is asking you to do something illegal? It's crazy. She's crazy. You can't let yourself get pulled into something like this out of your own sympathy and good-heartedness."

"I suppose you're right. That's basically what Lucy told me, too."

"You told Lucy?"

"Today at lunch. Not in as much detail as I've just told you. But she also told me I shouldn't get involved."

"Lucy is a smart woman. Listen to her. And I may not be a rocket scientist, but I have a bad feeling about this. I think you should burn that letter and forget about it."

Janina sighed and leaned against Jim. He pulled her close, and she closed her eyes. "You're right, of course. I'll do that. I'll get rid of the letter."

Tomorrow. She'd get rid of the letter tomorrow.

Maybe.

CHAPTER 3

Janina made it home in time for lunch, her face streaked with dried tears and dirt. Fortunately for her, Maddy was intent on fixing lunch when she came inside. Janina had time to make a dash for the bathroom and clean herself up a bit before her mother saw her and asked questions. Questions she couldn't answer, just like the ones her mom had asked Justin at the hardware store.

Only she couldn't turn her mom's thoughts away like Justin apparently could.

"Janina," called Maddy, "I have your lunch ready."

"Okay, Mom," she shouted over the sound of the bathroom tap. "I'll be out in a minute." She splashed water on her face, and then rubbed it dry with the hand towel. Her eyes felt swollen and sensitive. She looked in the mirror, and the red rims seemed to jump out at her. No way to hide it when you've been crying.

Questions that couldn't be answered. There seemed to be an awful lot of those lately. Justin knew things before they happened. He could change what people were thinking of. And music, music coming out of a switched-off radio.

Yeah, when Justin was around, a lot of questions came up.

"What happened to you?" asked Doug conversationally as Janina sat down at the kitchen table.

Janina froze. She had known he'd notice. It was obvious. Now, when they asked the inevitable question—"What have you been crying about?"—what should she tell them? She looked at him, eyes wide, and said nothing. Maddy swiveled around, curiosity furrowing her broad face. Doug pointed to her hands, which still carried bandages from yesterday's spill in the driveway.

Janina looked dumbly at her hands, not comprehending at first, then she took a deep breath of relief. "Oh, that. I was roller-skating yesterday and fell down in the driveway. Didn't you notice last night?"

"Nope," Doug replied around a mouthful of sandwich.

Maddy raised an eyebrow and turned back to the sink. "Did you put some Bactine on it?"

"Yes, Mom," Janina lied, and then fell silent, waiting for further questions. None came. Maddy and Doug both seemed satisfied.

Janina concentrated on eating, but her mind was going at light speed. How could Doug have missed her red eyes? Or was it not as obvious as she'd thought it was? Maybe he had noticed and didn't want to say anything more in front of their mother. It was hard to tell what Doug was thinking sometimes. And then, there was her reaction to his question. She'd jumped like a startled rabbit. How long would it be before one of them noticed how strangely she was acting?

The remainder of lunch passed without any further awkward questions. Doug wolfed down his sandwich in minutes and ran off to play ball with some friends. Janina finished hers more slowly before returning to her bedroom for a cursory and unsuccessful check of the radio. Afterwards, frustrated and bored, she wandered off outside. The weather was hot and still. Everything seemed subdued. There weren't even any birds singing—unusual for summer—and the hum of a distant lawn mower hung heavy in the humid air. Janina found some matchbox cars in a cardboard box in the corner of the garage and carried them off to the shade of the forsythia hedge that separated their back yard from the Christians'. She played with them in a bored, distracted way for several minutes while wondering how she could ever have found matchbox cars interesting, despite it being all of three weeks ago that she had last played with them. After about fifteen minutes, however, she had dug out a tunnel underneath one of the forsythia roots and had begun sweeping clean a road for the cars. Maybe they weren't so bad after all. By the time a half-hour had passed, she was totally absorbed. Her attention was so completely captured that it took her a while to become aware that she could hear voices. In fact, the voices were quite close and must have been going on for some time before she became conscious of their presence.

Once she began to attend to them, she recognized them both instantly. She sat there for a moment, ears pricking like a cat's. A red toy truck dropped from her hand unnoticed as she strained to pick up the words in the hot, heavy air.

"... really don't think Tom will understand, but I suppose you'll have to tell him anyway."

"What do you think he'll say?"

"I don't know. He's hard to predict that way."

Janina got down on her belly and crawled toward the hedge on elbows and knees like a soldier under heavy fire. She wriggled under the arching branches of the hedge, moving slowly so that she didn't make them rustle too much. She knew the word *eavesdropping* and that listening in on others was impolite at best. At least that much of her mother's moralizing had sunk in. However, she also recognized her own curiosity as insatiable. She knew that it was more satisfying in the long run to give into it immediately rather than engage herself in some sort of protracted internal argument and risk missing the interesting stuff.

Janina pushed her way into the middle of the hedge and lay there on her stomach in the damp leaf mold. She peered through the green branches already knowing who she'd see. Kathy was sitting on her back porch, her elbows on the picnic table, and her chin resting in her hands. The pose, so innocent and childlike, seemed to heighten the sense of grace that always flowed from her. Justin, dressed in his typical jeans and t-shirt, was standing, leaning against one of the upright beams that supported the awning. Even seen at a distance through a network of forsythia branches, he looked skittish.

"Maybe it's best if I disappear without telling him," Justin was saying.

"That's hardly fair to Tom. I think you need to tell him, or at least tell him what you can." Kathy's voice had a plaintive note. "Are you sure you have to go?"

"I'm sure. They're getting close. I know it. If I stay here, I'm at risk, but so are you all. If I go, I think you'll be all right. They may ask you some questions, but it's me they're after."

"Can't you hide?"

Justin's answer was blunt, almost derisive. "Where?"

"I'd offer to hide you, but Tom would never agree. He'd never knowingly do anything that was against the law."

"But it's not really...."

Kathy's voice was soft but quite distinct. "That's how he'd see it. I know him, remember."

"It doesn't make any difference, anyway," Justin said wearily. "This is the first place they'd look."

"Isn't there anywhere else?"

Justin leaned his head back and closed his eyes. "No. Nowhere. God, I'm so tired of this. But I'm going to have to run for it. Again."

Neither one spoke again for some moments. Kathy's next words were so quiet that Janina wasn't sure she'd heard them correctly, and it took a moment for their meaning to register.

"Justin, take me with you."

There was another long pause during which Janina was sure that the little gasp she'd given had been overheard. Neither Kathy nor Justin turned her way, though. She momentarily closed her eyes in relief.

Finally, Justin spoke, and again his voice sounded tired. "You don't know what you're asking."

"I wouldn't be a burden to you."

"I know that. That's not it. It's not the burden, but the danger to you that I'm thinking of. If you understood it, really understood it, you'd never ask to come along."

"I think I do understand. And I'm still asking."

"What about Tom? What about your home, your friends, your village? You'd give all that up for a life on the run, the dangers of which you don't even understand?"

Kathy turned toward Justin, her eyes pleading. "I can't say I was ever truly happy with my life, but three weeks ago, I was at least satisfied. Now... now, it seems so dull, so lifeless. I love Tom, but it's almost like loving a brother. He's always there, he provides for me, he never denies me anything. But there's no brightness, no excitement, no life. Just the house, the store, and being stuck in this little village until I grow old and die." Kathy's voice had a bitter edge.

"Don't disdain stability. You have no idea how much I want what you've got."

Kathy gave an ironic laugh. "Neither of us wants what we've got. A pity we can't trade."

"Look," said Justin. "You'd better get back to the store before Tom starts to wonder where you are. What did you tell him?"

"Don't worry, I told him I'd forgotten my lunch and had to come back to pick it up. There were only a couple of people in the store when I left. He won't notice if I'm gone a little longer than I should be."

"I'm supposed to be at the store today at two o'clock. What time is it?"

"One-fifteen. Justin, I love you."

Once again, there were a few moments of silence before Justin said simply, "I know you do."

"Do you love me?" Kathy's voice was eager, pleading, almost desperate.

"Kathy, don't ask that."

"Do you?" Kathy persisted.

"If I could, I would. I can't do any better than that."

"Please take me with you."

"I can't put you in that kind of danger."

"You're not putting me in danger. I'm asking to be put in it."

"No. You've got a life here. I don't have anything to offer you besides what will probably be the shortest escape attempt on record. I've got to tell Tom, soon. And then...." His voice faltered, just for a moment. "Just remember me when I go. I may have to go quickly without saying goodbye. Don't ever forget me."

"I won't, ever." Kathy stood up and gave Justin a kiss on the mouth. Then, she turned and went into her house. Janina blushed scarlet from her hiding place inside the hedge.

Justin stood for a moment, still leaning against the beam, and then turned and went down the steps into the back yard. He circled around the back of the house toward the end of the hedge, and then along the side of the Christians' house toward the street. Janina froze, trying to be as still as she could, crouched in the shadows of the hedge. Justin continued to walk steadily until he was even with where she was hiding. Suddenly, he turned toward her and gave her a quick wink, almost too fast to notice. Instinctively Janina ducked. It was too late, of course, and she only succeeded in scraping her cheek against a branch. By the time she had recovered her wits sufficiently to peer out along the hedge toward the street, Justin had already disappeared.

CHAPTER 4

What was wrong with her?

That question kept echoing through Janina's brain as her car, virtually on automatic pilot, swished smoothly northward along New York State Route 93. She was a very, very sick person. Obsessive-compulsive disorder. Pretty soon she'd be washing her hands fifty times a day and returning home from work five or six times before class starts to make sure that she'd turned the stove off.

In fact, work was where she should have been this morning. She had seen Jim and the kids off, gotten dressed in her work clothes, made her lunch, and put her book bag together. None of them knew, though, that she had left plans for a substitute on her desk the previous afternoon, and that even before she left school she had called the substitute registry and arranged to be absent. A personal day. It was all quite legitimate, she told herself. She was allowed three personal days per year. She just hoped that Jim wouldn't wonder where this one had gone. The school district, in an unusual gesture of understanding, allowed all teachers three days for personal reasons, including "mental health days." There was nothing wrong with her taking one today, right?

Except today wasn't a mental health day. It was a mental illness day. She'd even deceived her family and employer about it.

But, she rationalized, she was doing it. So, she may as well accept that.

She slowed to a standstill at the traffic light in Lemoine, about halfway between Guildford and Hazleton. Lemoine was so small that it made Guildford look like a metropolis—a stoplight and a convenience store were the only signs of civilization in evidence. The light turned green, and Janina pulled away from the intersection. Her face was set. She had to accept that she wasn't going to turn the car around. Time to stop beating herself up and simply get on with it.

And what exactly was it she was going to do? What was she trying to accomplish? Those questions were bouncing around inside her skull like an interior version of the water torture.

But the answer was obvious. She was going to see Kathy in an attempt to put an end to this matter once and for all.

Immediately, this initiated a chorus of panicked thought. This *wouldn't* end it, whatever Kathy said. This was only the beginning. She was drifting out to sea, caught in a rip tide….

"Oh, shut up," she said aloud and switched the radio on with the volume turned up loud.

Janina's relief following her conversations with Lucy and Jim two days earlier had been short-lived. She had gone to school the next morning feeling much lighter. Her classes had gone well, and she'd found out that her budget for the next school year had passed the principal's scrutiny relatively unscathed. Then, lunch time came around.

The usual odd assortment of faculty, with the addition of Martha Alport, were in the faculty room. When Janina entered, there was the typical babble of conversation, and Janina set her lunch down as she sat next to Alice Jackson, who taught math. Alice gave her a smile before returning to listen to Wanda, who was holding forth from the opposite end of the table.

"I am still *appalled* at the O. J. Simpson verdict," she was saying with tremendous gusto. "I mean, the man is as guilty as they come. The race issue has nothing to do with it. He killed his wife, pure and simple."

"The jury didn't think so," Lucy said curtly.

"Don't you think there may have been more to the story than the media reported?" asked Alice. "We certainly didn't get the whole story. After all, there were weeks and weeks of testimony, and all the nightly news gave was a five-minute synopsis."

"If there had been more, the news would have included it," said Wanda firmly. "Believe me, he was guilty. For the most part, I'm a believer in the American justice system, but this time it screwed up."

"The system didn't screw up," said Lucy. "Money talked, that's all."

"Of course!" said Wanda explosively. Lucy winced, probably more at having been found in agreement with Wanda than anything else. "If anyone from the middle class killed their spouse," Wanda continued, "they'd end up in jail for life."

"Or in an insane asylum," added Martha quietly.

The comment cut effortlessly through the hum of conversation. Even through Wanda's strident chatter. Janina's head snapped up, her eyes staring and mouth open in surprise. Martha was already looking back down at her lunch tray, a faint smile on her graceful lips. Janina glanced around at the others to see how they had reacted. It seemed that none of them had. Had no one else heard it?

Wanda was still in full cry. Alice was still listening to her intently—Alice was one of the only people nice enough actually to listen when Wanda talked. Lucy was giving deliberate attention to a fairly disreputable serving of cafeteria apple crisp.

Her expression stated clearly, *This lousy apple crisp is far more interesting than you are, Wanda.* Janina was no longer listening, either, but needed to expend no effort to do so. Her brain had popped into high gear.

Every time she tried to let this go, something like this happened. She was fated to obsess about this for the rest of her life.

After her mind raced for a few minutes, she forced herself to calm down. Wanda probably had just told Martha about the Christian case, so it was fresh in her mind. Or maybe she grew up around here and heard about it herself. It certainly got enough publicity.

In any case, it was ridiculous to let a stray comment get her all upset again.

But it was already too late, and she knew it.

☆☆☆

She had sleepwalked through the remainder of the school day. She watched herself with a kind of weary surprise as she called the substitute registry and wrote out her plans. The actions felt fated, as if she had no control over what she was doing. Then she had called Hazleton Institute to ask about hours for visiting.

Now, she was in her car driving north. Even the radio blaring couldn't drown out the insistent questions. What had Martha meant by mentioning insane asylums? Maybe she really was strange like the kids seemed to think. That comment had to be aimed at her.

Awesome. Now she could add paranoia to the list of maladies she was suffering from. She was becoming a walking encyclopedia of mental illness.

A few more houses began to be in evidence along the road,

and there was a sign saying "Reduced Speed Ahead." Then, about a hundred yards further on, a nice wooden sign, surrounded by tulips in full bloom, saying "Welcome to Hazleton. Inc. 1803."

Yes, welcome to Hazleton. Come here and you'll never leave.

It was hard to picture this as a real city with ordinary inhabitants, just like any other city. Yet it was an ordinary city. Ordinary except for that one complex on the east side of the city, the one surrounded by the ten-foot chain-link fence with the razor wire.

For several miles, Janina followed the small road signs that said simply "Institute" above an arrow, until she could see the squat, blocky institute complex in the distance. It was set nearly a half-mile back from the road, and in that vast expanse there was nothing to break the monotony—no trees, not even a shrub, just acres of close-cropped lawn surrounded by the fence. No, there was no way to escape from this place. If a rabbit moved in there, it would be immediately obvious.

Janina drove to the single, gated entrance and pulled up alongside the guard's cubicle. An unsmiling man in uniform slid back the window as Janina rolled hers down.

"I'm here to visit someone," Janina said.

The man pulled out a clipboard. "Your name?"

"Janina Vannoy."

He jotted it down. "Who are you here to see?"

"Katherine Christian."

"I'll radio down to the office. You can park in Lot C, off to your left. There should be plenty of open spaces. You need to check in at the office in the front, and they'll send someone to accompany you to the women's block."

"Thanks."

The man responded by sliding the window shut. Janina drove on into the parking area, wondering again what it must have felt like for Kathy to take this ride knowing she wouldn't be leaving.

Ever.

Janina pulled into a parking space, picked up her purse, and locked her car. She immediately scowled at herself for this last action. Who would be able to steal her car here? But she nevertheless left it locked. She then got out and began to walk toward the office.

The stillness surrounded her like a blanket. Even the birds seemed to avoid the grounds of Hazleton Institute. The noises of the village were left far behind. The silence was almost unearthly, and the dull thuds of her simple, flat-soled shoes against the asphalt were unnerving. The walk seemed to take longer than she expected. Everything was magnified in this place— sounds, distances, even her own emotional responses. She finally reached the barred, glass-fronted door and pushed it open.

The interior was brightly lit with fluorescent lights. A single armed guard sat at the desk. He didn't look up as she entered. Janina felt that in some oblique way this meant that he was expecting her. She was quite certain that if she'd walked in unexpected, he'd have looked up a lot quicker.

Finally, the guard looked up from his papers. "Janina Vannoy?" he said, in the same flat, unemotional voice the first guard had used.

Janina nodded.

"I've called for a guard to bring you to the women's quarters. When she arrives, I'm afraid you and your purse will have to be searched. It's standard procedure, you understand."

Janina nodded again. The guard looked back down, his information delivered. No inclination to small talk in this place, it seemed. However, Janina was not left standing long. Within a minute, a door at the rear of the room opened, and a uniformed woman stepped through. "Ms. Vannoy?" she said.

Janina replied, "That's me."

"You can come with me."

Janina followed the woman through the door, which was locked after they passed through it.

"I'm afraid you'll have to be searched," the woman said, but at least her voice had a note of sympathy. "And I have to go through your purse. But we've called ahead, and Mrs. Christian will be waiting for you when we get to the visitation room."

The guard took Janina into a small side room furnished only with a table and a chair, but like the front lobby awash down to the farthest corners with the brilliant white fluorescent light. There, Janina's purse was emptied, and nothing being found more dangerous than a bottle of extra-strength aspirin, she submitted to being frisked. This guard seemed more human than the other two had been. As she was patting down Janina from head to toe, she said, "Shame we have to do this, almost makes it seem like you're the criminal for coming to visit someone. But you know, we can't take the chance."

"I understand," said Janina.

The guard then led her down a long, echoing hallway, through two doors, and then to the door of a side room. At this point, the guard said, "Please remain seated opposite Mrs. Christian the entire time you're here. Don't stand up. Don't attempt to cross to her side of the table. When you're ready to leave, call the guard in attendance, and he'll call me down to accompany you back." With this, she opened the door.

It was a big, open room. Yet another armed guard stood next to the door across the room, the one that Janina supposed led into the cell block. There were a number of tables and chairs, all empty except for one.

At this one sat a slender woman. She looked far younger than Janina expected and far smaller than Janina remembered—dressed in the institutional green cotton dress, her dark hair faintly streaked with gray and still up in her characteristic knot. Janina crossed over to the table and sat down. She heard the door close behind her.

"Kathy?" she said, her voice a hoarse croak.

"Janina," said Kathy, and reached across the table and clasped both of Janina's hands in a tight, almost painful grip. "I knew you'd come. I knew it."

"I'm so... so sorry...." Janina began, and though she kept control over her voice, the tears spilled over down her cheeks and onto the marbled Formica of the table. "This place, it's so horrible."

"One gets used to it. For me, the hardest thing has been that there's no music, no art, or anything to keep my mind going. And I miss everyone. I missed Tom especially at first. But I have a few friends here. Like I said, it's not so bad once one gets used to it. Tell me... oh, tell me everything! What is your life like now?"

Janina took a deep breath. She wouldn't start sobbing like a child. She couldn't. "I'm a music teacher at the high school in Guildford. I'm married and have three children."

"Three children... it's hard to believe. I knew you were married when I heard your name was Vannoy now. What does your husband do?"

"He's a veterinarian. He bought Dr. Carlisle's practice when he retired."

"Oh, wonderful! And your children... how old? Boys or girls or both?"

This was surreal. They sounded like two old friends who had just met on a street corner.

"Two girls, twelve and seven, and one boy, nine."

"I remember when you were that age. Hard to believe you've got children of your own. How are your parents? Do they still live in the same house?"

"Well, my father died six years ago. He had a heart attack out working in his garden, as you'd expect. He was gone before the ambulance even got there. My mother couldn't keep the house and yard up, so she sold it and now lives in a retirement community with her sister in Allenton."

"My goodness." Kathy gave Janina's hands another squeeze. "One always pictures things staying the same, even though of course they never do. Somehow being in here makes the whole world seem like it's in stasis."

"I can see how it would."

"I'm very sorry about your father. He was a fine man."

"Thanks. I know. I miss him terribly."

Suddenly Kathy smiled, and the corners of her eyes and mouth crinkled into a hundred fine lines. "I can't tell you how glad I am that you came."

"I got your letter," Janina said.

Kathy looked alarmed. "Don't mention that." Her voice dropped to a whisper. "They don't know I sent it."

Janina glanced up at the guard whose blank expression gave no sign of his having overheard. Still, Janina lowered her own voice to a near whisper. "You wanted me to do something for you."

"Yes." Kathy's eyes became distant as if she were lost in memory.

Janina waited, but the other woman didn't reply for some time. All expression had faded out of her face. She seemed to have lost touch with where she was and who she was with. The grip on Janina's hands slackened.

"Kathy?" said Janina gently, and the animation returned to Kathy's face. She looked at Janina, smiled again, and her hands tightened once more.

"Yes. I need you to find something for me."

"A necklace. You mentioned a necklace."

"Yes. It's still in the house, I'm sure of it. I lost it the night Tom died. I need it back."

"What does it look like? Where in the house is it?"

"Justin gave it to me. He keeps coming to me in dreams. Saying, 'Find the necklace, Kathy. I can't reach you unless you have the necklace.' He's the one who told me to write to you,

you know." Kathy smiled up at Janina again, as if what she had said was the most reasonable thing in the world.

Janina resisted the impulse to pull her hands out of Kathy's tight grip. Jim and Lucy had been right. She was crazy, and Janina had been crazy to come here.

She had to get out of there.

When she spoke, she kept her voice steady with an effort. "What does this necklace look like?"

Kathy's right hand let go of Janina's left, and it began to sculpt the air as she spoke. "It's a fine silver chain. Hanging from it is a little silver ball inside a spherical silver cage with five bars. It jingles if you shake it. Justin told me it was a family keepsake of his." Her face clouded. "I... dropped it the night Tom died. It rolled away, fell through the grating near the kitchen door, and went down the heat vent. It must still be there."

Janina stared in silence at Kathy. Kathy's eyes met Janina's, and the intensity in them was overpowering. "Please, you must find it. Then, either bring it to me, or...." Here her voice dropped even further. "Even better, give it to Leo Carson, and he'll get it to me. He's my friend here. He's one of the nurses. He lives in Emerson. You could give him a call, and then meet him to give it to him. That would probably be safer. If you come here again, they may start to suspect."

They? Who were "they?" But once again, she avoided saying what she was actually thinking. Finally, she asked, "Kathy, I should probably remember, but I don't. Who is Justin Lazarus?"

There was a moment of silence, and then, to Janina's horror, Kathy began to laugh, quietly at first, and then more energetically. "I really have no idea," she finally said, her slim body quaking with laughter.

Janina felt a shudder vibrate down her spine. "What... what do you mean? I thought you knew him...."

Kathy stopped laughing, but her eyes were bright, and she wore a broad smile. "I do. I do think I know him. But you can't ever *really* know him. Not unless he wants you to. You knew him too, Janina. But now you don't know him either, do you? You don't remember because he doesn't want you to remember. I will know him better soon. Right now, though? No, I really don't have any idea who he is."

Janina stared at the other woman for a moment, her face frozen, but her eyes registering panic. With an effort, she pulled her hands away. "I have to go," she said hoarsely.

Kathy's smile vanished. "The necklace, Janina. Please," she said in a rough whisper.

Janina motioned to the guard. She was trying to keep the desperation out of her motions and her voice, but she felt that she had to get out of there, now, or she'd go insane herself. The guard nodded and spoke quietly into his walkie-talkie.

"I'm not crazy, Janina." Her hands knotted into hard fists. "I know I sound crazy. They all thought I was crazy, but I'm not. I'm not." Kathy reached out toward Janina again with both hands.

Instinctively Janina recoiled, pulling her chair back, and the legs squawked against the tile floor. The guard frowned and began to walk toward them. At the same time, the woman who had conducted Janina into the visitation room unlocked the exit door, walked in, and strode briskly to the table.

"Are you ready to go, ma'am?" she asked.

Janina nodded, still staring at Kathy as she stood up. Kathy was still stretched out across the table, and she looked up at Janina pleadingly as she turned away. Her expression was pathetic, despairing. The guard conducted Janina to the exit. As she unlocked it to allow Janina to leave, to escape this horrible place of insanity and fear and deadly boredom, the last thing Janina heard was Kathy's voice rising to an unsteady shout. "Janina, please, remember what I asked you...."

Then, the door shut, and the voice was cut off like someone had flipped a switch.

CHAPTER 5

"I'd better get these clothes out early before it's too hot for me to stand," said Maddy, more to herself than to anyone else. Janina was eating a bowl of Cap'n Crunch as she wondered what she was going to do with herself. The heat the previous night would have made sleep difficult even if she hadn't been emotionally jangled, but the combination had made for an uncomfortable and unrestful night. She'd awakened at six-thirty, a good hour and a half earlier than usual, and had gotten up immediately. The tangled and sweat-damp sheets were hardly inviting. She was eating breakfast by seven.

Maddy, of course, was already up by the time Janina walked into the kitchen, yawning and blinking. No matter when Janina got up, Maddy seemed to have been up for hours already. Janina was beginning to harbor doubts that her mother slept at all.

Janina poured herself a bowl of cereal, added milk, and commenced crunching solemnly and silently.

"What are you brooding about?" demanded Maddy suddenly.

"Nothing," replied Janina, looking up with as much sweetness and innocence as her fatigue and her worries would allow.

Maddy frowned, not satisfied. She seemed to consider pursuing the matter further for a moment but apparently decided against it. Then she made her pronouncement about the necessity of hanging out laundry early and walked ponderously out of the room.

The fact was, Janina *was* brooding. The events of the previous weeks had been bad enough, but the conversation she had overheard the previous day had given a new, and possibly dangerous, twist to the whole affair. She hadn't understood it all, but one thing was clear. Justin Lazarus was trouble. While he was around, everyone and everything was in peril. Worse than that, it seemed that all of her thoughts and feelings had grown double edges overnight. She had felt an immediate pang of sympathy for him, but even so, part of her wanted him gone as soon as possible. She felt that anyone that Kathy was in love with must be inherently okay, but at the same time she had watched enough television to recognize a love triangle when she saw one. She had a rather surprising protective urge toward Tom, who certainly looked like coming off worst in this particular geometry. And finally, she felt a twinge of simple excitement about being connected with something as storybook as a pursued fugitive. However, that was tempered by an equal amount of pure, unadulterated fear.

She finished her cereal, and feeling emotions far more ambivalent than any she had yet experienced in her ten years, she wandered outside to help her mother hang clothes. It was one of the few chores she enjoyed. For some reason, handing her mother those strange, springy wooden pins was almost fun. None of her toys and games were at all appealing, and this would give her something to do. Plus, she knew that winning points with her mother wasn't easy. Helping with chores was a sure-fire point winner.

Maddy had hardly started when Janina joined her, and after

the initial "I've come to help," and "Oh, good, I could use some help around here occasionally," there was little in the way of conversation from either of them. Twenty minutes passed, the thermometer steadily rose as the pile of laundry steadily diminished, and neither felt inclined to say anything.

Then, the sound of a car—a big car—made Maddy turn her head. A large, dark blue, expensive-looking sedan pulled into view as it slowed in front of their house. The driver squinted out of the window and seemed to be reading the house number. He evidently realized his mistake, and then accelerated slightly, finally braking to a stop in front of Tom and Kathy's house. There was a pause, followed by the sound of two heavy car doors slamming.

"Now, who on earth can that be at seven-thirty in the morning?" wondered Maddy aloud. The forsythia hedge blocked their view of the house, but as Janina could have told her mother, it didn't do much in the way of screening voices.

There was a knock on the door of the Christians' house. Then a pause before the sound of a door opening.

There were murmurs of voices, and Maddy and Janina both caught the word "FBI" Maddy said, "Oh, dear God," in a hushed voice. She looked back at her laundry, fidgeted with a damp bed sheet, and set it back into the laundry basket. Her face redder than usual, she stammered, "Oh… Janina, I... uh...." and then spied the matchbox cars Janina had left by the hedge the previous afternoon. The triumph in her face was unmistakable. "Just look at those toy trucks you left all over by the hedge yesterday!" she crowed, speaking unusually quickly for a lecture. "You two kids, you never take care of your toys. I am so tired of having to clean up after you both. You'll work me to death yet." She then veritably trotted over to the hedge.

Janina tried not to smile and followed her mother over. It was sometimes convenient that there was at least one thing the two of them had in common. Maddy knelt on the grass, carefully picked up the matchbox cars, dusted them off on her apron, and deposited them very gently in her apron pocket. Neither one spoke.

"... trying to find the whereabouts of Justin Lazarus," a male voice was saying.

"I'm sorry, I don't know," said a female voice. It was Kathy. She sounded near the breaking point but was controlling it. "He isn't due in to work until eleven o'clock. I'd expect he'd be home."

"Where is home?"

"He lives in an apartment somewhere in the village. Surely that's easy enough to find out. Why are you asking me?"

The response was blunt. "Let us ask the questions, ma'am. Do you know where his apartment is?"

"All of our employee records are at the store. I'm sorry, I don't know where he lives."

"Might your husband know?" The voice had taken on a hint of a threat to it.

There was a moment's hesitation. "Perhaps. But he's not here now. He went out early to pick up some rabbits one of the local farmers is trying to sell. He'll be in the store by eight-thirty."

"Thanks." The voice sounded anything but thankful.

There was a sound of retreating footsteps, clopping hollowly on the wooden front stairs, and simultaneously the door of the house closed. Two car doors slammed almost as one. Then there was the low, coughing roar of a big engine being started.

"My goodness," said Maddy, under her breath. "FBI." Then she seemed to be aware that Janina was watching her intently. "Shameful the way you two treat your toys," she added, breathlessly, quickly scooping up the last two cars and dropping them unceremoniously and un-wiped into her apron pocket.

Alarm bells sounded in Janina's head. It was a new, startling sensation that came from all directions at once. She felt compelled irresistibly to... to do what? She wasn't quite sure, but she knew that this compulsion was strong enough to make her jump from a cliff if that was its aim. Almost without willing it, she said, "Can I go ride my bike, Mom?"

Maddy got up and walked back toward the unfinished laundry. "Yes, you can. Just watch the traffic and stop at stop signs...." The remainder of the lecture—which this morning seemed strangely devoid of its usual vigor—was lost on Janina, who had bolted for the garage as soon as she had heard the first word.

☆☆☆

The tassels of her handlebars flickered in the speed of her pedaling, and the heavy, humid air flowed over her body fast enough to feel almost comfortable. Janina was heading toward Main Street as fast as she could push her little bicycle.

But why? The question tumbled through her brain like a leaf on the wind. Why was she doing this?

Then the answer came, seeming to come from somewhere outside of her own mind. Of course, she knew perfectly well why.

To warn Justin.

Why did she want to warn Justin, though? Why did she feel like she didn't only want but *needed* to? This question propelled her mind into a cloudy region where she couldn't feel sure of anything. But she did know that she had to do it, and fast. She also somehow knew that this was not the last time in her life that she would feel this compulsion.

She braked to a standstill before crossing Main Street where she pedaled slowly across the crosswalk. She scanned the cars parked along the street in front of Lars's bicycle shop. No dark blue sedans. She coasted up onto the sidewalk, onto the grass, and hopped off her bike. She propped her bike next to the wall of the bicycle shop and stood there a moment, pondering her next move.

There had to be a way to get up to the second floor. Was it by going through the shop? She doubted it. Lars would not want a renter to have access to his merchandise at all hours of the night. So, how did you get up there?

She walked slowly along the front of the still-closed shop and just past it noticed a little recess with a small gate. She had probably seen it hundreds of times, but it had somehow never registered. She had never thought to ask where it might lead. But surely that had to be it. She reached up to unlatch it.

"Hey, you, where you think you're going?" A strident voice cut through Janina's thoughts, and she whirled around looking both guilty and terrified. She expected to see one of the men from the blue car, even though she had only had a fleeting glimpse of one of them, quick enough that she probably wouldn't have recognized him. Instead, she saw the glowering face of Lars Nilsson surrounded by his alarming mass of curling hair.

"I... I'm going up... I'm trying to find where Justin lives," Janina squeaked.

Lars's voice was as bristly as his beard. He didn't like children and suspected them all of being up to no good. "What for?" he asked, and it was nearly an accusation.

Her brother Doug, who had several unpleasant run-ins with Lars but had come off relatively unscathed, would have probably replied, "None of your damned business." Janina, though, didn't have Doug's age or self-assurance. She did, however, have a quick mind honed to an edge by years of evading her mother's prying. "My mom asked me to deliver a message to him." She hoped it sounded more plausible to him than it did to her.

Lars's bright blue eyes narrowed for a moment as if trying to come up with a reason why this was unacceptable. Apparently finding none, he said, "Through the gate and the door, then up the stairs." He then turned, unlocked the door of his shop, and went inside, re-locking it behind him.

Heart pounding, Janina reached up again to unlatch the gate, swung it open, and stepped into the narrow alley that opened beyond it. She let go of the gate to let it swing smoothly shut. The latch clicked once back in place. She stood for a moment, looking around her. The closing of the gate shut out the noise of Main Street. She felt suddenly alone, cut off and trapped in the bottom of a narrow rectangular brick box with a slice of sky for a roof.

At the far end was a door. Janina walked down the alley and opened it. Beyond was a dimly-lit staircase rising into a vague, shadowy space without any definition. Anything, she felt, could be up there. Climbing a staircase is a simple thing, perhaps, but it was one of the bravest things she had ever done to walk inside, let go of the door—which also swung shut behind her—and begin to ascend the steps.

She had only reached the third stair by the time her eyes had adjusted to the darkness, and she could see all the way to the top. The stairs ended on a shallow landing, beyond which there was yet another door. Justin's door. Upon seeing it, she was galvanized into action, sprinted up the remaining steps, and began pounding on the door.

"Justin! Justin! It's me, Janina. You've got to let me in. I have to talk to you!"

There was no sound of footsteps, but in moments the doorknob suddenly turned. Justin stood there barefoot but in his typical t-shirt and jeans. Janina knew immediately that he was scared. Seeing her here meant something to him. Did he know already what she was going to tell him? It wouldn't have surprised her.

Despite the fear that showed clearly in his face, Justin smiled at her. "Hi again. What's up?"

The words spilled out of her mouth with almost no conscious

volition. "You've got to get out of here. Two men showed up at Tom and Kathy's house this morning. They said they were FBI, and they were looking for you."

Justin's eyes went blank for a moment. Then, he knelt down in front of her. He reached out and took her by the shoulders, gently, but irresistibly. "What else did they say? What else did you overhear?"

Janina looked squarely into Justin's clear gray eyes and without hesitation said, "Kathy said that she didn't know where you lived, but that it was somewhere in the village. She said that Tom would be at the store at eight-thirty, and that he would know, that he would tell them. It's been enough time that they're probably there now. You've got to get out of here."

"You're sure she didn't tell them where I lived?"

Janina nodded.

Justin released her shoulders and rocked back on his heels. "Well, that gives me a little bit of time, at least." He stood up. "Thanks, Janina. You've really helped me a lot. I have to go now...." He paused. "I'll try to come talk to you one more time... down by your pond, maybe. If I can. But if I don't see you again... take care of yourself." He started to retreat into his apartment, then his face clouded. "Oh. And Janina?"

She looked up at him.

"Those men who talked to Kathy...." His voice trailed off. He seemed to be trying to decide what to say.

"What about them?" asked Janina finally.

"They're not from the FBI Don't talk to them. They're dangerous."

He reached out and gently touched her hair. Then, with a swift, graceful motion, he stepped into his apartment and shut the door.

CHAPTER 6

Janina didn't want her husband to come home.

In fourteen years of marriage, that was the first time she had ever felt that way. She wasn't mad at Jim. In fact, the reason for her feelings had very little to do with him at all. The problem was that she knew how perceptive he was. She was upset, terribly upset, by what had happened earlier that day at Hazleton Institution, and she knew that all she'd have to do is open her mouth for him to know something was wrong. Then he'd ask questions. And then what?

Should she lie and further widen the rift that this situation was creating between Janina and her family? Or tell him the truth—that she had taken a personal day to go see Kathy, which she had specifically told Jim she wouldn't do? Neither answer seemed a viable option.

The more she tried to work her way through this maze, the more entangled she became.

Maybe there was no way out.

So when she heard the door open, and then the kids shouting,

"Hi, Dad!" she cringed.

This was it. He'd know, surely he'd know as soon as he walked in the kitchen.

But he didn't. He came in, gave her a smile and a kiss, stirred the pot of soup on the stove, and asked if his help was needed. She told him no, everything was under control and dinner would be ready in about a half hour. Then he went off to read the newspaper.

Janina stood there for nearly a minute, not sure whether to be elated or disturbed by the fact that he hadn't noticed her black mood. Either she was hiding it better, or he was becoming used to her being distraught.

"I am cracking up," she finally murmured while leaning against the counter and staring blankly at the ribbons of steam curling up from the soup pot. "Pretty soon I'll be joining Kathy in the nuthouse." But saying that just brought back the memory of Kathy, the real Kathy, in that horrible, empty visitation room, reaching out toward Janina across the Formica-topped table in desperation, and that added another dimension to her dark dismay.

But whether she was right about her family becoming used to her moodiness, or because of her determination not to let her cheerful mask slip tonight, no one that evening seemed to notice that anything was wrong. Dinner, homework, and bedtime all swirled around her like a noisy torrent, and then, quite suddenly, the house was quiet. The kids disappeared into their respective bedrooms. Jim was stretched out on the couch reading a veterinary journal. Janina sat in the recliner, staring unseeingly at the newspaper. She was thinking with equal measures of pride and shame about how she had played her role with conviction and had successfully avoided any suspicion that things were not as they should be with her.

Then Jim looked up, over the tops of his reading glasses, and said, "You look a little tired tonight, honey." Janina responded by bursting into tears.

She was hardly aware of being bundled into his arms and virtually carried onto the couch. Jim pulled her against his massive chest, and she melted into him, sobbing and darkening his shirt with her tears. Finally, the tempest had largely passed, and Jim asked, his voice gentle, "What happened today?"

This brought a fresh round of tears, but they were fewer this time and over sooner. Jim, who was not really used to seeing his wife fall to pieces, simply sat and held her and didn't say anything more.

"Jim," Janina finally said, "I went to see Kathy at the Institution today."

She felt a momentary stiffening of his body, but he said nothing.

She then told him about her visit, the prison-like atmosphere, the cold, emotionless guards, being searched, the sterile, fluorescent-lit rooms—and then of her conversation with Kathy, the seeming sense of it at first, and how it had degenerated into what could only be wild fantasies.

"Oh, my God, it was so horrible," she finished. The tears were once more fighting their way to the surface. "She acted so reasonable, so much like the old Kathy. But she... she was...." She gulped and tightened her embrace of her husband's middle. "That place, it was hideous. I can't imagine what it would be like to be there. I just can't imagine it."

There was a silence, and then Jim asked, his voice still quiet, "Do you think that you can let it go now?"

"Oh, I don't know. I feel this compulsion, Jim. It's like it comes from somewhere outside of me. I don't understand it, but it's almost impossible to ignore. When we talked—and when I talked with Lucy—I really had decided to destroy the letter and forget all about it. But I couldn't. It's like there's something that won't let me let this go." She paused, and then added, "It scares me."

"What are you going to do now?"

Her voice almost a whisper, Janina said, "I feel like I need to go look for the necklace."

"You know that's illegal."

"Oh, I know that. But I don't know if I can stop myself. God, I'm so confused."

"Did she say why she wanted it?"

Janina frowned. "She said that it had been given to her by someone named Justin Lazarus." She paused, her frown deepening. "That's another thing. I have this feeling that I should know who he is, that I *do* know who he is... but I can't remember. I can't remember him at all." There was another pause, and then she said, "I think I'm going crazy."

He ignored this last comment. "But she didn't say why the necklace was important?"

"No."

Jim seemed to sense that he shouldn't question her any further. He pulled her close, and she closed her eyes and relaxed into him. After a few moments, he said, tentatively, "Well, you know I hate giving advice, but I really think that you need to come to peace with this."

Janina's eyes snapped open. She said, with a touch of anger, "That's what I've been trying to do. For weeks now."

Jim's voice was soothing. "I know. But now you've seen Kathy, and you've seen that she isn't like you remember her. She really is insane, whether or not she killed her husband. Anything she asks you to do needs to be seen in that light. You need to close this affair and get on with your own life."

Janina sighed again, and said, "I know. You're right. You, and Lucy, are both right. I should never have gone. Seeing her just made it a hundred times worse. Now that I've seen her, maybe I can let it go."

"Good. I'm glad to hear you say that. For right now, I think it's time for us both to go to bed. And no more unscheduled personal days, okay?" He gave her a little squeeze. "At least next time when you do something foolish, take me along."

It was midnight. Janina was standing in her bathrobe on the back porch of the Christians' house. In one hand she held a small claw hammer, and in the other she held a flashlight. She hadn't the slightest idea of how she had gotten there. She remembered being led up to bed, undressing and climbing under the covers, and her husband holding her close as she slipped off into sleep more easily than she had in days. Then, without warning, here she was, her bare feet cold and wet with dew, leaving tracks on the stairs that showed dark in the silvery moonlight.

Janina peered into the dark windows, then into the small rectangular window in the back door. There wasn't sufficient light to see anything more than black shadows. She rattled the door handle, but of course the door was locked. There was a thin, almost inaudible thought of *What on earth am I doing here?* before she struck the window in the door with the hammer.

In the stillness of the night the sound of the glass shattering was far louder than she had expected. Somewhere nearby, a dog barked, then subsided. Janina stood, frozen to the spot, expecting the lights to come on in the neighbors' house—her parents' old home—but nothing happened. She waited for about five minutes, but the silence was unbroken. So, she slipped the hammer into one of the deep pockets of her bathrobe, reached in through the broken window, and unlocked the door. Then she opened it and stepped inside.

She switched on the flashlight, taking care to aim it at the floor. She found herself in the broad, open kitchen floored with linoleum patterned with yellow rectangles. As a child, she had been inside this house several times, and memories came flooding back to her—cookies and tea with Kathy and her mom, sitting in one of the cane-back kitchen chairs and swinging her legs a good two inches off the floor. She could almost hear their conversation now, as if a memory of it were trapped in this room, echoing down the years.

She looked around her. Two doors led out of the kitchen. One, she recalled, was the door to a pantry, and the other opened into the living room, but she couldn't remember which was which. She tried one and found herself facing rows of empty shelves. She shut it, went to the other one, and the beam of her flashlight swung silently out into the darkened living room.

This was where it happened twenty-five years ago. Was it true that houses remembered violent acts that were committed in them? This one certainly seemed peaceful enough. You'd never guess.

The beam of the flashlight ran over armchairs wearing old gray slipcovers like linen shrouds, and a couch draped with a swath of cloth which made it, in the dimness, look like some great, sleeping animal. The dark, shiny hardwood floors were relatively dust-free. Janina guessed that the house had recently been cleaned because it was being sold. The flashlight searched the corners of the room. Where had Kathy said it would be? In a heat vent along the wall that separated the living room from the kitchen.

In the end, the vent turned out to be virtually under her feet, right next to the door by which she had entered the room. She knelt on the floor and tugged at the metal grate. With a creak of protest, the grate came loose, and she pulled it out and set it on the floor next to the vent. Janina aimed the flashlight down into the rectangular opening, wondering how far down the duct went.

It turned out that the vent made a right angle a little more than an arm's length underneath the floor. Surely, anything that had gone down the vent would still be there, caught in the bend.

Janina eagerly turned the flashlight this way and that, but all that she saw was the dull, dusty surface of the galvanized duct.

Maybe someone else had found it. Maybe it had been gone for years.

Or maybe it was never there at all.

As that alarming thought was passing through her mind, she caught a glimpse of something a little brighter on the dull metal floor of the duct, right at the point where it disappeared into the dark reaches of the heating system. She leaned forward, training the flashlight beam on it, and squinted down into the hole. The object was slender, irregular in shape, and glittered slightly. It was hard to tell what she was seeing. It could be a necklace, or it could simply be a stray piece of wire.

Janina lay on her stomach and reached her arm into the vent. The tips of her fingers touched the object, and she felt the roughness of tiny links. Immediately she knew what it was.

It was a thin metal chain.

She gave a little cry of triumph, and her index finger and thumb came together over it before she lifted it up. It was unusually heavy for its size. When she had retrieved it, she brought her legs underneath her and sat cross-legged on the floor while shining the flashlight into the palm of her hand to see what it was that she had found— what Kathy thought was so important.

It was, as she had thought when she touched it, a fine silver chain, strangely untarnished by all the years it had spent down in the depths of the heating vent. Hanging from it was a tiny pendant. It, too, was made of silver. Five thin wires, shaped to form a spherical cage, joined together at the top into a loop through which the chain passed. Trapped within the cage was a little silver ball about the same diameter as a pencil eraser. It made a faint, sweet chiming noise as it moved inside its cage.

"It's beautiful," said Janina aloud.

At the same time, she became aware of the risk she was

taking by lingering here. She quickly slipped the necklace into her robe pocket, making sure that it was not the same one occupied by the hammer. Then she fitted the grate back into the vent opening, rose, and walked back into the kitchen, shutting the living room door behind her. She crossed the kitchen, noticed the glass on the floor for the first time, and opened the door onto the back porch, stepping carefully to avoid cutting her feet. She relocked the door, and walked down the stairs, where she discovered that she'd cut her foot anyway. She wondered momentarily when it had happened and felt a vague surprise that she hadn't been aware of it.

She walked down the brick pathway along the back of the house, and saw her car parked at the end of the driveway. It was only then that she realized that she had had no memory of where she had left the car, or indeed of having driven here at all. If the car had not been in the driveway, she would have been at a complete loss, and would probably have walked home, barefoot and clad in her bathrobe.

The keys were still dangling from the ignition. Without turning on the headlights, she started the engine, and then backed down the driveway. She pulled out into the street, put the car into drive, and drove away. She waited until she had reached the first stop sign before turning on the headlights.

She drove the rest of the way home, feeling suddenly drained of thoughts and energy. She was nearly asleep on her feet by the time she pulled the car into her garage. Stumbling drowsily from the car, she shut the door as quietly as she could. She opened the door into the kitchen noiselessly and padded across to the staircase leading up to her bedroom. She slipped off her bathrobe and climbed into bed beside Jim, who thankfully seemed to have once again slept through her nocturnal restlessness. Within thirty seconds, she was asleep herself.

CHAPTER 7

Janina rode her bicycle home slowly and cautiously. She shied like a skittish horse when she saw a dark blue car at the corner of King Street and Haskill Road, but it turned out to be only Mrs. O'Neal, her curly red hair tied back with a scarf into an untidy snarl. She waved and grinned as Janina passed her. The car, far from the sleek, shiny machine driven by the FBI men, was an old Buick with gaping rust wounds above the wheel wells and looked like it contained about seven children—although they were in constant motion, and it was difficult to tell. Janina smiled back wanly and continued to pedal up King Street past the Sorensons' house, then the McMillans', and finally up to her own driveway. She coasted into her garage, dismounted, and walked into the house.

Janina felt disoriented, punch-drunk. She felt like she remembered feeling when, in the grip of a January cold, she had been given a cup of sticky green fluid by her mother and had downed it without a word, her submissiveness a better indication of her illness than any thermometer. It had been Nyquil, and she had fallen asleep within fifteen minutes, but not before spending an amazing interval where she alternately felt like the room was spinning, she was spinning, or both.

Today she remembered that strange green stuff and how it had made her feel and recognized the similarity in how she felt today. The difference was that today her body felt fine. Today it was all in her head. It was like her brain had been slapped silly and then given a double dose of Extra-Strength Nyquil.

She walked through the kitchen. Her mother was on the phone, chattering so busily that she didn't even notice Janina's entrance, nor her bemused expression. Janina heard a sweep of conversation brush past her, fading in and out as she first approached her mother, then passed her as she headed off down the hall to her room.

"... well, Georgia, I'm sure I don't know, but I know I heard the word 'FBI' And you know what that means.... They were looking for that boy that works for Tom and Kathy. Justin Something-or-Another.... That's right, Lazarus. I'll bet it isn't his real name, of course. You know, the first time I set eyes on him, I knew something wasn't right.... Oh, no, I can't believe it either.... Of course! Kathy surely must know where he lives. I think she must have been covering up for him.... Well, yes, you're right, Georgia, they will find him sooner or later. Hopefully sooner.... Yes.... No, I have no idea what he could have done, but it must have been serious...."

Janina went into her bedroom and closed the door. Her mother's voice continued as a faint, rising and falling murmur in the background, in which no words were discernible. She sat down on her bed, staring blankly in front of her, for some time.

Within ten minutes, the fog had begun to clear, and she looked around her as if noticing where she was for the first time. She wondered how she had gotten to her bedroom. Wasn't she just outside listening with her mother to the two strange men talking to Kathy in such a threatening fashion? She remembered them getting in their car and driving away. Then, it felt as if she had blinked her eyes and here she was, sitting on her bed.

So, Justin was in trouble with the police. She found the idea a little sad but hardly surprising given his strange, frightened behavior the two times he had spoken to her previously. She supposed that she should warn him that the men were after him. She glanced at the clock on her desk. It was almost nine o'clock. Kathy had said that Tom would be at the store by eight-thirty, and he would surely have given them Justin's address. It was pretty likely that Justin had already been arrested and was handcuffed in the back of that big blue car. It was too late to warn him. No point in it now.

Janina wondered what he could have done. Her understanding of the criminal justice system was mostly gleaned from watching *Dragnet* and *The Mod Squad*, but it was light years away from anything in her actual experience. The entire village of Guildford was policed by one man, Officer DeRosa, and his job seemed to consist mainly of catching speeders and preventing teenage pranks. Real crime was virtually nonexistent. Many people in Guildford didn't even lock their doors when they left their houses for the day.

Still, she did understand that if the FBI. was after you, you must have done something really bad. This was out of Officer DeRosa's league. These people meant business. They weren't part of the village. They were people from outside who could come into the village and take away someone if they'd done something really bad.

So, what really bad thing had Justin done? Janina had a hard time imagining Justin doing something of that sort, something like the crimes that Sergeant Joe Friday was always solving—murder, theft, arson, assault. Could that gentle, innocent young man really have done something like that?

Janina stood and walked out of her bedroom. The house was already becoming oppressively hot and stuffy. The heat and humidity had been building for several days, and now it was at levels more typical of the Deep South than upstate New York. It was, in a word, miserable. The windows were open, but it hardly seemed to matter. The air wasn't moving at all. Perhaps if the sliding glass door at the back of the living room had been opened wide, it would have been better, but it had no screen—Doug had put a football through it earlier that summer, and it had never been replaced. Her mother didn't like to leave it open because it let flies in.

Maddy was getting ready to vacuum the living room floor. Her broad face was damp and ruddy with the heat, but even when she was deathly sick, she never stopped doing housework. She certainly wouldn't let a little thing like a muggy day stop her. Janina wondered, not for the first time, why she felt it was so important to keep the house spotless. Neither of the children cared. Leonard would probably have said something if he did, but truthfully he hardly seemed to notice. The vacuum cleaner began its shrill howl, and Janina made her escape into the comparative silence of the back yard.

She spent most of the rest of the morning idling, pitching rocks into the pond, trying to catch the big bullfrog that lived near the cluster of pink waterlilies on the far side, and making little boats out of the bark of a fallen pine tree from the woods behind their yard. She kept looking up, hoping that she'd see Justin walking towards her, and then wondering at herself for wishing it. She also wished she could have warned him in time. He'd scared her, upset her, and mystified her, but for some reason she still liked him. It saddened her to think of him captive like a rabbit in a hunter's snare.

Lunchtime came, and then at one o'clock her father returned home cheerful as always. Janina listened as Maddy recounted the entire story about the visit of the FBI men at Kathy's house. She found it mildly funny that her mother framed the entire story in such a way as to disguise the fact that she'd heard the whole thing because she'd been eavesdropping. Leonard chewed thoughtfully on his ham sandwich, occasionally interjecting, "Well!" or "You don't say!" but otherwise not commenting. Maddy finished with a triumphant declaration, "Amazing that Tom and Kathy hired a criminal to work for them!"

Janina felt a sudden desire to defend Justin but fortunately caught herself in time.

"Well, now," said Leonard. "They didn't exactly say he was a criminal."

"Why else would they have been looking for him? Just tell me that."

"Maybe they wanted him for questioning. Maybe he knows something about a case. You never can tell."

Maddy seemed put out. "Leonard, all I can say is that I've spoken to him, so I should think I know what he's like. You're entitled to your own opinions, of course."

Janina wanted to interject that only two days ago Maddy had been saying how nice Justin seemed to be, but once again she wisely remained silent.

Leonard finished his glass of milk. "You may be right, Maddy," he said mildly. He considered for a moment, and then his face clouded. "Have you noticed that we've got Japanese beetles on the roses again?"

Maddy was on the verge of what would have undoubtedly been an acidic comment regarding the relative importance of fugitive criminals and Japanese beetles. The doorbell rang, though, and she never got to make it. Still looking at her husband with a pinched and peevish expression, she said to Janina, "Janina, go answer the door. It's probably Georgia. She said she'd be coming by this afternoon. She must have left the library early today."

Janina dutifully got up and trotted into the living room, went to the front door, and without hesitation swung the door wide open. She expected to see the severe, angular face of Mrs. Petrie, the head librarian and her mother's best friend, but Georgia Petrie wasn't there. Janina froze like a cornered mouse. Her mouth was open, but no sounds came out.

Standing at the door were two men in dark business suits. One was tall with brown hair graying at the temples and thick wire-rim glasses that made his blue eyes look far larger than they were. The other was shorter and heavier with dark hair and a face smudged with an early case of five o'clock shadow. This man carried a shiny black clipboard under one arm.

"Is your father or mother at home?" asked the tall one. He didn't speak loudly, but his voice held an implicit threat like the sound of thunder in the distance.

Janina found her own voice, but it came out in a stuttering squeak. "I... I'll... get him... them."

She backed up, keeping her eyes on the men who made no move to enter the house. When she felt she'd put sufficient distance between herself and them, she turned and fled into the kitchen.

Her parents were both still in there. Her father was at the sink where he was washing his lunch dishes, and her mother seated at the table.

"Well, where's Georgia?" Maddy demanded.

Janina ignored her mother completely. "Dad?" Her voice was still a fluttery tremolo, and her father turned toward her, frowning. He seemed to take in her distress—her pale face, her fast breathing—but he didn't seem sure how to respond to it. Finally, all he said was, "Yes?"

Janina gulped. "Dad, there are two men at the door. They want to talk to you."

The significance of this was immediately obvious to both him and Maddy. Leonard hesitated. "To me?" To Janina's amazement, he sounded frightened.

Maddy said in exasperation, "Well, Leonard, don't keep them waiting for heaven's sake!"

Leonard put down the towel he had been using and left the room. Maddy followed, her curiosity evident in her every move. Finally, so did Janina, but she would get no closer than the doorway between the kitchen and the living room. When she turned the corner, she could see the two men and her father standing at the door.

"Are you Leonard Starcevich?" the tall man, who seemed to be the leader, was asking.

"Yes, I am."

"Mr. Starcevich, we're from the FBI" Both men flashed badges at him, and then the taller man handed him a business card, which Leonard took and frowned at for a moment. "We're trying to locate a man named Justin Lazarus. We'd like to ask you a few questions. Would that be all right?"

"I suppose it would."

Janina's eyes widened. They hadn't caught Justin after all! She felt a surge of relief and lightness of heart, and then immediately forced herself to attend once more to what the men were saying to her father.

The tall man was still speaking. "Your wife's name is Madeleine, and you have a daughter named Janina?"

"Yes."

The shorter man looked down and began writing on his clipboard.

"Do you know Justin Lazarus?"

"I don't know him. I mean, I've seen him a few times. I know he works for Tom Christian, but I don't know that I've ever even spoken to him." His voice sounded hesitant, uncertain.

Maddy, on the other hand, who had tried unsuccessfully to get a glimpse at the business card her husband was holding, moved to the side and behind him and was nearly pawing the ground with impatience. It was with obvious difficulty that she held her tongue and let her husband speak.

"He's been seen on your property," the tall man was saying,

staring at Leonard with those odd, cold blue eyes.

Janina felt the last of the blood drain from her face. The room felt like it was spinning again but for a completely different reason this time. Someone had seen them talking? How was that possible? What did it mean? And... most frightening of all... if they knew that she had spoken to him, would these men want to take her away, too?

"Well, I'm sure I don't know anything about it," said Leonard. "I certainly have never seen him come onto my property."

The tall man gestured with a minute nod of his head toward Maddy. "How about you, Mrs. Starcevich?"

Maddy stepped forward, very nearly shouldering Leonard aside in the process. "I've seen him at the hardware store, of course, but not on our property. I don't know what this Justin Lazarus is wanted for, but you need to understand that we have nothing at all to do with it. We're law-abiding people, Mr... uh, Mr.?" She ended on a question, her eyes bright and eager.

"I have no doubt that you are, Mrs. Starcevich," said the tall man. He ignored Maddy's implicit question. "How about your daughter?"

Maddy's expression became even more righteous. She responded, "Of course she hasn't seen him here," in such declamatory tones that Janina momentarily doubted her own memory and wondered if perhaps her mother might not be right.

"Perhaps we could hear it from her?" the man persisted. His voice was flat, cold, and impossible to deny.

Maddy's eyebrows rose. Janina saw her expression, and immediately realized, *My mom is scared, too*. The thought left her doubly terrified. Even her mother seemed to have met her match in these men. Maddy turned and said, "Janina, come here. You don't need to be afraid. They have a question they'd like to ask you."

Janina felt that she had to force her legs to move and was sure that the effort would show in her face. None of the four people watching her, however, showed any sign of noticing her distress. Her parents seemed scared on their own behalf, and it didn't seem to enter their minds that Janina might possibly have been the one who had spoken to Justin on their property. She finally made her way to the door.

In the past when Janina had spoken to strange adults, their voices became gentler and softer. When the FBI man spoke, though, his tone and manner became even more subtly threatening. "Do you know who Justin Lazarus is?" he asked, staring at Janina with his flat, impassive blue eyes.

Janina stared back at him, not certain if she would be able to answer. It was with something like astonishment that she heard her voice saying, "Yes, I know who he is. He works for Tom and Kathy." Her voice sounded tremulous, but this man didn't care. She was quite certain that it was all the same to him if he left her sobbing and miserable.

"Have you ever spoken to him here on your parents' property?"

Again, the magnified blue eyes probed her. "No," she finally said. "I only saw him at the hardware store."

The men exchanged a momentary glance, and then the tall man turned his attention back to Leonard. Janina once more became a nonentity. "Thank you. I think those are all the questions we have for now. However, Mr. and Mrs. Starcevich, we want you to know that this man, who is using the name of Justin Lazarus, is dangerous. He is extremely dangerous. If you see him, you should not attempt to speak to him, and you especially shouldn't try to apprehend him. Simply go to the telephone and dial that number on the business card. Our office is down in Colville, and we can be out here within twenty minutes. It is essential that you understand this. Your daughter, too."

"Of course, we understand it," said Maddy eagerly. "As I was saying before, you need to know that we are law-abiding citizens and have every wish to...."

The tall man cut her off with a single small gesture of his hand. A chilly smile crossed his lips, but it did not touch his eyes and was quickly swallowed up. "I am aware of that. You have not been accused of anything and don't need to defend yourselves. I am giving you a warning, not an indictment." Again, there was a moment's exchange of glances between the two men. "Good day, Mr. Starcevich, Mrs. Starcevich."

"Good day," echoed Leonard.

The door closed.

There was a moment's silence, and then Maddy snatched the business card from her husband's hand. "Paul S. Trowbridge, Federal Bureau of Investigations," she read aloud. "Well, I don't know how it seemed to you, Leonard, but I definitely think that man believes we're guilty of something!"

"Now, Maddy," Leonard said, "he said that he knew we were law-abiding...."

Maddy cut him off with an impatient noise. "Well, maybe. Now what I want to know is, why was this Justin Lazarus on our property? Trespassing, but why? I'll bet that he was up to no good. And who can have seen him and told those men? I'll bet it was that Pauline McMillan. That woman is never happy unless she's sticking her nose into someone else's business."

"Maybe Kathy or Tom told them," Leonard said, but he sounded unsure. "You said the FBI men talked to Kathy and Tom first. Why would they have talked to Pauline at all? What does she have to do with any of this?"

"I know Kathy didn't tell them, because, well, I was...." Maddy stumbled, flustered for a moment, and then continued. "I *told* you, Leonard, that I had heard what they were saying to Kathy. They were talking loud enough for anyone to hear."

"Then maybe Tom told them."

"Maybe," replied Maddy but didn't seem convinced.

Janina silently turned and walked back through the kitchen,

down the hall, and into her room.

Dangerous. That's what they'd said. He was extremely dangerous. Don't speak to him.

She sat down on her bed for the second time that day. Almost without thinking about it, she reached out and picked up her stuffed bear and held on to him. Comfort from anywhere was welcome at this moment. It was obvious that her parents were not going to be able to provide it. They'd been thrown off balance by this themselves.

Was Justin dangerous? He'd saved her from being hurt at the parade. He'd always seemed nice....

But no, he hadn't. He'd scared her good a couple of times. Maybe they were right about him.

Was he dangerous? And how would she know?

How could she possibly be sure?

All of a sudden, she was sure. She didn't know how. She pictured Justin, clad in his old t-shirt and jeans, his smile like spring after winter, and then Mr. Trowbridge with his strange, expressionless blue eyes and icy demeanor. It was obvious whom she believed.

Justin. She believed Justin.

Janina frowned, her eyes squinting as if she were trying to stare right through her closet door. In reality, she hardly realized what she was looking at, because the sudden decision to trust what Justin said had deflected her mind into another track entirely—a track that brought her face-to-face with a question that was straight from a nightmare, and then left her there.

If Justin was the one who was telling the truth, then those two men weren't from the FBI He'd said himself that they weren't. But if they were not from the FBI, then who were they?

CHAPTER 8

The clock radio went off, a burst of discordant notes that Janina vaguely recognized as some recent number-one hit song. She opened her eyes and switched it off, letting the renewed silence flow over her.

She yawned and stretched as her brain began to activate—a process that was never complete before breakfast. What a strange dream she had. Something about breaking windows in Kathy's old house and pulling up heat grates. She swung her legs out of bed, and when her left foot touched the floor, she winced slightly. She crossed her legs and turned the sole of her foot upwards. There was a small cut, reddened and tender to the touch, on the ball of her foot.

Her eyes widened, and her mouth opened slightly, her heart drumming against her ribs. She turned and looked at the floor at the foot of the bed, knowing already what she would see—her aqua-green bathrobe crumpled into an untidy heap.

She stood, limped over to the robe, and picked it up. It felt heavier than it should have, and one pocket was distorted by the shape of some narrow, dense object. She reached into it and pulled out a small claw hammer.

"Dear God," said Janina quietly.

She turned the robe around in her hands to frantically reach into the other pocket. After feeling about in it for a few seconds, she drew out a slender silver necklace with a pendant shaped like a cage with a ball in it.

"What on earth am I going to do with this?" she said. No one, including herself, volunteered an answer.

Janina dropped the hammer into her dresser drawer and pulled several pairs of socks over it. She'd have to remember to retrieve it later and return it to the garage. Then she rehung her bathrobe in the closet, and after some thought, she placed the necklace around her neck. It looked fragile, and Kathy evidently valued it highly. It wouldn't do to damage or lose it, whether or not she ever actually had the opportunity to give it to Kathy. She certainly didn't want anyone, Jim or the kids especially, to notice it and comment on it. Better to have it remain hidden along with her knowledge of where and how she had found it.

As Janina was dressing for work, she slipped on her blouse over Kathy's necklace. After a moment's thought, she selected a second necklace to wear on the outside.

Her work day proceeded without incident, class following class. She thought periodically about the events of the previous night, but they still seemed unreal. She had to fight with herself not to label the memories as a weird dream, and it was only the occasional soft chime from the little caged ball lying against her skin that reminded her that what had happened was not, could not be, a dream.

Between second period jazz chorus and third period select chorus, Janina was hurriedly rearranging her sheet music in preparation for the new group of students when a pleasant voice behind her said, "Excuse me."

Janina turned to see Martha standing beside the doorway. She was dressed in a simple flower-print dress, her long, straight blond hair pulled back with a dark green silk scarf. She smiled fetchingly, and said, "Sorry to disturb you between classes, I'm sure you've got a million things to do...."

Janina smiled in response. "No, no problem. I was just getting my music ready to go. Some days I don't know how I keep it all straight as to which group is learning what."

"I can't imagine how you do it." Martha's tone was so warm that it didn't sound like flattery. "Wanda told me that she wanted me to do some observing of other teachers, even teachers outside my own subject area. She said that you really work wonders with your select chorus and thought I might like to watch you for a period. If this isn't a good day...."

"No, it's fine," Janina said. It wasn't uncommon for student teachers to observe a variety of classrooms other than their own assignment, although Janina did have a momentary pang of wonder about what could have gotten into Wanda, who hardly had a kind word to say about anyone. "We're practicing for a concert—the last one of the school year—and we're working on a piece called the *Geographical Fugue* which we'll be performing. It's the most difficult thing we've ever attempted, and it's probably pretty different from anything you've ever heard before. You can sit at my desk if you like, and we can talk afterwards."

Martha smiled. "Thanks. I'd love to."

The late bell rang, and Janina began the warm-up —"Monday my mother makes me Mexican munchies." Martha's lovely smile flashed out at the sweet harmonizing on the nonsense words, eliciting a significant amount of surreptitious drooling on the part of the bass and tenor section. Then the rehearsing began, and Martha's attention was unwavering. She seemed entirely captivated.

Janina had her planning time during fourth period. When the bell had rung and the students filed out, Martha stood up and walked to her. "Wow," she said, the admiration apparent in her voice. "Wanda was certainly right. I've heard college choral groups who weren't this good."

"Oh, come, now." Janina felt a blush rising in her cheeks. She picked up her director's score and closed it. "They have a long way to go."

"Well, no doubt to your ears, but to someone like myself who loves music but doesn't know a whole lot about the technical side of it, they sounded splendid. When is the concert? I must make a point of going."

"May 27th."

"How did you hurt your foot?"

The question was so unexpected that Janina just froze, gaping at the other woman in silence. Finally, she said, "What did you say?"

Martha's kind expression didn't waver. "I said, how did you hurt your foot?"

Janina stared at Martha, unable to contain the jet of cold fear rising inside her but determined not to let it show. "I cut it on a piece of broken glass. How did you know?"

"I noticed you limping."

Janina's heart hammered against her chest. She had hardly walked anywhere all period. And she was not really limping in any case. She knew, she just knew.

But how?

"It's only a little cut." Janina kept her voice even with an effort. "One of my kids broke a drinking glass and evidently a chip of it got missed when we were cleaning up. I found it with my foot this morning."

"That's the pits. I did that once. The worst part was that I didn't realize it at first and left little spots of blood all over the house. It would have been easy for any bloodhound to track me down." She laughed merrily.

Could she have left bloody tracks in Kathy's house? She

tried, with little success, to force a smile. "Thank you for coming in this morning. I'm sure my students liked having a chance to give a little pre-performance for an appreciative audience."

"Oh, it was my pleasure entirely. In fact, I'd love to come back and observe again."

Janina nodded, feeling that her smile was fading around the edges. When was this woman going to leave?

Martha seemed to be aware of Janina's discomfort. "Well, I've got to get back to the keyboarding room. I've taken over Wanda's fifth period, so I've got to make sure I know what I'm going to do with them." She walked to the door and then paused. Her smile flashed out again, full of sweetness and innocence and playfulness in exactly the right proportions. "Oh, I forgot to mention, that's a lovely necklace you have on."

And then she was gone.

Janina felt like she'd been punched in the solar plexus. She sat down on the piano stool and looked down at the simple little necklace she was wearing on the outside of her blouse—a small gold-plate maple leaf sent to her by a Canadian friend the previous Christmas. She lifted it and let it dangle from her hand.

This? Surely she couldn't have meant this.

She let the necklace drop, and as she did, she knew with certainty that Martha had not meant that necklace at all. She knew. Quiet desperation settled over her. Martha knew what she'd done. She knew how she'd cut her foot. And she knew about Kathy's necklace.

There was no rational way Martha could know any of that.

But she did.

Janina didn't eat lunch in the faculty room that day. Martha would have been there with her sweetly innocent smile and her razor-edged comments alongside her air of quiet intelligence and strange ability to know things she should have no way of knowing. No, there was no way Janina could face eating lunch at the same table as Martha.

So she ate her brown-bag lunch at her desk in the music office, wondering how on earth she had let herself get so deeply entangled in this strange affair.

The necklace seemed to weigh heavily around her neck. Now that she had retrieved it—almost against her own will—from Kathy's house, she felt that she had to do something with it. But what? The only option seemed to be to try to get it to Kathy. Janina knew she couldn't just keep it herself. To lie to Jim that she had bought it at the Marrakesh Bazaar, a curio shop down in Colville, and begin to wear it as casually as she wore her other inexpensive jewelry? No, that was impossible. There was some indefinable air of importance, of seriousness, about the necklace. To treat it like a piece of cheap costume jewelry wasn't an option.

So how could she get it to Kathy? It would be impossible to give it to her in that huge, empty room without the guard seeing her. Also, in her current emotional state, Janina wasn't sure she could face going back in there again.

Suddenly she remembered something that Kathy had said. There was someone who might be able to help. She'd mentioned him in her letter, too. What was it that she had said? Something about a male nurse....

The words suddenly came back in a flood, and she could picture Kathy sitting at that table, so frail and slender, and hear her voice....

"... Even better, give it to Leo Carson, and he'll get it to me. He's my friend here. He's one of the nurses. He lives in Emerson. You could give him a call. Then, meet him and give it to him. That would probably be safer...."

That was it. Janina could give him the necklace, and it would be off her hands. It could hardly be dangerous to meet this friend of Kathy's somewhere neutral away from the institution and hand it over to him. Then Leo Carson could run the risks. He would be far less likely to get caught anyway, because he worked in the institution where talking to an inmate, or even giving her something, would hardly be looked upon as unusual.

Janina reached out, picked up the telephone, and dialed information, trying not to think of the last time she had done this, only two weeks ago—it seemed like years—and had ended up in a bitter conversation with Tom Christian's sister.

"What city?" came the inflectionless voice at the other end of the line.

"Emerson."

"Go ahead."

"Leo Carson."

There was a pause, then, "Please hold for the number," followed by a click, and then the computer recited his telephone number. Janina jotted it down. She pushed down the lever to cut the connection, then dialed Leo Carson's telephone number.

There were four rings, a click, and a deep, resonant male voice said, "You have reached the home of Leo and Ellen Carson. We're not here right now, but please leave your name and number and we'll get back to you right away."

Janina hung up. Explaining this to an answering machine would simply have been too difficult.

It was eight o'clock that evening, and Janina was beginning to realize that there wouldn't be an opportunity to make a phone call from home without being overheard. When she had left her parents' home and gone away to college, she had decided to abandon her penchant for secrecy. In the absence of her mother's prying, she hadn't felt as if she needed it. While she and Jim were courting, secrecy had seemed to be the antithesis of love, and this had reinforced her determination to be open. As a result, it had never occurred to her how difficult it would be in her current setting—small house, intelligent husband, three aware and curious children—to do something surreptitiously should the occasion ever arise.

She and Jim finished cleaning up the dinner dishes. Jim vanished into the study, and the kids dispersed to their various rooms to complete homework and to play. The house was quiet except for the distant thrumming of Brendan's radio playing music so raucous that it made her brother's sixties rock sound like Gregorian chant. Janina moved stealthily into the kitchen and picked up the telephone. Then, she began to dial Leo's number.

It was only after a single ring that the word, "Mom!" blasted out from somewhere near, and Janina hastily hung the phone up, her pulse rate and her frustration rising simultaneously. Katie came into the room wearing a scowl that would have curdled fresh milk.

"Mom, I went into Brendan's room to borrow his colored markers, and he told me to get out of his room. Then he called me a name."

"What did he call you?" Janina asked gently.

"He called me 'butt face.'" Katie was near tears.

Janina went up and hugged her daughter, and then knelt on the floor, looking at her at her own eye level. "That wasn't a very nice thing to say, was it?"

Katie shook her head.

"I'll bet you're pretty mad about that."

Katie nodded. "And I didn't even do anything to him."

"I know. Would you like me to talk to him?"

Katie considered, and then her jaw clenched in determination. "No, I will." She gave her mom another hug before she walked out of the room. Janina heard Katie begin to yell before she even got near Brendan's room. "I don't like it when you call me names, so don't call me names, Brendan, you stupid poop head!"

Janina sighed, and then walked out of the kitchen towards the study.

Jim was sitting at his desk, updating some of his patients' files. The light from a small crook-neck lamp spilled over a disordered spread of papers and file folders headed with names like "Wainwright, Bubbles," "Warren, Mitzi-Pie," and "Fredericks, Quigby." Janina smiled, giving a quick word of thanks, as she had many times in the past, that people didn't give their children the same sorts of strange names that they gave their pets.

"Jim?" she said, putting a hand on his shoulder. "I realized that I forgot some papers from my music theory class at school. I need to run down and get them. Can you hold down the fort?"

Jim looked up and smiled. "No problem. Have Katie and Brendan resolved their difficulties?"

"Temporarily, at least. Katie objected to being called 'butt-face.'"

"Imagine that."

"I wonder if Brendan's ever going to figure out that Katie is not someone who takes insults lying down?"

He chuckled. "Couldn't tell you."

Janina leaned over and kissed him. "I'll be back in a few minutes. Shouldn't take long."

As she backed her car down the driveway, Janina reflected on the little fracas between her children. The thought crossed her mind that if ever she could untangle herself from this whole mess with Kathy, the day-to-day trials of raising children would seem easy by comparison. And not only easy—wholesome. Name-calling, fights, whining about chores, all of them seemed positively healthy and normal compared to the labyrinth of secrecy and unreality that Janina had been trying to navigate through during the past few weeks.

She drove the two miles to school, down the driveway of the campus, and into the empty teachers' parking lot. The windows of the high school were dark except where they were streaked with the reflection of the floodlights that illuminated the lot. Janina pulled into a space near the door and turned off her engine.

She got out, walked to the entrance, and unlocked it. The empty hallway stretched out in front of her. After hours, the custodians turned off all but every third bank of lights, which swathed the halls in an eerie half-illumination that concealed as much as it showed. Janina's footfalls echoed as she walked down the hall toward the choral room.

She unlocked her room and turned on the lights. After a moment's thought, she relocked the door and quietly closed it. Then, she went into her office and sat down at her desk where she picked up the phone and dialed.

It rang only twice before it was answered. A female voice said, "Hello?"

"Hello, may I please speak to Leo Carson?"

"Who may I say is calling?"

"My name is Janina Vannoy. We have a mutual friend."

"Hold on a sec."

There was the sound of the phone being put down, and Janina could hear the woman say, "Leo? It's for you. Some woman who says she knows a friend of yours."

A moment later, the receiver was picked up, and Janina recognized the deep voice of the man who had recorded the answering machine message she'd heard earlier. "This is Leo Carson speaking."

"Hi, my name is Janina Vannoy. I was wondering if you had a moment to talk." Janina hesitated, then decided to plunge on ahead. "I'm a friend of Kathy Christian's."

There was a moment of silence on the other end. "Oh. Did she give you my name?"

"Yes. She said I should contact you if I ever needed someone who could... help her."

"What kind of help are you thinking of?" The voice was tinged with suspicion but remained friendly.

"Well, Kathy has told me about... about something that happened in her past. She says she needs me to give her something that she lost… to get it back to her…." Janina faltered and became silent.

There was no response for a moment. She assumed that he had decided that she was crazy and was simply trying to figure out how to get off the phone gracefully. His response took her completely by surprise. "I know all about her story. You need to understand that. You also need to understand that I believe her."

"I...." Janina swallowed. "I think I do, too, but I'm not sure why. It seems crazy."

Leo laughed softly, a warm, inclusive laugh. "Ain't it the truth."

"But you still believe her."

"Well, now... I'm sorry, I've forgotten your name."

"Janina. Janina Vannoy."

"Well, Janina, I do what's called listening to my heart. I know that Kathy isn't insane. When she says that she has been contacted by her friend Justin, I guess I have to believe her."

"She said that Justin has contacted her?" The incredulity was plain in her voice.

"She didn't tell you? She didn't tell you about Justin?"

"Only hints. She said she dreamed about him. But I didn't think...." She stopped suddenly, realizing that she was about to say, "… that it had really happened," and wondering how this man would react if she so blatantly dismissed what Kathy had said.

Once again, the man's voice remained friendly, but by an infinitesimal degree, it became more guarded. "Then it's not for me to say. But I think a lot of Kathy, and I'd go a long way to help her. What is it she wants me to do?"

Janina paused, thinking of her words before putting them together. "She wants me to give you a necklace. It once belonged to her. She says she needs it."

"Do you have it?"

Janina touched her blouse and felt the tiny cage press against the skin on her chest. "Yes."

"Oh, then that's no problem. I could meet you and get it from you. It wouldn't be hard for me to get it to Kathy."

"You'd do that?"

"Surely. Tomorrow is Saturday. My shift doesn't start until noon. Where do you live?"

"Guildford."

"Of course. That's where Kathy was from, isn't it?"

"Yes. I lived next door to her."

"Well, well. Anyhow, we could meet at the 7-Eleven in Lemoine. That's on the main road and just about halfway. Sometime tomorrow morning, maybe. How's eleven o'clock?"

"Fine."

"Okay, then, let's consider it done."

Janina took a deep breath. Maybe, just maybe, she was reaching the end of the labyrinth. "Sounds great. Thanks."

"No problem. And, Janina?"

"Yes?"

"She is telling the truth, you know."

"I think I know that," Janina said, her voice thoughtful. "I think that I always have, even if I haven't wanted to. I'll see you tomorrow."

"Bye."

Janina replaced the receiver, and after sitting for a moment, her eyes distant, she stood up. She picked up the nearest stack of homework from her music theory class—so as to have something to show for her trip, should Jim ask—and then turned out the light in her office. She opened the door to the classroom, switched off the classroom light, and stepped into the hall, pulling the door shut behind her.

Then she turned and found herself only about a foot away from the smiling face of Martha Alport.

"Working late?" she asked, her voice merry.

Janina gave a little gasp and dropped her papers. They separated and drifted toward the floor where they scattered like leaves in a breeze. Janina didn't make a move to retrieve them but simply stared at Martha, frozen to the spot.

Martha frowned. "Oh, I'm sorry, I didn't mean to startle you. I was just here working late myself, and I saw the light on in your room. Thought I'd pop down and say hello." She knelt down on the floor and began to scoop up papers.

Janina reached down to help her. Her mind was racing. She had passed Wanda's room on the way in. Had the lights been on? She didn't think so. And there had been no other cars in the faculty parking lot. Although Martha could have conceivably parked elsewhere or even walked to school if she lived close enough.

Within a few moments they had the papers reassembled.

"Here you are." Martha handed her stack to Janina. "Good night, and I'll see you tomorrow. I hope you haven't been pulling late-nighters like this too often lately. Bodes no good for the sleep cycle."

Janina's heart raced. All she could think of was escape. She backed up along the wall, her spine scraping painfully along the textured surface. Martha seemed not to see anything odd in Janina's behavior but continued to watch her, a faint smile on her lips.

When Janina had gotten about ten feet away, she turned and walked away as fast as she could. It was only iron will that kept her from running. Still, she couldn't help looking over her shoulder twice, and each time, Martha was still standing there by the door to the choral room, becoming more and more indistinct in the half-light.

Janina turned the corner, and about thirty feet further on saw the door into the parking lot. At this point she could not control herself and began to run. Her footfalls reverberated around her. It sounded as if a mob of mute pursuers were just behind her giving chase. She reached the door and turned the handle. The night breeze blew into her face. She slowed to a walk, breathing heavily, and heard the door click shut behind her. Only then did she turn to look back, half expecting to see Martha's face peering through the window in the door, still wearing her cheerful smile, but there was no one there.

PART 3
THE HUNT CLOSES IN

CHAPTER 1

After the FBI men left, Janina spent the rest of the day inside her house. She was, for the first time in her life, afraid to go outside.

Both of her parents seemed to be unaware of her fear. They were too immersed in their own cares. Both Leonard and Maddy had grown up in small towns themselves. Leonard in the village of Hennen near the Pennsylvania border, which was even smaller than their own village. Janina could remember him calling it "Guildford with fewer stop signs" when they were on their way to visit her grandparents for Christmas. Maddy, on the other hand, had grown up right in Guildford itself. Janina sensed that neither had ever seen an FBI man anywhere besides on television. The sight of not one but two right here on their own doorstep was enough to overturn their expectations about what village life should be like as completely as it had Janina's.

They didn't react the same way, however. Over lunch, they had talked in hushed voices about the situation. Leonard was mostly distressed that Tom and Kathy's hired hand could have turned out to be such a bad seed. Dangerous—that was what the men had said. And he had looked like such a nice boy. Ever since the Vietnam protests had started in earnest five or six years earlier, there were these young people. What did they call them? Hippies. With their protests, ragged clothes, long hair, and drugs. Where was it all leading to? But this Justin, now... well, it just went to show that you really couldn't tell. Other than the fact that his hair was a little on the long side, he surely seemed like a personable fellow, not that he'd had the chance to talk to him much. No, you just could never tell.

Maddy's contribution to the conversation, on the other hand, focused on how places changed. Her family, the Larkins, had been one of the first families to settle in Guildford nearly two hundred years ago. Guildford was supposed to be stable, quiet, and crime-free. Not like other places. New York City? Sure. Anything could happen in New York City, and did, from all she had heard. But not here in Guildford. Not right on her front step, flanked by Leonard's neatly trimmed viburnum bushes. Not right out where all the neighbors could see.

Janina listened with only half an ear to their conversation. She, too, had her own very different concerns. This intrusion of the unaccountable into the quiet lives of the Starcevich family struck a wedge between them. None could quite understand what the others were feeling, and it drove them apart and kept them that way.

So the day, with its unusual heat and humidity and its unusual visitations, passed and drew to an end, settling into a clear but hazy night. The air was so laden with moisture that only a half-hour after sunset the grass was shimmering with dew. The sky went through a painter's palette of blues, darkening from azure to lapis to ultramarine to indigo, and a few stars began to flicker their way into the sky.

Janina retired early but couldn't get to sleep. It was still uncomfortably hot in the house, even with the windows open, and the warmth between her body and the sheets felt miserable. She rolled over, trying to find a cooler spot on the bed, only to find that within minutes the new spot was as sweaty and hot as the old one had been. Finally, she gave up and, with a little sigh of exasperation, sat up.

At that moment, there was a tap on the window screen. After the first startled split-second, Janina realized what it must be—a June beetle, smacking itself silly against the screen. It happened all summer, and yet it still scared her every time. Foolish. She turned around and looked at the window expecting to see the big brown beetle crawling drunkenly up the screen. Instead, she found herself looking into a man's face.

She gave a sharp little intake of breath, her heart thudding in her chest. She prepared to scream the house down. Then she realized that it was Justin, and her fear was immediately overturned in an unexpected transport of joy such as she had not felt since the afternoon she had discovered music. She jumped lightly out of bed and ran to the window.

"You're okay! They didn't catch you!" she whispered.

Justin smiled. "Not yet. I've been hiding in the woods."

"I'm so glad." Janina's face clouded. "The men came to my house. They asked about you. They asked if we'd seen you here on our property. I told them no."

"They knew I'd been here." It wasn't a question.

Janina looked at him closely. "Justin, who are they?"

"I don't think you'd believe me if I told you."

"Tell me anyway."

Justin seemed to consider for a moment, then said, "Can you come out to the pond with me for a few minutes? I'd like to talk to you, and if we keep talking here, your parents will hear. Can you open the screen?"

Without hesitation, Janina pulled the latches and lifted the screen. She climbed out onto the sill, and Justin reached up and caught her beneath the armpits in order to help her down. Her feet were cooled by the dew on the grass, and she left dark footprints in the silvered lawn.

When they had gotten a little way away from the house, Justin said, "I'm leaving tomorrow. Probably for good. If I don't get caught, that is."

"Where to?"

"I don't know. Away. I've been running for a long time, and I've got to run again. They've caught up with me. I'm not sure where I'll go yet. I guess I'll know when I get there."

Janina looked up into his face and into his clear, friendly eyes. "Why are they after you? What do they want to do with you?"

Justin looked away. "I don't know why, really. I mean, I do, but I don't really understand it. As far as what they want... they want to kill me. Plain and simple." There was fear and sadness in his words, but his voice remained level and controlled. "They probably want to hurt me quite a bit first, too."

Suddenly, Janina felt a surge of hot tears welling up, and she held them back with an effort. Even so, one escaped and trickled down her cheek to join the dew on the grass. "I hate them!" she said vehemently.

"So do I."

They had reached the pond, which lay still in the starlight. Its surface was flat and smooth. Justin looked down at Janina, and suddenly smiled—a smile sweet enough to break your heart. "Look, I didn't get you out of bed to make you all upset. I just came to say goodbye and talk for a little while. But maybe now that we're out here, I can show you something."

"What?"

"We have to wait for a few moments. It's still a little early."

Justin leaned against the willow tree, seeming to melt into the shadows. Janina felt oddly conspicuous. She slapped away a mosquito that droned past her ear and looked around her. A wisp of cloud blew past, but the stars flickered quietly in a sky largely clear of obstructions. They were facing south where Sagittarius and the Scorpion hung low in the sky. The Scorpion's tail was brushing the long line of trees that formed the edge of the woods in which Justin had been hiding.

Finally, Janina grew fidgety and impatient. "What is it you want to show me?"

Justin stepped forward, and his arm lifted to point his finger toward a spot a little above the horizon. "There."

"What?"

"Look at that red star. I think it's the one they call Antares. The eye of the Scorpion. Now, do you see a white star, up and a little to the right of it?"

"Yes."

"That's it."

Janina's reply had an edge to it. She was confused and also becoming a little scared again, but she wasn't sure why. "That's what?" she demanded irritably.

"That's my home."

Janina continued to stare at the star. The words didn't sink in. How could anyone live in a point of light? It sounded like one of those silly nursery rhymes or poems that she had only recently begun to outgrow—"'Now cast your nets wherever you wish, never afeared are we!' So cried the stars to the fishermen three, Wynken, Blynken, and Nod...."

Then, gradually, the significance of what he was saying began to dawn on her. Janina felt a thrill of fear vibrate down her spine, and she took a reflexive step backward.

"But...." she began, then faltered and became silent. The only sound was the crickets and frogs, and the whine of an occasional mosquito. Janina continued to stare at him, but he turned his face away gazing off into the night sky. Finally, she was able to extract a single question from the muddle of confusion in her brain. "How did you come here?"

Justin didn't move. "That's not important," he said, his voice quiet. "What's important is that I have to go. Soon."

"Those people who are chasing you. Who are they?"

Justin turned. His gaze was intense, but his voice was steady. "It's enough for you to know that they won't rest until they find me. And I've got to go before they hurt or kill someone else, someone innocent. They've done it before."

"Why are they chasing you?" Her voice was pleading. "They said you did bad things, and you're dangerous."

Justin gave a soft laugh. "Do you know what the word *perspective* means?"

Janina shook her head.

"It means how you look at things. That it all depends. Look, Janina, suppose I'm a hunter. I'm trying to shoot a deer, so I can feed myself and my family. Now, to me, what I'm doing is justified. There's no reason that there's anything wrong with what I'm doing. Right?"

"I guess so."

"But look at it from the deer's point of view. To the deer, the hunter is a murderer, and someone who takes life unexpectedly for no apparent reason. Even if you could explain the reason to the deer, it wouldn't understand. The fact that the hunter needed food wouldn't make any difference. The hunter would still represent nothing but blood, pain, and senseless killing. All it would want to do is escape. Do you understand?"

"I think so."

"It's the same here. The ones who are trying to find me. Maybe to them I really do seem dangerous. Maybe to them, their reason for wanting me dead is reasonable and justifiable. But for me... I'm the deer trying to escape from the hand of the hunter."

Janina felt her heartbeat quicken, and she glanced around her anxiously. She half expected to see dark-suited men watching them from the other side of the pond, men with icy smiles and flat, expressionless eyes, cold as nickels. "You should run away," she said, her voice urgent and intense. "Now. Tonight."

"I can't. I won't be able to leave for another day, at least."

Janina scowled at him. "I'd ask you why, but you'd just say again that the reason wasn't important."

Justin replied to her scowl with a broad smile. "You're probably right. But I do have two reasons for staying, and there's no reason why I can't tell you one of them. I have to give your friend Kathy something."

As always, Janina's curiosity overrode her sense of etiquette. "What is it?"

Justin reached inside his shirt and pulled out a slender chain that was hanging around his neck. Attached to it was a little wire cage containing a silver ball.

Janina reached out to touch it and listened to its soft, bell-like chime. "It's beautiful."

"Yes. But it's also useful." He knelt on the wet ground and held the little pendant out in front of Janina's eyes where it caught the starlight and shimmered as it turned slowly on its chain.

"What does it do?" Janina was captivated by its simple beauty.

"Have you ever heard of a homing beacon?"

She shook her head.

"It gives off a signal. Sort of like when a police car turns on its siren. You can hear it and know where it is. It's a tiny signal, but if you know how, you can figure out where it's coming from."

"Why do you want Kathy to have it?"

Justin looked at her, still smiling slightly, but his eyes were melancholy. "Kathy doesn't belong here."

Janina's eyes widened in an almost comical expression of astonishment. "You mean, Kathy too... she comes from...."

His smile flashed out, his white teeth catching the starlight. "No. I don't mean that. What I mean is that she doesn't belong here in Guildford. She isn't happy here."

"She's always looked happy to me. And what's wrong with Guildford?" she added a little defensively.

"Nothing's wrong with Guildford. But it's not right for everyone. I don't know if I can explain, because I'm not sure I understand it all myself. All I can say is that she's not happy. But you know that. You heard what she said." He looked piercingly at Janina, and she blushed.

"She asked if she could come with you. And you said no."

"That's true. I felt like I couldn't do that, not with... them... so close. But this necklace will allow me to find her, if later... if she decides she still wants to go with me. If I'm still alive, and if it's safe... or at least safer. Maybe one day I can come back and get her."

The silence fell between them again as heavy as the damp air around them. Janina looked troubled.

"What are you thinking?" Justin finally asked.

"Justin...." she said quietly. "What about Tom?"

He looked away. "Just like some places aren't for everyone, sometimes people don't... belong together. Tom's a good person. I know that. But I also know that Kathy and he don't fit together. I don't want to cause him pain, but Kathy should be able to do what she needs to do. I just want to give her that opportunity...." He stopped. "You probably don't understand, you're too young."

Janina's scowl returned. "I *hate* it when people say that. Just because I'm ten doesn't mean I'm stupid."

Justin's somber expression suddenly transformed into a grin, and he laughed merrily. "Sorry. I should have known better. Janina, do you remember a few days ago when you asked me how I know things?"

"Yes." A few days ago? Was that all the time that had passed? It seemed to Janina as if that conversation were ages ago, and the years before Justin's arrival another lifetime.

"When I first saw you I knew that you were the right person to help me, and that I could trust you. You've got an ability—to know what's real and what's not, between what's good and what's not. All you have to do is listen to your heart, and you know what to do. Don't ever lose that ability or let other people talk you out of doing what you know you must do."

"But I feel so confused," Janina began, and then stopped.

"But you still do what you know is right. You warned me this morning, and I got away before the men came."

"I did?"

"You did."

"I don't remember doing that," she said, her voice bewildered. "Why don't I remember it if it only happened this morning?"

Justin looked away. "It's safer that way."

"What do you mean?"

"What you don't remember, you can't tell anyone."

Another little tremor of fear fluttered down the back of Janina's neck. "How did you do that? How did you make me forget?"

Justin still did not meet her eyes, and an uncomfortable silence descended.

Finally, Janina asked in a small voice, "Will I ever remember what happened?"

"Perhaps. When you need to, you will."

"When will that be?"

"I have no idea. A long time from now, probably. But for now, I hope...." He looked at her closely, his face becoming serious. "I hope you have a life where no one ever takes the people you care about, and who care about you, away from you."

"I don't know if there really is anyone who cares about me." She didn't say this with any self-pity. She simply said it.

"There will be one day," said Justin cryptically.

"How do you know?" demanded Janina, but he didn't respond. He simply stood up and walked back toward the house. She followed, padding barefoot across the wet grass.

"I've got to go. I've spent as much time here talking to you that is safe. If they caught you here with me... I don't want you to get hurt. I may not see you again."

"I know."

They had reached Janina's window, which opened blackly into the house. He said, "I wish I had something to give you, but I don't."

Janina turned to face him. "That's okay. I hope you get away."

He smiled. "So do I." He placed his hands under her arms and lifted her onto the sill. She swung her legs over and clambered into her bedroom.

"Good luck."

"Thanks," he said quietly and was gone.

Janina stood at her open window, gazing out into the darkness, for quite a long time. After only fifteen minutes had passed, her memory of her conversation with Justin was already becoming dreamlike. It hardly seemed real any more. She leaned out of the window to see if she could still see his star above the eye of the Scorpion, but it had already set.

That was when she noticed the tracks in the grass, showing darkly against the glittering dew. Two sets of tracks. Both hers. One set going out and one coming back. That was all. The rest of the dew-drenched lawn lay untouched and silver in the light of countless stars.

CHAPTER 2

Saturday morning dawned bright and clear, as beautiful a May day as anyone could want. By the time Janina woke, Jim was already gone to his Saturday morning walk-in clinic. She lay in bed, staring at the ceiling, lost in her own thoughts. She still felt shaken from her experience the previous evening. The sense of unreality, of having stepped into a dream, would not leave her.

What was Martha trying to do to her? She gave a shudder. The truth was, Martha scared her. No, scared wasn't strong enough—Martha terrified her. How did she know the things she did?

More to the point, what was she going to do next?

Janina sat up abruptly. The top of the blanket slithered from her shoulders and crumpled up in her lap. Well, for better or worse, she would be done with it after this morning. She was going to give the necklace to Leo Carson, and he would give it to Kathy. That would be the end of it. Whatever created this weird bond between Kathy and her, it would be done and over with after today.

Janina got out of bed and pulled on a sweatshirt and a pair of old jeans. She then retrieved the necklace from her underwear drawer and slipped it over her head. She paused for a moment and lifted the chain in her hand, holding the pendant in front of her.

Why on earth did Kathy want this? It was pretty, but there had to be more to it than that. Janina swung it gently. It caught the sunlight streaming in through the bedroom window and glittered brightly.

Of course, Kathy was crazy. Who knew why she wanted it? Maybe even Kathy herself didn't really know.

That thought struck her as sad, and she sighed as she slipped the necklace inside her sweatshirt before going downstairs.

All three children were up by the time Janina got downstairs—a highly unusual occurrence in the Vannoy household. Katie and Brendan were arguing loudly about who should get the last of the Life cereal. Each of them had ahold of the box and were tugging back and forth with such vigor that any cereal inside seemed likely to be soon reduced to an inedible powder. Sarah, as usual, was watching the two of them with detached amusement with an air of being above such immature squabbling.

Janina's entrance into the kitchen was greeted with a chorus of shouts.

"Mom! It's not fair! Brendan is going to eat all of the Life cereal, and he knows it's my favorite. I don't like any of the other kinds of cereal, and he's so mean!"

"I had it first. She thinks that she can just barge in and grab it from me!"

"Brendan, give it to me!"

"Why should I? You're a spoiled little brat! You always get your way!"

"Okay, okay," Janina said, trying to keep her voice mild and impartial. "Why can't you share it?"

"I had it first!" shouted Brendan. "There isn't enough!"

"But you know that I hate Cheerios, and that's the only other kind we have!" Katie's voice was nearly a shriek.

"So?" Brendan snarled.

"How much is left?" Janina interjected.

"Not enough for her to get any!" said Brendan in an aggrieved tone.

She picked up the box, went to the cabinet, got two bowls out, filled each with cereal nearly to overflowing, and put what was left back in the box and in the pantry. She silently handed Brendan and Katie each a bowl. They sat down, somewhat chastened, and began to eat.

Janina was getting a cup of coffee when Katie said, through a mouth full of cereal, "When are we going to Kristie's party?"

Janina turned around, cup in her hand. "What?"

"Kristie's birthday party. It's today. You said last week you'd bring me there."

Janina didn't respond for a moment. "Um," she said, and went to the fridge where the invitation was hanging by a magnet. "It starts at ten-thirty." She glanced at the digital clock on the stove. "That's an hour from now."

"Awesome," Katie said, and returned to her cereal.

Janina had completely forgotten about that. Jesus Christ, her own daughter was taking second seat to Kathy and her affairs.

But the obsession wasn't as easily argued down as that. Her next thought was to wonder if she could get Katie to the party and still have time to meet Leo at eleven o'clock.

It was only a twenty minute drive up to Lemoine. Plenty of time. She could relax.

The thought seemed to come from somewhere outside her own mind, and her relief at this realization was an almost physical sensation of pleasure. She thought, with some sense of confusion, she didn't simply want to get the necklace to Kathy—she had to.

But why?

Janina and Katie left at a quarter after ten. Katie's friend Kristie McPhee lived right in the village, only a half-mile away. Katie sat in the passenger seat with a large, brightly-wrapped present in her lap. Her usual intense, serious expression was replaced by happy anticipation of fun, games, and cake. Janina pulled up to the McPhees', signaled a left turn, and waited while three other cars coming the opposite way passed her.

And that was when, giving an idle glance further down the street, she saw Martha sitting in the driver's seat of a sleek gray Mercedes parked underneath a maple tree about four houses up.

It was only a glimpse, but Janina was certain. The back of a blond head sank almost instantaneously beneath the level of the headrest.

Martha knew she'd be there. But how? Did she have a tracking device on Janina's car?

Moving on auto-pilot, and trying not to show any alarm to Katie, Janina turned left down a long, shaded gravel driveway that circled around to the back of the McPhees' house.

There were about five other cars there already, and Kristie's friends were already running around in the back of the yard, yelling and laughing with a wild abandon that would have put most boys' parties to shame. Katie got out, slamming the door behind her, tossed the present on the back deck, and without a word of farewell to her mother, joined the pack while whooping with delight.

Janina got out with her stomach clenching, and walked toward the house like she was sleepwalking.

What should she do now? Could she leave her daughter here with that woman so close? What if she tried to abduct Katie?

A reassuring thought came to her. Martha couldn't do that in front of all the other kids and parents. Plus, Katie already didn't trust her. She said so in the library. If Martha tried anything—probably even if she simply showed up—Katie would not hesitate to give the alarm.

But she still couldn't shake the feeling of horror at having Martha so near her daughter. And Janina wouldn't be at home—ten minutes away—if something happened. She'd be miles away and nowhere near a phone. She'd be helpless to stop Martha if she should be inclined to try anything.

Once again, a voice, seeming to come from elsewhere, replied with comforting words.

Katie would be safe. It was the necklace Martha wanted. She'd follow Janina.

But then how could she get to Lemoine without Martha knowing?

"Hi, Janina," said a warm voice.

Janina snapped out of her reverie to realize she'd almost walked right into Barb McPhee, Kristie's mom. She managed a smile. "Hi, Barb. Sorry, I was woolgathering."

Barb smiled back. "About something good, I hope?"

"Actually, I was wondering how…." She stopped, and then swallowed before she went on. "My car is having problems. It's been overheating when I drive it more than a few miles, and I have to run an errand up to Lemoine. Is there any chance I could borrow your car? It'd only be an hour and a half or so."

Where in God's name had that idea come from? It was like she wasn't in control of her own brain….

But Barb was saying, "Sure, no problem! I'll be here with the girls for the next couple of hours, and Bill has his car if we need it for some reason. It's no problem. Let me get you the key."

Barb returned in less than a minute and handed her the key while pointing out a grimy, forest-green station wagon. "Ignore the junk all over the floor. It hasn't been cleaned in ages.

Cleaning out the car isn't on my radar most days."

Janina nodded, said a rather weak thank you, went to the car, and climbed in. She backed up and then turned forward down the driveway, the gravel scrunching under the tires.

When the nose of the car came around the side of the house, and the gray Mercedes came into view, Janina slithered down into the seat and turned her head away. It was hard to resist the impulse to look, to see if Martha's innocent eyes were staring at her. She could picture Martha's face, the corners of her pretty mouth turned upward in a wicked little smile as she reached down to start the engine and follow her. But Janina forced herself to remain turned away in hopes that the fact that she was driving a different car would be enough to fool her. She turned right out of the driveway, drove to the end of the block, and only then looked into the mirror.

The Mercedes was still sitting parked by the side of the road.

Janina let out a long breath of held air. She turned left toward Main Street, and the car went out of view behind a house. She kept driving, came to the first stop sign, and stopped to wait to see if the Mercedes would turn, following her.

Nothing.

She drove the next block a little faster, still looking for any sign of pursuit, and the next one faster still. She made herself lift up on the accelerator. It'd do no good to get pulled over for speeding.

It was only after she got onto the highway, heading north to Lemoine, that she finally was able to relax a little. But at that point, she began to wonder. What did Martha want with the necklace? Why was it so important to so many people? How had Janina become a pawn in this weird game?

No matter. She didn't have to understand it. When Leo took the necklace, it'd be over.

Her mind wasn't ready yet to leave behind the dark, paranoid track that it was locked into, though. Who was this Leo Carson?

She honestly didn't know. When she'd called Leo, a woman had answered the phone. Janina had assumed that it was Leo's wife. The answering machine message had said that she had reached the home of "Leo and Ellen Carson." But suppose that there really was no such person as "Ellen Carson." Maybe that woman had really been Martha. Maybe Leo and Martha were in league to get the necklace, and....

"And what?" demanded Janina aloud, interrupting the stream of wild, hysterical thoughts. Ridiculous. Once again, she was letting her imagination get the better of her. Leo was just a nice man trying to do a favor for a poor woman who had no friends, no hope, and no future.

And what about Martha? Well, realistically speaking, what had Martha actually ever done to Janina? Nothing. She'd made a passing comment about insane asylums during lunch. She'd noticed that Janina was limping.

Maybe she *had* been limping. She certainly couldn't remember for sure.

What else? There'd been the comment on Janina's necklace. Then last night, she'd startled her in the school after hours and made some kind of comment about working late. Now, she happened to be near where a friend of Katie's was having a birthday party.

What, exactly, was wrong with any of that? Weird coincidences, at worst. But no harm done, not even a threat of harm.

She was getting paranoid. That was all there was to it. She really had to get this under control, or she'd start suspecting everyone of being one of "them."

She checked the rearview mirror. About a quarter of a mile back there was a battered farm pickup, but that was all. She'd half expected to see the gray Mercedes gaining on her, and Martha's face wearing a gleeful grin as the distance between them diminished.

Apparently, she had given Martha the slip. But still, she sped up a little.

About twenty minutes later, Janina pulled into the parking lot of the 7-Eleven in Lemoine. There was no problem finding it, even though she was unfamiliar with the village—a laundromat and a video store were its only other businesses. She sidled into a parking space between an old SUV and a shiny maroon pickup truck and turned off the engine. There was no sign of a gray Mercedes anywhere. She leaned back in the seat, feeling the tension in her body finally unwind.

She checked her wristwatch to see she was five minutes early. Now what? Should she wait for someone to come up to her car, and say, "Janina Vannoy, I presume? Can I have the necklace?"

She switched on the radio and listened to the end of an intricate Handel flute sonata on the Colville station, although the signal was a little fuzzy up here in the hill country. The owner of the SUV, a harassed-looking young woman with a baby in a stroller and a two-year old girl in tow, came out of the store, loaded her kids in, climbed into the car herself, and drove off. The truck's owner, a swaggering twenty-year old with over-long blond hair and tight jeans, came out a moment later. He gave a sidelong glance at Janina, pulled off his t-shirt to expose a well-muscled chest covered with tattoos, and climbed in. The engine roared to life, and then he pulled out, his wheels spinning alarmingly in the gravel of the parking lot. Over the next ten minutes, they were regularly replaced by other customers. She wondered at the steady flow of people in and out of this little convenience store so far from anywhere.

At ten minutes after ten, a nondescript and somewhat rusty blue sedan pulled into the space next to Janina's. The door opened, and a huge bear of a man stepped out—six-foot-four, probably two-hundred-and-fifty pounds, prodigiously bearded, and with arms nearly as big around as one of Janina's legs. He glanced around the parking lot for a moment, and then catching Janina's eye, he broke into an infectious smile. Janina smiled back and got out of the car.

"Janina Vannoy?" said the man. "I'm making a guess, of course, and if I'm wrong you'll think I'm a nut."

"No, I'm Janina. You must be Leo."

"That's me." Leo's huge hand engulfed Janina's smaller one. "I'm glad we connected."

"Me too."

They stood there, each looking a little uncomfortable, for a moment. "Well, I'd better give you the necklace," Janina finally said. "Really, I want to get it off my hands. It seems to bring me nothing but bad luck." She pulled the necklace out of her sweatshirt and slipped it over her head. She held it out to Leo. There was a momentary thought of, *Don't trust him! Don't give it to him!* But she forced herself to drop the necklace into his open palm. When she did, relief flooded through her. She knew she could trust him. She'd known all along this was the right thing to do.

Leo broke into an easy grin, and he dropped the necklace into the pocket of his windbreaker. "Now, don't you worry. I'll get this to Kathy. I know she'll never forget that you helped her."

"Helped her to do what?" asked Janina. "That's what I don't understand. I don't know why she wants this necklace. She just said she wanted it."

Leo gave her an appraising look, and then smiled again. "Well, since she didn't tell you, I don't know that I should. All I can say is maybe you ought to keep your eye on the newspapers for the next few days."

Janina didn't know quite how to respond to that. In the end, she said, "Okay."

"I've got to get going." Leo gave her another massive handshake. "Thanks. This means a lot to me, too. Kathy's a good person. She really is."

"I know."

He turned, and then paused with his hand on the handle to his car door. "I get feelings about people, sometimes. My grandma always used to tell me that I had the second sight. Now, I don't know about that, but I do know that I know about people. When they're telling the truth and when they're not. Who can be trusted and who can't. You know, there's a lot of people out there who can't be trusted, but there's a lot who can, too."

"I trust Kathy," said Janina, a little defensively.

"I wasn't talking about Kathy. I was talking about *you*. I know that I can trust you." He smiled at her. "Now, you just need to trust yourself. But, like I said, I gotta go. Thanks again. And watch those newspapers."

Janina watched him drive away, feeling a little giddy. Trust herself? It wasn't bad advice. At least, the necklace was gone, too.

It was over.

She touched her shirt, feeling the place where the necklace had been. She'd only worn it for a day and a half, but she already felt a little strange without it.

She got back in her car, pulled out of the parking lot, and then onto the highway, heading south, toward home.

Still no sign of Martha.

Of course there was no sign of her. Janina felt strangely like laughing. Why should she show up? She was just weird, not psychic. There was no reason to be afraid of her any more.

The twelve miles from Lemoine back to Guildford seemed to fly. The thought, *I'm done, it's over*, kept dancing about in her mind, and by the time Janina reached the sign that said "Welcome to Guildford," she was in a lighter mood than she had been for weeks.

She pictured Leo going to work and slipping the necklace to Kathy. Kathy's eyes shining as she looked at it, the keepsake which had been given to her years ago by that strange man whose name kept coming up everywhere Janina looked. Justin Lazarus. Just who, exactly, was he? In all her involvement with this strange business, she had never gotten a good idea of who he was and exactly how he fit into all of this.

Had Kathy been having an affair with him? She exited the highway, heading toward the village center. At this point it didn't matter much, but it would explain why she wanted the necklace. Maybe it had been a love triangle that resulted in Tom's death. Sad, but after all these years, Kathy had surely paid enough and deserved to have a least one little remembrance of happier times.

She turned off Main Street, heading back to the McPhees' house. Her heart gave a little jump as she made the right turn onto Church Street, and she looked past the McPhees' driveway where the big sugar maple overhung the street.

The gray Mercedes was gone.

She turned into the driveway and pulled to a stop behind the house. The girls, from the look of it, were still going strong, wearing party hats and playing a game of what looked like tag in the wide, treed backyard. Barb and a couple of the other parents were sitting in lawn chairs with cups of coffee. Barb grinned and waved as Janina got out.

"Thanks so much for the loan," Janina said. "I really appreciate it."

"Not a problem. There's coffee in the kitchen. Help yourself."

"That's okay, I've already had my two cups." Janina sat in a lawn chair and stretched out her legs. "How's the party been?"

"No crises. I think they're having a great time." Barb's eyebrows went up. "Oh, Janina, I almost forgot. You just missed a friend of yours."

"Oh?" Janina smiled questioningly.

"Yeah. It couldn't have been ten minutes after you left. She said she'd seen you drive up and wanted to say hi. She seemed really disappointed when I told her you'd left. She said you worked together."

Janina opened her mouth, but her voice seemed to have dried up and blown away.

"She said her name was Martha Alport. She told me to tell you that she was really sorry she'd missed you but would definitely catch you another time."

CHAPTER 3

When Janina woke the next morning, the heat and cloying dampness were, if anything, worse than it had been during the previous few days. The sky was overcast and looked heavy and sullen. This spell of Deep South weather in the Northeast was unusual not only for its intensity but for its duration. While there were often scattered hot, humid days during summer, it had been a number of years since it had been this uncomfortable for this long.

Everyone was irritable, with the possible exception of her father. The only thing that ever put him in a bad mood was when he'd planned to spend the afternoon in the garden and something got in his way. Maddy groused and sniped at her husband and children over breakfast, and even Doug's usual equanimity seemed to have evaporated. In fact, breakfast ended when Doug accidentally dropped his cereal spoon on the floor.

Maddy gave an exasperated snort. "Will you kids please be more careful? You've splattered milk all over the floor. You seem to think I have nothing better to do than to clean up after you."

Doug snatched the spoon from the floor. "I didn't do it on purpose," he said, his voice low and snarly. "And I didn't ask you to clean it up."

"You keep a civil tongue in your head, Douglas Starcevich," Maddy growled back.

"I will if you will," Doug said under his breath.

"You're not too old for a good swat on the backside if you can't learn some respect," she said, turning back to the sink.

Doug sent a withering glare in her direction, picked up his bowl and spoon, and walked to the sink where he dumped what was left of his cereal.

"Look at how much cereal you've wasted!" Maddy shouted at his retreating back. Doug, though, only responded by walking out of the room.

Leonard looked uncomfortably around him. "Now, Maddy, maybe you were a little hard on Doug," he began.

"Don't you start. If you had to work to keep this house clean, you'd understand." The accusation was clear in her voice. "I've got enough to do without cleaning up after other people's carelessness."

Leonard seemed to know a losing battle when he saw one. Within two minutes, his dishes and silverware had joined Doug's in the sink, and Leonard himself had followed Doug out of the kitchen.

Janina knew better than to enter this fray and prudently decided to leave Maddy to her mood. She quickly finished the rest of her breakfast and went outside through the sliding glass door into the back yard.

Nothing was moving—not a stir of wind, a bird, or an insect. The whole world seemed to be holding its breath. She walked out to the pond and sat on the grass, staring out past it to the woods beyond in a bemused sort of way.

Where was Justin? Had they finally caught him? The somber

thought slipped across her mind.

Either way, she'd probably never see him again. The fact that she might never know which, though, was horrid.

The morning crawled by as lunchtime came and went. The afternoon stretched out ahead, flat and featureless. The sky, if anything, grew heavier, but there was no rain to promise an end to the oppressive heat.

There was no one around except Janina and her mother. After breakfast, Leonard had escaped to work. Doug had also vanished early on to the safe haven of a friend's house. Maddy spent the morning stomping around the house with a thunderous expression on her face, and Janina avoided her, although the inevitable contacts resulted in their fretting each other and snapping at each other until their nerves were stretched to near breaking.

Leonard returned at around three o'clock, saw that the emotional temperature of the household had not improved since morning, and wisely decided to attend to spraying the rose bushes despite the heat. Janina joined him, and they discussed the depredations of Japanese beetles for a few minutes as Leonard waged his own small chemical warfare against the foe.

Finally, the conversation lagged. Leonard, content as usual with his own thoughts, didn't seem to notice, but finally Janina said, "Dad?"

"Hmm?"

"What do you think Justin Lazarus did that those FBI men are trying to catch him?"

Leonard considered. "Well, I don't know. But for the FBI to be involved, it must be something serious. They did say that he was dangerous, too."

"He didn't seem dangerous to me."

"I must say, I thought that myself. But you know, not everything is what it seems. They say that Billy the Kid was just an innocent-looking teenager when he committed his first murder. And some of the gangsters back in the twenties and thirties were handsome men to look at, not people you'd think were criminals. In fact, there was one called 'Baby Face Nelson.'"

"But, Justin couldn't really be dangerous, could he? He always seemed so nice...." This last statement wasn't completely true, but she couldn't say why without further explanation.

"Well, you just never know," Leonard said. "You can't tell about people."

There seemed to be no good answer to that, and Janina subsided into silence.

She remained outside for the rest of the afternoon. She spent a while trying to catch frogs in the pond, but the frogs seemed to have departed to cooler locales because there were none to be found. She thought about getting out the matchbox cars again but didn't know where her mother had put them after picking them up the previous morning. Janina certainly didn't feel like going inside and asking. In the end, she just wandered. Aimlessness seemed to be becoming a part of her normal routine. She didn't like it. Much to her surprise, she found herself looking forward to the beginning of school, which was four weeks away.

She was called in to a tense and cheerless dinner at five o'clock. Maddy's mood had, if anything, darkened further since that morning. The heat in the house was positively stifling, especially after an afternoon of Maddy using the oven and the stovetop for preparing dinner. Janina escaped as quickly as she could to the comparatively fresh air outside.

The sky was darkening early, promising rain and a possible relief from the heat wave. There was a slight breeze, which lifted the damp lock of hair plastered to Janina's forehead and gave her spirits a momentary uplift as well. The breeze also carried voices. The voices were coming from the direction of Tom and Kathy's house.

"... have a hell of a lot of nerve...." was all she caught before the breeze died into stillness and the voices passed into a distant buzz.

Janina's ears perked up, and she trotted over to the forsythia hedge. However, once there, she still could hear nothing but an angry sounding murmur. Then, a high, desperate voice rose up into a shout, "No, Tom, please! You can't!"

Janina's eyes widened, and her heart began to pound. She looked around to see if anyone else had heard, but there was no one else outside. Everyone seemed to have retreated into their houses. There was another shout, but no words were understandable.

That was all Janina could stand. She ran around the end of the hedge and up to the living room window of the Christians' house, which faced toward the Starceviches' yard. The window stood open with only a screen over it to keep out flies. Janina stepped into the little garden that lay against the foundation of the house. There she stood on tiptoe and peered inside.

There were three people in the living room standing in a long, narrow triangle. Justin and Kathy formed the base and were standing close together near the door. Kathy had something in her hand. Both of them were facing Tom, who stood at the apex of the triangle, near the door into the kitchen.

Tom was holding a gun.

Justin looked like a cornered animal. He was clearly terrified. Kathy's face was not visible from where Janina was standing, but her body was frozen into immobility. Tom was speaking.

"Kathy, go and get the card."

"No," she said. "Tom, I won't do it."

A bitter smile crossed Tom's face. It was the most emotion that Janina had ever seen him show. "Now I see which way the wind is blowing. I'll get it myself." He looked at Justin. "Those FBI. men gave me a card with their number on it. I'm going to call them, and they'll come collect you, and that'll be that."

"Tom, please," Kathy pleaded. "Just let him go."

He turned toward her, his eyes hard as flint. Then something in him, something that had been stopped up for years, seemed to burst. He began to shout at her. "After all I've done for you, that's how you repay me? By taking up with the first young drifter that comes along. And the fact that he's a criminal makes no difference to you?"

"He's not a criminal...."

"You're so sure. How do you know? What lies has he been telling you?" He gestured with the gun. "It doesn't matter. I'm done with the both of you. I gave you my good name...."

"Tom, stop!"

But Tom wouldn't stop. Once the floodgates to his invective had been opened, there was no closing them. "My family took you in. What were you? Pregnant and homeless. Your own family didn't want you. We took you in, and I fell in love with you and gave you my name...."

"Tom, don't you think I love you?"

He laughed. Janina had never heard a sound that seemed to hold so much anger and betrayal. "Love? You don't love me. You love your art, your music, your image of being several cuts above your country hick husband. You love it that everyone wonders how I could have ended up marrying someone like you. They don't see you as you were when I first saw you."

Kathy was sobbing, but Tom didn't seem to hear.

"Nothing I ever did was good enough. I took care of you when the baby died. I gave you a home, a place in the community, and security. But none of it is good enough. The first common criminal who comes along, and you're accepting his gifts."

"It's not like that, Mr. Christian," Justin said, but Tom cut him off.

"Well, why don't you tell me how it is, you filthy wife-stealing bastard!" Tom crossed the room toward Kathy in three strides, grabbed her hand, and pried it open. There was a brief struggle, and Janina saw Tom's hand clenched around a slender silver chain with something small and bright hanging from it. "If you're not my wife's lover, then why would you give her this?" His voice had risen to a scream. Without waiting for an answer, he slung the necklace toward the wall behind him. It struck the wall near the door in the kitchen, but Janina couldn't see where it landed.

At that moment, everything exploded into motion. Tom had lowered the gun aimed at Justin to throw the necklace, and Justin leaped forward to grab his arm. Kathy caught the gun, and Tom dropped it. It skittered across the floor.

Janina turned and ran for home faster than she had ever run.

She burst through the door into the living room where her parents were watching television. The door struck the doorstop with a crash and rebounded so hard that it nearly shut. Startled, both of her parents looked up. Undeterred, Ed Sullivan on the television went on introducing the next act.

Maddy's intended derisive comment about opening doors gently was cut off by a near-hysterical torrent of words from Janina. "Dad! You've got to come, quick! Tom's got a gun, and Justin's there. Tom's going to kill him!"

Leonard jumped up out of his recliner and bolted for the door. "Janina, you stay here!" he said in a voice more commanding than any of them had ever heard him use. Maddy, struck speechless for once, didn't move.

Leonard had just run outside when all three of them heard the sharp report of a single gunshot. Janina heard her mother give a little shriek behind her, and cry out, "God have mercy!"

Janina found herself running out of the house, despite her father's command. She sprinted around the front end of the hedge and along the sidewalk to the Christians' front walk. She saw Leonard vaulting up the steps onto the front porch before he reached the door and stood frozen. Janina came up quietly behind and peered around him.

The front door was standing wide open. There were only two people in the living room. Tom was lying on the dark, shiny hardwood floor, his blue work shirt drenched in blood from a small ragged hole through the front pocket. Kathy was sitting on the floor next to him, staring at him, her face emotionless, saying over and over, "Tom, I'm sorry, oh, I'm so sorry, Tom, I'm so sorry...."

In her lap rested a gun. Her fingers were still loosely coiled around it.

Leonard seemed to become aware for the first time that Janina had followed him there. He turned a white face toward his daughter. "Janina, go tell your mother to call the police and an ambulance."

Janina backed up. Then, she turned and ran back down the front stairs and down the sidewalk towards home. Her mother met her at the door. "What happened?" Maddy asked, her face a study of tension between fear and curiosity.

"Tom's been shot," Janina said. "Dad said to call the police and an ambulance."

"Oh, dear God, no." Maddy turned to run towards the phone, snatched up the handset, and began to dial.

Janina returned to the Christians' house. She found her father kneeling next to Kathy, telling her that she should tell the police the truth about everything. Kathy wasn't responding but was still sitting on the floor staring blankly at her husband.

Janina went up to them. Leonard saw her and tried to motion her away, but Janina once again ignored him. "Kathy?" she said, her voice quiet. "Kathy? It's me, Janina."

Kathy looked up, her eyes flat and expressionless.

"Kathy, where's Justin?"

Kathy's gaze met Janina's briefly, but her expression didn't change. "Who is Justin?"

The ambulance came and paramedics carried Tom out on a stretcher. They were working on him as they took him, giving

Janina hope that he might still be alive. Minutes after the ambulance came, the police arrived. Officer DeRosa of the Guildford Police Department was followed by another car with "Stephens County Police Department" written on the side. Leonard and Janina were asked to leave the house. The three policemen talked briefly to Kathy within. Leonard and Janina, standing on the porch, could hear the murmur of words, mostly that of male voices.

By this time, a small crowd of neighbors had collected on the sidewalk. Expressions varied from curiosity to fear. Janina saw Pauline McMillan, who lived on the other side of the Starceviches, talking excitedly to someone. Then, Pauline looked up, and said, "Leonard! Leonard, what happened?" Leonard either didn't hear or simply ignored her.

Within a few moments, the three policemen came out. The two from the county police were ushering Kathy along with them. She still looked distant and disinterested, but as she passed, Janina saw with some measure of horror that they had handcuffed her. They directed her into the back of their car, and then got in and drove away.

Officer DeRosa came up to Leonard.

"God help us, Tony," said Leonard, his voice weak. "What the hell has just happened here?"

Officer DeRosa shook his head. "Maybe you can tell me. I've got to take your statement, Leonard. Can you describe what you saw?"

"Well, I didn't see it happen," Leonard said. "Janina came in saying that Tom had a gun and was threatening someone. So, we came running back, and we heard a shot. When we came in, there was only Kathy there, and Tom was lying on the floor."

"And Kathy had the gun in her hand at the time?"

"Yes."

The policeman turned to Janina and knelt next to her. He attempted a smile but failed miserably. It was clear that he was badly shaken. "Hi, young lady."

"Hi, Officer DeRosa." She herself was near tears but struggled to control them.

"Now, I just need you to tell me what you saw tonight. Okay?"

Janina took a deep, hitching breath. "I was outside, and I heard them arguing. I came over to look into the window, and I saw them in there. Tom was holding a gun, and Kathy and Justin were standing near the door."

Officer DeRosa looked up from his notebook. "Justin?"

"Justin Lazarus," said Janina. "He works for Tom and Kathy. Tom was pointing the gun around while Kathy was saying, 'No, Tom, don't.' Then, Tom yelled some stuff at Kathy I didn't understand. Something about a baby and Tom giving her his name."

Officer DeRosa glanced at Leonard who shrugged and said nothing.

"I got scared and ran to get my dad. Then we heard the gunshot. When we came back, Tom was lying on the floor and Justin was gone."

"Say, Tony, maybe you ought to know something about this Justin Lazarus...." Leonard said. Janina looked up at her father, her eyes terrified and pleading.

No, Daddy, don't tell him. Don't tell him about the FBI men. Don't tell him....

But Leonard either didn't understand what she was trying to tell him or ignored it. "Yesterday we got a visit from the FBI saying that they were looking for this Justin Lazarus."

Officer DeRosa's eyebrows shot up, and he made a notation in his notebook. "Is that so?"

"Yes, they gave me a card with a telephone number on it. Down in Colville. Said they had an office there."

Officer DeRosa looked up. "What?"

"They said they came from the FBI office in Colville."

"That isn't possible. There is no FBI office in Colville. Not that I know of, anyway."

Leonard looked taken aback. "Well, I don't know, Tony. But that's what the men said. They had badges and all."

"That doesn't mean much. Could have been fake. Do you still have the card?"

"Yes, I think so."

"Why don't you go get it, and I'll give it to the county police."

As he was speaking, a second county police car with lights flashing pulled up in front of the Christians' house. Officer DeRosa went over and began to talk to the men who got out of the car as Janina and her father went back home to retrieve the card. Several neighbors came clamoring up, asking questions, but Leonard ignored them all and returned to his house.

Maddy was standing at the front door, looking out. "Leonard, for God's sake, what happened?"

"Tom's been shot," Leonard said bluntly.

Maddy turned whiter than she was already. "By who?"

"I don't know. When we came in, Kathy was sitting next to him holding a gun. But Janina saw this Justin Lazarus in the room before Tom was shot."

Maddy's voice rose in triumph. "I knew it! I knew it! He's killed Tom. I knew they were right about him. He's the one who's killed Tom."

"Maddy, will you just shut up!" Leonard shouted. "You don't know what happened over there, so just shut up!"

Maddy's voice was cut off as if she had been slapped.

"Now, where is the card those FBI men left?" Leonard demanded.

"By the telephone," said Maddy. Janina could not recall ever hearing her mother sounding so meek.

Leonard retrieved the card and went back outside. This time, both Janina and Maddy followed.

There was yellow plastic tape saying, "Crime Scene – Do Not Cross" surrounding the Christians' front porch.

Leonard wordlessly handed the business card to Officer DeRosa, who was standing with the other policemen by the cars parked along the road. DeRosa glanced at it, and then handed it to one of the other officers.

There were still a number of neighbors and other onlookers standing in tense little knots along the sidewalk, and Maddy went over to join them. Janina heard her voice clearly over the murmur of conversation.

"... killed by his hired help. Some young drifter named Justin Lazarus...."

Janina felt something cool brush her face. Then, again, this time striking her hand. A sudden breeze made the police barrier tape flutter and twirl. Within moments, rain began to fall, a silent, streaming rain falling in veils and sheets from a leaden sky.

CHAPTER 4

Sprays of rain spattered the window. The wind whistling forlornly in the trees was the first sound Janina heard when she woke up. She opened her eyes and saw runnels of rainwater streaming down the window glass. Strange how fast the weather could change in May in upstate New York. Saturday and Sunday had been beautiful, clear, and cool. Now it was Monday morning, and it was windy and raining. Probably forty degrees from the look of it. Janina thought about the Marshalls, a retired couple who lived next door and prided themselves on their gardens. Their huge, formal bed filled with a painter's palette of peonies was sure to be ruined by now, the flowers face down in the mud. It would almost be painful to look at it.

Monday morning—rain, wind, and spoiled gardens notwithstanding—Janina somehow couldn't feel upset this morning. She got up, showered, and dressed in a spirit of unrestrainable cheer. She was looking forward to being at work. She was looking forward to the last concert of the year, which was a week from Tuesday. She was even looking forward to the little routines of school and home that had occupied no part of her thoughts recently. It was nice not to have to worry about Kathy anymore. Her compulsion, never far from her mind in the past couple of weeks, was now completely gone.

Also, Martha had no more reason to stalk her. Whatever she was trying to do, it was too late now. The necklace was gone.

Jim walked into the kitchen to give Janina a goodbye kiss as she was pouring herself a cup of coffee. She was singing a snatch of a Gilbert and Sullivan tune as he entered, and when she noticed him, she looked up sheepishly.

"What is that, anyway?" Jim asked, grinning.

"'Poor Wandering One,' from *The Pirates of Penzance*. It's been years since I've sung that. I'm having to la-la a bunch of the words because I can't remember them all."

"Of course. I knew I recognized it. If I had time, I'd join in. I could be that old fellow, what's his name? The Very Model of a Modern Major General. Although I don't think I can sing that fast."

Janina grinned. "You'd make a much better Frederick. Or the Pirate King. Someone who can sweep a young girl off her feet. You certainly do that to me."

Jim encircled her waist with one arm, tipped her over backward, and gave her a sloppy kiss while Janina attempted to fight him off with little success.

"You are such a beast," she said after he had set her back on her feet.

"Comes from working with beasts all day. And it's nice to see you in such a good mood."

"I've been pretty awful lately, haven't I?" Janina looked rueful. "I'm really sorry."

"Don't apologize. I've been worried, that's all."

"Well, I'm feeling much better, and I think it's going to be permanent this time." Her face became serious. "I'd like to talk to you about it, but let's wait until we have more time, okay?"

"Sure." He gave her another kiss, and then said, "Gotta go. Have a good day at school."

"I will. Keep them critters in line."

"You do the same," said Jim.

Janina heard her husband saying goodbye to the children. He had to roll Brendan out of bed to do so, and she heard Brendan's wail of distress all the way across the house. She smiled to herself. The sweet little routines, which had been subsumed into the weirdness of the past few weeks, were again becoming the focus of her life. And that was the way it should be.

By the time she drove to work, the rain was coming down so hard that even though she had the windshield wipers on full speed, she still could hardly see. The tires hissed on the wet pavement, and the gusts of wind rocked her little car as she drove down the main street of Guildford toward the school. When she arrived, she found that the parking lot had turned into a miniature lake. She had to sprint from her car to the entrance to avoid getting soaked. Her umbrella did little good because the majority of the raindrops seemed to be using the wind to defy gravity— blowing horizontally under and around all the obstructions set up to block them. She dashed inside, pulling the door shut behind her.

She was running late today. It was already seven forty-five— only fifteen minutes until first period began. A small number of students were milling about in the halls as she stood on the mat and watched her with some amusement as she was closing up her umbrella and attempting to brush the water from her coat and book bag.

Once she had shaken off what rainwater she could, she walked down the hallway toward the music wing, her wet shoes squeaking on the tile floor. When she turned the corner, she looked down toward her room and saw that there was someone leaning against the wall next to the door.

Janina's heart went into a sudden, terrified staccato. It was

Martha, standing in the same place as she'd been Friday night when she'd given Janina such a fright.

She forced herself to continue to walk at a normal pace as her pulse thundered in her ears.

She'd thought this was all over. But it wasn't.

And then, the more rational part of her mind reassured her. Martha had no claim on her now. It was of no importance whether she really was mixed up in the business of Kathy and Tom because Janina was done with it.

As Janina approached, Martha gave her a gentle, harmless smile. "Hi."

"Hi," replied Janina warily.

"Can I help you with any of that?"

"No, thanks, I've got it."

Martha's face became serious. "I know you're just getting here. You haven't even set your stuff down yet. But I need to talk to you. It'll only take five minutes."

Janina put her book bag on the floor and unlocked her door. "Sure. Come in."

She sure as hell was going to leave the door open.

As Janina took off and hung up her raincoat and umbrella, Martha began to talk to her. She spoke in a rapid, prattling fashion that didn't seem to fit with the clipped, succinct phrases she'd always heard her use in conversation before.

"I'm sorry if I scared you Friday night. I wasn't myself. It just struck me as funny that you were here on a Friday night, and so was I. I know that you must have thought it odd that there I was, hanging around outside your door. But all I really wanted was to talk to you. And since I didn't get to talk to you then, I thought I'd catch you now before class starts. It's about something that has been on my mind lately."

"Oh, really?" said Janina in a noncommittal tone.

Okay, this woman wasn't scary. She was just nuts.

"Yes, well, you may have noticed that I don't really seem like

I fit as a business ed student teacher."

Janina pulled a stack of music out of the piano bench and set it down on the music stand. "What do you mean?"

Martha leaned over the back of the piano, resting her chin in her hands in a manner which no doubt would have seemed fetching to most males. Janina, now that she was over her first fright, was beginning to be irritated. Maybe if she just kept messing about with her sheet music and answering her in monosyllables, Martha would get the idea and leave.

"It's a little hard for me to explain. So, I don't think I will. Let's just say that I don't belong here."

"You don't?"

"No. In fact, I sort of need to go somewhere where I... fit in better. Where I really belong, you might say. But there's something I need before I go."

Janina looked up, her brow furrowed with annoyance. Okay, enough was enough. "What are you talking about?" she demanded, her voice uncharacteristically sharp.

Martha gave a demure little sigh. "The necklace, Janina. I need you to give me the necklace."

Janina froze, her eyes wide. Martha's face didn't change. The guileless blue eyes continued to watch Janina with the same blithe simplicity as always. Janina stared back. For a moment, neither of them said anything.

"The what?" Janina finally croaked.

"Oh, now, let's not act more foolish than you really are. I could have taken it from you Friday night, but I thought it might have been more prudent to wait and see what you were going to do with it. Then on Saturday, you gave me the slip while you were at your daughter's friend's house." She wagged her finger playfully. "You really had me wondering what had happened to you until I realized that you had switched cars. In any case, I think we can both agree that the chase has gone on long enough. Give me the necklace, and I'll go away. We can forget any of this happened."

"I don't have the necklace," Janina said, trying to keep her voice calm.

"Really, Janina, there's no use in your lying. I know about your little excursion to retrieve it. You really must be more careful, you know. You could have been cut badly. Not to mention getting yourself in serious trouble." The mock compassion, so cleverly acted, made her words seem horrific.

"I'm not lying. I really don't have it. Look." She pulled on the collar of her blouse and tipped her head sideways to expose her neck.

"Then I'm sure you won't mind going back home on your prep period to get it for me." The threat, thinly veiled at best, was beginning to show through.

Much to her own surprise, Janina suddenly felt a flood of calm wash over her. She'd told herself she was done with this affair.

So be done with it. Finish it. Now.

"What do you want it for, Martha?"

The other woman smiled. "Nothing you need to concern yourself with."

"I'm just curious," Janina persisted. "If I have to give it up, you might at least tell me what it's for."

One eyebrow went up, and she gave Janina an appraising glance. "Very well, I suppose I owe you that much. You might say I'm going to use it to trap a fox." She smiled, seeming to enjoy the image. "A very, very wary fox who has needed catching for a long time."

"I wouldn't have thought of you as the fox hunting type."

Martha's smile faded. "Don't play games with me, Janina. Give me the necklace or tell me where it is."

"I really don't know where it is."

Martha's guise was slipping. Her eyes flashed with anger. "You're lying."

"No, I'm not. I don't know where it is because I don't have it any longer."

There was a moment of silence. The two women locked in each other's gaze. Then Martha gave a slight frown. The dawning realization that Janina was telling the truth showed itself in Martha's eyes as astonishment, then fear. "What do you mean, you don't have it any longer? Who has it?"

"The person that it really belongs to."

Martha stared at her. "That's impossible."

"No, it's not. What's impossible is that you'll ever get it now."

"How did you get it to him without my knowing?" she demanded. "We've been watching…."

Janina shrugged. "Honestly, Martha, that's none of your damned business. Besides, who is 'we?'"

Martha ignored the question. "I don't believe you." Her voice was rough-edged with panic. "What you're saying isn't possible…." She trailed off, a helpless realization dawning in her expression. It was the first time Janina recalled ever seeing her show any emotion other than self-assurance. "You did it when you switched cars," Martha said, the blood draining from her face.

Janina picked up her stack of sheet music. "You play around with figuring out what happened if you want to. But do it on your own time. I've got a class to teach, and it's starting in five minutes."

Martha's face was white except for two spots of high color in her cheeks. For an instant Janina thought she was going to strike her. In the same moment, Janina realized that her fear was gone. She was simply angry. Angry as she had never been before.

She took a step toward Martha. "Are you going to leave my classroom under your own power? Or do I have to call the office and have them phone the police? Whatever stupid game you're playing, Miss Alport, it's over. Whatever you want that necklace for, it's out of my hands and out of yours. Go tell your friends who have been 'watching' that it's over." Janina slammed her stack of music down on the table. "Now get the hell out of my classroom."

Martha's lips narrowed to a thin, bloodless line, and panic and fury seeming to compete in her eyes. Panic won. She snarled, "We'll still find him," and then spun on her heel and stormed out of the door. On the way out, she nearly bowled over an early student who took a step backward, almost dropped his books, and swore under his breath. Janina ignored that but walked over to the door and leaned out into the hall watching Martha's retreating form. It was only then that a thought crossed her mind.

Twice she'd referred to "him." What "him" was she talking about? Was it Leo, or someone else?

About halfway down the hallway, the formidable bulk of Wanda was approaching. Janina winced. Martha and she were on a collision course.

Martha stopped her headlong flight approximately three inches away from Wanda's face. From her expression, Martha was clearly seething with fury, and Wanda stared uncomprehendingly up at her student teacher, whose behavior had so suddenly and inexplicably altered from her previous warmth and calm competence. The students in the hall turned away from their lockers and their conversations. One by one every student fell silent, staring at the women in astonishment.

When Wanda spoke, it was in her typical stentorian tones, which rang even louder in the almost palpable silence in the hallway. "Miss Alport," she announced severely, "I've been looking everywhere for you! You've got two students down in the classroom who need to set up times to practice drills. I told them you should be there since they're your responsibility. I didn't know what I should tell them to do."

There was a moment of total silence as Martha stared down at Wanda. Then her features contorted, and she hissed, "You can tell them both to go to hell, and you can take your practice drills and stick them up your fat ass."

Martha swept off down the hall and out of the door into the parking lot, leaving Wanda standing in the middle of the hall, her mouth wide open, and for once totally speechless.

There was a moment's stunned silence, and then every student in the hall began either talking or laughing uproariously. Wanda turned a brilliant shade of crimson and beat a hasty retreat to her classroom. Within minutes, everyone in the school knew that the lovely Miss Alport had told Mrs. Corliss what most of the students, and many of the faculty, had wanted to tell her for years.

Janina withdrew back into her room, went to the piano, and sat down on the bench. She looked a little stunned. The student who had almost been knocked down by Martha's exit looked at her in concern.

"Are you all right, Mrs. Vannoy?"

Janina looked up and gave him a smile—weak at first—but finally a real, honest smile. "Yes, Mark. I'm all right. A little shook up but all right."

And she was, too. No more need to lie.

She really was.

CHAPTER 5

The rain fell all night, drenching the dreaming world with a steady, enveloping downpour. The streets glistened in the glare of the streetlights, and water chuckled down the gutters and into the storm sewers. Through it all Janina slept, absorbed in melancholy dreams about looking in the woods for someone who was lost as the rain sheeted and swirled down from the gray-black sky. Dark, wet tree trunks surrounded her. Raindrops hissed and pattered their way through the branches and onto the leaf-strewn ground beneath. She finally came upon a clearing in the forest, a circular area of open grass. In the center, stood a young man who smiled and beckoned to her. There was a brilliant flash of light. She recoiled and covered her face with her hands. Then, the darkness became complete, and when she opened her eyes, she was alone in the wet night.

She woke to find sunshine pouring through her window from a crystalline blue sky. The air coming in through the window screen felt cool and fresh for the first time in many days. She sat up and yawned.

It had to have been a dream. All that stuff about Tom getting shot, and her running after Justin in the woods. It had to have been a dream.

But when she went into the kitchen, her mother was standing at the sink holding a tea towel. She wasn't drying dishes like usual. She was standing there, motionless. Janina watched her for nearly a full minute, but Maddy didn't move.

"Mom?" Janina began, then faltered and fell silent.

Maddy turned to face her, and then walked over to the kitchen table and sat down. "Janina, honey," she said in a quiet voice. Her hands twisted the towel convulsively, but she seemed to be unaware that she was still holding it. "Tom's dead. He died on the way to the hospital."

When Janina spoke, her voice lacked any trace of emotion. She felt she was somehow beyond emotion, although she knew that she would feel it all later, perhaps much later. "Where's Kathy?"

"I haven't heard. In jail, I suppose. She never came back last night."

So, it had been real after all. Tom was dead, Kathy was gone, and the house next door was empty.

The phone rang pretty much continuously all morning. Reporters from the Colville newspaper, Channel 6, and Channel 11 News wanting to know when Leonard would be home so they could interview him briefly. Also, Georgia Petrie, Pauline McMillan, and several other curious neighbors wanting to know exactly what had happened. Every time the receiver was set down, the telephone sang out its shrill call again.

Janina watched her mother curiously through all of this. Maddy, normally one of the executive directors of Guildford's gossip network, seemed to have lost all of her enthusiasm for explaining the events of the previous night. Her initial crowing about knowing who was responsible for Tom's death had been very short-lived. Janina recalled that after she'd gone to bed, she'd heard her parents arguing in the living room. This was a very infrequent occurrence. Leonard seemed to look upon most battles with his wife as not worth fighting. But this time, she could hear his voice, angry and stern, although the distance and the closed doors muffled the words. Only once did she hear his voice rise up loudly enough for her to clearly discern the words, "Don't treat these people's lives as if they were raw materials for your damned gossip factory!"

It was impossible to tell whether it was the fight that had occasioned the change in Maddy's attitude, or the simple realization that what had happened in the house next door was final, tragic, and irrevocable. Whatever the cause, Maddy's conversations with nosy neighbors and friends were succinct and, from their points of view, undoubtedly unsatisfying.

Leonard returned at about three o'clock, and almost at once the reporters began to arrive. Leonard was questioned and interviewed. He responded in as vaguely sympathetic a fashion as he could manage, always trying to keep Janina's name out of it. Only when the reporter from the Channel 11 News asked, "Now, Mr. Starcevich, how did you come to discover the shooting? Did you go to investigate when you heard the gunshot?" did Leonard slip and say, "No, I was already on my way over there when I heard it." The reporter frowned.

"How did you know that there was a fight going on in the Christians' house?"

Leonard looked startled and then mumbled something about overhearing them arguing.

The reporter seemed to accept that but continued to press for more information. "Do you know what they were arguing about?"

"The Christians were very private people," Leonard answered with some degree of asperity. "If there was a quarrel between them, I'm sure I don't know what it was nor was it any of my business."

The last of the reporters were gone by four-thirty, and Maddy was in the kitchen fixing dinner. Leonard sat slumped in his recliner as he dozed, exhausted by the events of the past day. Janina was watching *Gilligan's Island* with such a serious expression that anyone would have thought it was high drama, but in reality, her thoughts were miles away from the escapades of Gilligan and the Skipper. Her mind was trying to locate three people who had, for varying amounts of time, been fixtures in her life.

Tom—where was he this evening? Janina went to the Guildford Roman Catholic Church with her parents on Sunday mornings, but she had never really quite believed the pious impossibilities that Father Morris and the parishioners spoke about during mass. Heaven. Where exactly was that? Wherever and whatever it was, heaven certainly didn't seem to have any impact on this world. Tom had bled his life away almost twenty-four hours ago, and the world still continued around them virtually unchanged. Maddy fried pork chops in the kitchen. Her dad slept in his recliner. The cars still passed by their house with common people going about on their common errands. Someone had died, and everything was still the same. How could that be?

Kathy was gone, too. Sweet, elegant Kathy, who played her piano in the evenings and ran the till at the hardware store during the day, was gone. Not quite as completely gone as Tom was but still gone. Had Kathy killed Tom? It was hard to imagine. But what else could "Tom, I'm so sorry" mean? What else could she have been sorry for? Janina thought again about the words— the harsh, bitter words Tom had shouted at her shortly before the bullet had torn his life away. The thought crossed her mind that maybe there could have been other things to be sorry about. Maybe a lot of things.

Lastly, where was Justin? Had Kathy really not remembered him last night? Being around Justin did do strange things to people's memories—Janina herself had evidently warned Justin about the FBI men, and she still had not the least glimmer of recollection of having done so. But where was he now? Surely the police were after him. Maybe he'd be joining Kathy in jail soon. But for now, where was he?

The doorbell rang. Leonard started up, clearing his throat and blinking in a dazed fashion. "Janina, could you get that?" he asked, his voice a little hoarse with sleep.

Janina went to the door and opened it with some trepidation, fearing what new and sinister person could be on their doorstep this time. However, it only turned out to be Officer DeRosa. He smiled kindly at her, although he was still obviously preoccupied. His eyes were grave.

"Evening, Miss Starcevich. Is your dad around?" Officer DeRosa always seemed to call Janina "young lady" or "Miss Starcevich," a habit she found to be simultaneously endearing and annoying.

"Sure, Officer DeRosa. I'll get him."

Janina trotted back into the living room. "Dad? It's Officer DeRosa."

Leonard heaved himself wearily out of his recliner and went to the door. "Hey, Tony."

"Evening, Leonard. I wanted to get back to you about that FBI card."

"Yes?"

Officer DeRosa seemed to be considering his words carefully. "Well, we don't know where those men were from, but they're not FBI The phone number on the card was disconnected only a day ago. It had been registered under the name of Paul Trowbridge, same as on the card. We've contacted the FBI—the real FBI, you understand. They said they have no one named Paul Trowbridge on their staff, and no one at all working a case in this area."

"So, who were those men?"

"Got me. And even more interesting, the FBI told us that they had never heard of anyone named Justin Lazarus. In fact, we can't find any records of anyone under that name. The Social Security number he gave to Tom on his job application is fake. So, it seems pretty likely that he was running from someone and was under an assumed identity."

"Could he be wanted under another name?"

"Possible. But those fake FBI men knew him as Justin Lazarus."

"That's true."

There was a pause. "Anyhow, Leonard, I wanted to let you know. I probably shouldn't have told you as much as I have, but I thought that maybe those two men might show up again. I thought you should be warned that they're not who they say they are. So, keep an eye out, okay?"

"I will. Thanks, Tony."

Leonard closed the door and turned wearily back to his chair. He found that Maddy was watching him from the door that led into the kitchen. She was still carrying a greasy spatula and wearing her apron. She looked confused, almost distraught.

"Who were those people, Leonard? If they weren't FBI, who were they?"

"Tony didn't know, and neither do I." Leonard sat down and smoothed back his thinning hair with one hand.

"Dear God, Leonard, isn't there anywhere safe anymore?" said Maddy.

Janina looked up. Maddy seemed to be waiting for reassurance, but Leonard was too exhausted to respond with more than, "I guess not."

Small clips of Leonard's interview with the reporters showed up on the Channel 6 News that evening, Leonard saying, "I can't imagine what must have happened. They always seemed like happy, ordinary folks," in a tone of diffuse distress that really didn't communicate anything.

The Colville newspaper ran a front-page story also quoting Leonard. The offhand notoriety of being quoted in so many different places at once seemed to increase his discomfort at being connected with the case at all. Dinnertime passed in near silence. Doug looked ill at ease, as if he didn't know what to say. Leonard was completely uncommunicative, and Maddy still sunk in her own depression.

Janina only interrupted the gloom and quiet once. She had tried to force herself to remain silent, but finally, she couldn't stand being caged with her own thoughts any longer. She asked, "What are they going to do to Kathy?" in a small voice.

Maddy put her hand to her face, her lips trembling, and looked at Leonard. "I don't know, Janina," her father finally said. "She'll probably be put on trial."

"What then?"

"Let's just wait and see."

"Maybe they only took her in to ask her some questions," said Janina, but no one answered. Leonard and Maddy just exchanged glances, and that was answer enough.

A week went by, then two. Maddy's mood gradually returned to normal, and when one morning she sniped at Doug for leaving his jeans on the floor and he fired back that wearing them wrinkled was the fashion these days, Janina almost felt relieved. She was beginning to realize that after a trauma things do eventually get back to normal.

Still, she had a hard time passing Tom and Kathy's house every day. Every time she looked at it, she felt a pang. The lawn had begun to be unkempt, but after about two and a half weeks had passed, someone mowed it—she didn't see who—and it was mowed regularly thereafter. The police barrier tape had been taken down a few days after Tom died. From all outward appearances, the house was perfectly normal. Every so often she would see a car in front of it, and the front door would stand open for a half-hour or so before the people would close it up and return from whence they came.

Then the beginning of school loomed on the horizon, blotting out other considerations. The newspaper articles came less and less frequently, and the death of Tom was a topic of conversation replaced by more mundane, but also more recent, events. Much to her own astonishment, Janina found herself within a few weeks unable to remember large pieces of the four-week period over which she had known Justin. His face was the first to go. One day she discovered, with a mild sense of puzzlement, that other than knowing that he had been young and male, she couldn't recall what he looked like. By the time school started, even the memory of his name was becoming fuzzy. It was several years before she stopped giving a little start every time she heard the name Justin, but within a month after Tom's death, she had already ceased to understand why.

PART 4

ENTRAPMENT AND RELEASE

CHAPTER 1

Three bells rang to signal the beginning of lunchtime at J. P. McMahon High School, and Janina quickly gathered together the sheet music left on the music stands in her room, retrieved her lunch bag, and headed off toward the faculty room. The halls were crowded with students rushing to and from classes. There was an almost tangible current of voices and laughter flowing with them and carrying them along. Janina marveled, as she had many times before, at how her tolerance for chaos had increased since she had become a teacher.

Of course, it was either learn tolerance or find a new career. Chaos in a high school was a fact of life.

The usual crowd was in the faculty room. Alice and Lucy discussing the reviews of a recent movie, Doris nibbling at a tuna sandwich and staring vaguely into space through her thick eyeglasses, the four men playing bridge at the table in the corner, and, of course, Wanda eating cafeteria chicken nuggets with relish while talking at the same time despite the fact that no one seemed to be listening—damn the torpedoes, full speed ahead.

Janina set her lunch down on the table.

"... and, so I called the education department at Colville College. Do you know what they told me?" Wanda was saying. "You'd never believe it."

Doris, the only one even pretending to listen, inclined her head in Wanda's direction. "What did they tell you?"

"They said that they had never heard of her! The papers that were sent into the school to assign her position were forgeries! Someone had even got hold of Colville College stationery! Even the person at the college who signed the thank you letter when I agreed to take her on had never heard of a Martha Alport. Not that I'm surprised," she added, her voice strident with indignation, "after the way she behaved a week ago. Of course, it was clear to me from the very outset that she wasn't terribly stable. Although I must say I was still surprised at what she did. Of all the nerve, to speak to me like that! And in front of students, right in the middle of the hallway, no less! It takes some believing, let me tell you."

"Do you know where she's gone?" Janina asked, attempting to make the question sound as offhand as possible.

Wanda snorted. "I have no idea, and I'll tell you, Janina, I really don't care. All I can say is that Colville College will have a long wait before I'll be ready to accept another student teacher from them. In my opinion, they should send me a letter of apology. Of course, we all know that it'll be a cold day in Hades before that happens."

Alice looked up from her lunch. "But I thought you said that the college had never heard of her?"

"It's their good name that's at stake," Wanda said in a self-righteous tone. "If I were them, I'd do whatever it took to get back into my good graces."

"But, Wanda," began Alice, "if they didn't even know...." Then Lucy caught her eye and gave a little shake of her head and a surreptitious wink. Alice trailed off into silence. Janina smiled and hid it behind a napkin.

"Now, Alice," Wanda said pontifically, "You know that I don't want to set a precedent in tolerating such behavior from my student teachers...."

Janina only half listened to the rest of the conversation. It was somehow refreshing to be able to be there and not be distracted or on edge. Even listening to Wanda's seemingly endless fund of opinions was a welcome change. The strange affair with Kathy was over and beginning to recede into memory. Although she still had not talked to her husband about it—she would soon, she told herself—it was already acquiring that air of almost comic melodrama that serious situations so often seem to gain in memory. Janina still found herself wondering about Martha's part in it, especially how she had known about the necklace, and why she wanted it. But she was finally feeling content simply to let herself not have all the answers. Her own life was more important.

She finished her lunch, dropped the remains into the trash can, and walked from the faculty room into the room that housed the photocopier. She had brought some worksheets for her music theory class with her to photocopy. She loaded them in, pressed a few buttons, and the machine reluctantly groaned to life.

As she was waiting, she glanced idly around the room. On a table in the corner, there was a copy of that day's *Colville Times.* Her eyes wandered over the bottom of the front page, which was all that was visible. She picked it up and unfolded it.

She read the headlines with only mild interest. "Colville City Council to Discuss Budget Items." "Nobel Laureate to Give Graduation Speech at Colville College." "Conflict Over Cellular Phone Towers in Foxcroft." She opened the paper up. At the top of the second page was a police photograph of a woman, her mouth unsmiling, her eyes vague and distant. Underneath was the caption, "Katherine Christian, 1971."

Janina took a sharp breath, and her eyes passed to a headline on the upper right, which was followed by several paragraphs of text—"Long-Term Inmate Escapes From Hazleton."

"Leo Carson was right," Janina said under her breath. "He said to watch the newspapers. He was right." Heart racing, she began to read, her photocopies forgotten.

HAZLETON – Katherine Christian, age 53, is reported as having escaped yesterday evening from the Hazleton Institution for the Criminally Insane. Guards report that she had been locked into her cell Wednesday evening as usual, but when the cell was checked in the early hours today, she was found to be missing. The cell door was still locked, and the guards claim to have heard nothing. The institution grounds and buildings have been thoroughly searched, but no trace of the missing woman has yet been found. Dr. Stephen Musgrave, the director of Hazleton Institution since 1989, has confessed that he is "at a loss" to explain Mrs. Christian's disappearance, which is only the third such escape since Hazleton was founded in the mid-1920's.

Mrs. Christian was responsible for the 1971 death of her husband, Thomas Christian, which shook the sleepy community of Guildford where the Christians were prominent citizens. Thomas Christian was the owner of a local hardware and feed store. On the evening of August 7, 1971, he was found shot in his home and died shortly thereafter en route to Colville Area General Hospital. Mrs. Christian was found next to him holding her husband's revolver and was taken into custody. Over the following next few weeks, she refused to answer any questions or respond in a rational fashion to anyone. She was eventually found to be sufficiently out of touch with reality to render her unfit to stand trial. She was institutionalized at Hazleton in October of that year and has been there ever since.

Police are currently scouring nearby woods and fields for the missing woman. It is not believed that she is dangerous, but nevertheless, she should not be approached if seen. The Sheriff's Department of Stephens County is asking that anyone with any information pertaining to her escape or current whereabouts to contact the police immediately.

"Are you done, Janina?" Mike Allen, who taught English, was standing behind her.

Janina whirled around. "What?"

"I was just asking if you were done." He grinned. "Sorry I startled you."

"Oh, no problem." Janina hastily gathered up her worksheets. "I got started reading the newspaper and forgot about what I was doing."

He put a sheet of paper on the copier screen and pushed the buttons to start it. He glanced over at the still-open newspaper. "What do you think of that woman escaping from Hazleton? I heard about it on the radio coming to work today."

"I think it's amazing that anyone could escape from a place like that," said Janina with feeling.

"You're not kidding. I hear she was from Guildford, but I didn't move here until 1980, so that's before my time."

"Yes," said Janina, "she was."

"I hope they catch her soon. We don't need any more crazies running around. We've got enough of them already in public office." He chuckled at his own joke.

Janina gave him a weak smile, and then left the room. She felt dizzy. She had to get back to her classroom, or she was afraid she was going to faint.

She made it—just—and walked into her office and collapsed into her chair. The room was spinning. She set her head down on her desk because she was afraid that she would fall out of her chair. The spinning was becoming intolerable. She grabbed the edge of her desk as she gave a weak little cry of panic and alarm.

Then, without warning, she felt like her brain was picked up in its entirety, turned around, and set back down into her skull. A shudder passed through her body as if her spine were a guitar string that someone had plucked. Then, with startling suddenness, the dizziness was gone like someone had shut it off with a switch. Memories—vivid, vibrant memories—began to flood her consciousness. She pictured herself as a child sitting underneath the big fir tree in the park, the one that had blown down in the storm two years ago. She could see the little Panasonic radio she had, and her stuffed bear sitting beside her backpack. And another memory of standing by her parents' pond at night, looking at the stars....

"Oh!" she said suddenly, and her eyes were wide and startled. She had a sensation like that of looking through a pair of unfocused binoculars when someone twists the focus knob before everything becomes clear. She also remembered—no, she saw— Justin Lazarus, his face as sharp and distinct as if she had just seen him minutes ago, dressed in an old t-shirt and jeans, blond hair tousled and shaggy, his clear gray eyes sparkling, and a broad grin on his face.

Everything suddenly made sense. Not only the events of the past few weeks, but the events during that strange four-week period in the summer twenty-five years ago. Events that she had not recalled for years—or ever recalled, perhaps. It was as if a veil had been lifted from a part of her life that had previously been hidden and inaccessible.

The bell rang, signaling the end of lunch and startling Janina out of her reverie. She stood up, gathering together her grade book and papers, and walked out into her classroom. The first students who came into her class looked at her a little oddly, as if they wondered why she was wearing that strange, mysterious little smile but were too polite to ask.

The rest of the day flew by. She returned home and welcomed the peace and stillness that greeted her as she walked in, knowing it would soon be shattered when the school bus arrived. She had about an hour and a half before Jim arrived to get dinner going and make some plans.

Janina pulled a CD off the shelf and slipped it into the player. Before pushing "Play," she turned the volume up to high. Moments later, the wild, thrilling trumpets and violins cascaded from the speakers, and the sweet, silvery voices, singing, "Magnificat, magnificat, magnificat anima mea Dominum...."

She felt transported into another part of her life. After so many years it was almost like another person's half-forgotten tale. She sat in the recliner, closing her eyes and letting the music wash over her, and began remembering.

Remembering and looking forward. Two sides of the same coin. The past was done and dealt with. Now it was time to turn and look in the opposite direction, toward the future. But before she did, there was still one more thing she had left undone.

There was the sudden tumult of her children running up the driveway. Janina smiled to herself. She pictured herself when Jim came home, giving him a kiss, and saying, "Jim, do you have time to listen? I'd like to tell you a story...."

CHAPTER 2

It was the last day of October, and the wind was stripping the sugar maples down to bare, gray branches. Drifts of yellow and bright orange tumbled across the fields and yards, catching what little light came from the overcast sky. There was a winter storm watch—the first of the season—and the weather forecast had predicted snow.

Janina sat in her fifth-grade classroom in Thomas J. Kraft Middle School, only half listening to Mrs. Clarke's explanation of how to reduce fractions. Most teachers were cutting the students some slack given that it was Halloween and their attention was elsewhere. However, Mrs. Clarke had evidently attended the fabled Old School, and today was no different than any other.

Janina was ordinarily a conscientious student even though math had never been a congenial subject for her. For some reason, she couldn't keep her mind on her work today. Unlike the other inattentive students in the classroom, however, for Janina it had nothing to do with trick-or-treating or the impending snowstorm. Her mind was replaying the conversation that occurred over breakfast, and Mrs. Clarke's rather nasal voice receded into the background.

Maddy had been scrambling eggs. Doug was already gone. He was in his first year of high school this year and had joined the JV soccer team. He had only found out afterwards that Coach Rice regularly scheduled practices at six-thirty in the morning. Leonard was munching his way through a bowl of cereal.

Maddy walked to the table, holding the skillet in a gloved hand, and slid some eggs onto Janina's plate.

"Leonard," Maddy said, "what do you think of the idea of moving?"

Leonard stopped in mid-chew. "Moving? Where?"

"Somewhere else in Guildford. Buying a different house."

"But why on earth would we do that?"

Maddy turned back to the stove. She seemed embarrassed. "I just can't bear living next to... that house anymore."

"But, Maddy. Nothing is wrong with the house. I heard that there'll be renters soon, so it won't be empty much longer." Leonard seemed completely taken aback.

"It's not the emptiness that bothers me," Maddy said earnestly as she dropped her spatula into a sink full of soapy water. "It's just knowing what happened there. Day after day. It's a reminder of it. A constant reminder." Her voice, which had up till now been unwarrantedly reasonable, suddenly regained a bit of its customary edge. "Besides, Leonard, it isn't you that has to be here all day, every day, watching that house and remembering."

"Now, Maddy, we have this house paid for, and it's a nice house. Not to mention the improvements we've put into it. I mean, the landscaping, the gardens...." The last words carried an overtone of pleading.

"I suppose you're right," said Maddy, meaning exactly the opposite. "You're right, Leonard. I'm sure my feelings will change. I'll just have to deal with it."

"Maddy, I don't mean that...."

"No, never mind." She gave a tight little laugh. "Case closed. You're right. We won't talk about it anymore."

But Janina knew that it wasn't closed at all. Cases seldom were closed with Maddy. Janina was sure—sure as if it had been engraved in stone—that they would eventually move out of this house where she'd spent her first ten years. It might be next year, or it might not be for five years. When Maddy stated her opinions, though, the family nearly always fell into line sooner or later.

"Janina?" She started and looked up. Mrs. Clarke was staring at her, frowning over the top of her glasses, and pointing at her with a piece of chalk. "Since you seem to find what is outside the window so interesting, why don't you tell us how to reduce sixteen-twentieths."

The day crawled by. When the final bell rang, Janina gathered her books together, donned her jacket, wool hat, and gloves, and stepped out into the windy world. The temperature was already dropping, and the clouds thickening. The promised snow looked likely to materialize. The happy thought *Maybe there will be no school tomorrow* flitted through her head, but her five years in the Guildford School District told her that realistically, the likelihood of a school cancellation was close to zero. The superintendent was from Buffalo and considered the amount of snow they got in Guildford to be trifling. He seemed to only be willing to cancel school when it snowed so much you couldn't *find* the school.

When she got home, she took advantage of the fact that her mother was vacuuming the bedrooms to fix herself a snack. Graham crackers and Oreo cookies sounded appealing, so she grabbed several of each. If her mom had been there, it would have had to be carrot sticks or something of the sort. Less palatable but more nutritious—especially given that it was

Halloween and there'd be candy aplenty that evening. Janina gave a surreptitious little smile at her good fortune.

Maddy had placed that day's *Colville Times* on the table, but it was unopened and unread. Janina idly looked over the headlines as she nibbled on a cookie.

Then, she turned over the first page, and there, on the upper right, a headline jumped out at her. She stared at it uncomprehending for a moment, her half-eaten cookie forgotten.

CHRISTIAN'S WIFE FOUND NOT GUILTY BY REASON OF INSANITY

Judge H. Terrell McKeown of Stephens County Court ruled yesterday that Katherine Christian, 28, of Guildford, was not guilty in the slaying of her husband, Thomas Christian, 30, by reason of insanity. Mr. Christian was found unconscious with a gunshot wound to the chest on the evening of August 7th and died in the ambulance on the way to Colville General Hospital.

Mrs. Christian was arrested for the killing the following day. Informed sources report that she brought much suspicion upon herself by refusing to talk to the police. Since her arrest, and especially during her trial, she has exhibited a great deal of bizarre and erratic behavior. The judge's ruling yesterday made it clear that he believed her responsible for her husband's death, but psychiatric testing indicated that she was sufficiently out of touch with reality to render her unable to understand what had happened.

The judge's ruling was met with anger from Joanne Christian, the dead man's younger sister. "She knows perfectly well what she did," Miss Christian told reporters outside the courthouse yesterday afternoon. "That woman has everyone fooled. She's no more insane than I am. She's covering for someone."

It is widely believed that a second person, a drifter traveling under the name of Justin Lazarus, was somehow involved in the slaying. Lazarus was in the employ of Mr. Christian and disappeared immediately after Christian's death. Inquiries were made, but there has been no information regarding Lazarus's whereabouts. Police report that there is no direct evidence to connect him to the killing, but that he is still wanted for questioning.

Judge McKeown has recommended that Mrs. Christian be institutionalized at Hazleton for an indefinite period.

Janina read it over once, then again. So, that was it. It was over. Kathy was gone. Locked up in Hazleton. She'd heard of that place. Among her fifth-grade comrades, people who acted strangely were told that they should be "sent up to Hazleton." Otherwise known as the loony bin, the crazy house, or the nut farm. She wondered briefly who this Justin Lazarus might be, but other thoughts crowded out any questions she might have about some unknown drifter whom she'd never heard of before.

Kathy wasn't crazy, was she? Had she really shot Tom? It didn't seem possible. But what other alternative was there? There hadn't been anyone else there that night, so who else could it have been? Janina could still picture Kathy sitting there, cradling the gun in her lap and chanting her apologies over and over to the unresponsive body of her husband. What else could those apologies mean other than that she had killed him and then regretted it?

Janina carefully refolded the newspaper, responding to her natural instincts toward secrecy. If her mom found out she'd read the article, it would get her all stirred up and would probably bring up once again the topic of moving to another house. No sense in disturbing the status quo.

She finished her snack and brushed the crumbs into her hand

and walked over to the trash can with them. She wondered what Kathy was doing right now. She pictured her sitting in a cell babbling to herself. Wasn't that what crazy people did? But Kathy wasn't really crazy. She couldn't be. Right?

It seemed inconceivable that she would never see Kathy Christian again, but at the moment, it certainly didn't seem likely. What would it be like to go visit her? She wasn't sure if she could do that, go into a place like that, even if it was allowed. It must be horrible.

Would Kathy ever get out? Janina was pretty certain that if you were sent to Hazleton, it was for good. There was no way out except to escape or die.

Escape. How would you escape from a place like Hazleton? She imagined armed guards patrolling the halls wearing huge key rings that were used to lock up the cells. It would take a miracle to escape from there.

Janina walked to her bedroom. Sitting on her desk was a little tape recorder—a long-term loan from the middle school chorus teacher, who had noticed Janina's love of music and decided to do something about it. Every week, Mrs. Lagrange gave Janina a new cassette tape with recordings from her own personal library of classical LP's.

Janina put this week's installment into the tape recorder, a somewhat scratchy, but still splendid, performance of Rimsky-Korsakov's *Scheherazade*.

A miracle. It would take a miracle.

The first haunting notes filled the room with shades of Arabian mystery.

Miracles were... well, not impossible, but so unlikely. So terribly unlikely.

But then, Janina had a thought. It almost seemed to come from somewhere outside of her, as if someone invisible had whispered it into her ear.

Strange things happen sometimes.

Janina looked out of her window as the first few flakes of snow began to spiral down from the sullen sky. It was a comforting thought, somehow.

Sometimes strange things really do happen.

Gordon Bonnet has been writing fiction since he was six years old, with a passion for storytelling and a deep love of the written word. He has always been fascinated with the paranormal, but his love of science, languages, and history also shows through in his writing.

He also writes the popular skepticism and critical thinking blog *Skeptophilia*, as well as producing the weekly YouTube *Skeptophilia* video. You can also follow him on Instagram at *@skygazer227*.

When he's not writing, he can usually be found running, making pottery, or playing music. He lives in rural upstate New York with his wife and three dogs.